POISON HEART

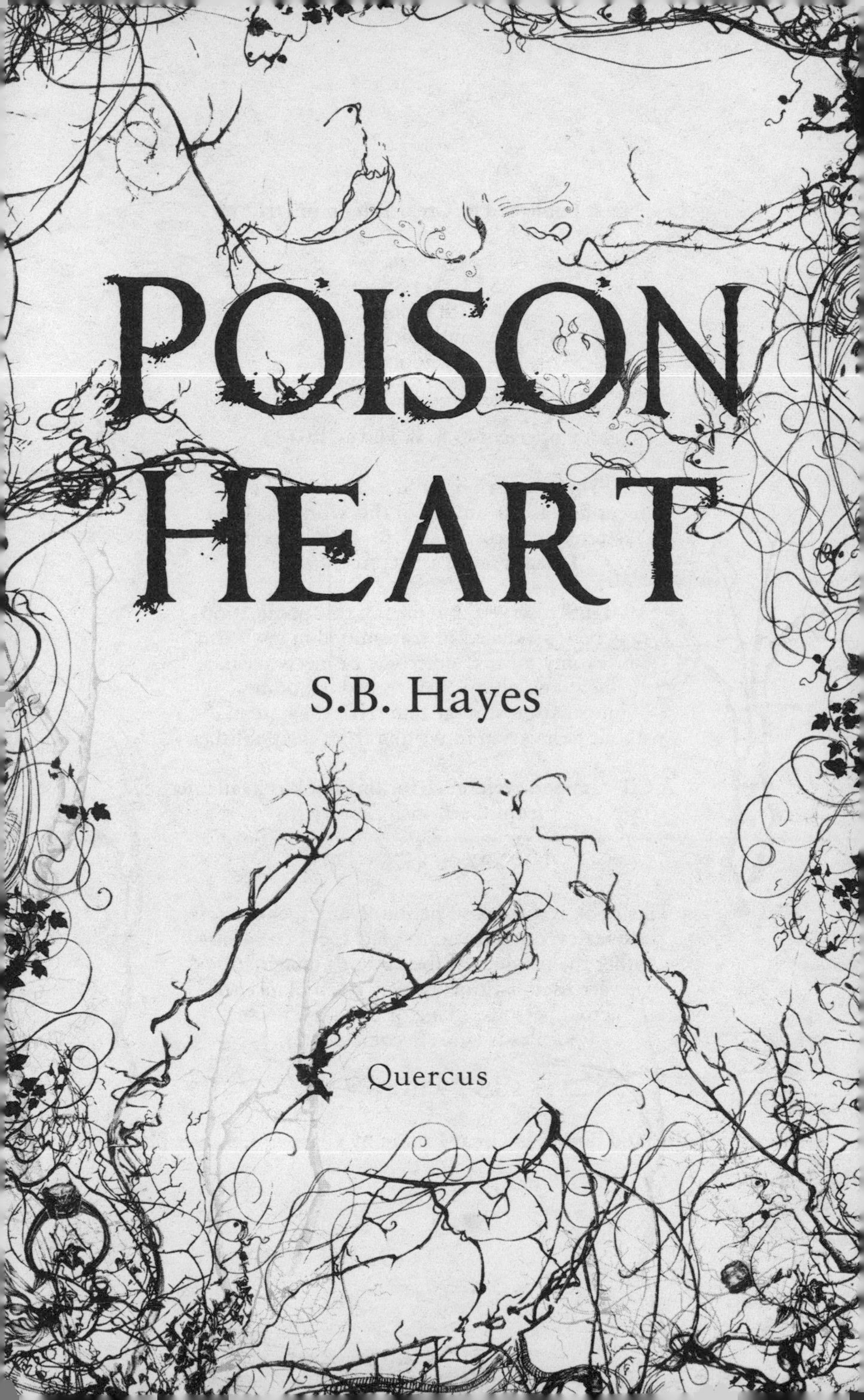

POISON HEART

S.B. Hayes

Quercus

First published in Great Britain in 2012 by

Quercus
55 Baker Street
7th Floor
South Block
London
W1U 8EW

A CIP catalogue reference for this book is available from the British Library

ISBN 978 0 85738 570 3

1 3 5 7 9 10 8 6 4 2

Printed and bound in Great Britain by Clays Ltd, St Ives plc.

For my husband, Peter, and my sons,
Michael, Christopher and Mark

Prologue

We were on the number fifty-seven bus when it happened – the moment that would change my life forever. The day wasn't anything special; it was mid-September, late afternoon, with the low sun blasting in and the smell of diesel filling the air. The hairs on the back of my neck stood up, one by one, and I just *knew* someone was staring at me. I couldn't see anyone, but I could sense them and – it was a compulsion – I had to look back. Slowly I turned my head to the left, where another bus had pulled up alongside. A girl had her nose pressed against the window. She had a heart-shaped face, full lips and straight brown hair, but it was the eyes that dominated. They were big and luminously green, just like those of a cat about to pounce. I put one hand on the glass and she did the same, in a perfect map of my fingers.

For some reason this made me think about my dream, the one I'd had since I was small. I'm entering a huge creepy house alone. I keep moving forward, past the giant front door with the peeling paint and coloured glass, through the porch, pungent with damp leaves, then into the hall of geometric blue and terracotta tiles until I'm at the foot of a winding oak staircase. I know I'm going to climb that staircase and I won't be able to wake up even though I'll be trying to. All my senses are alert; I hear every creak, feel each gnarl and groove of the banister and smell fruity decaying earth. Now I'm at the top, and the door in front of me is open but the corridor has suddenly doubled in length and I'm walking faster and faster, like running up an escalator the wrong way. It takes ages to reach the doorway at the end but I'm finally here, panting with curiosity.

There's a girl sitting in front of a dressing table looking into an elaborately carved set of three mirrors. Her back is towards me and I'm desperate to see her face, but she doesn't have a reflection. The three mirrors all reflect the room as if she's not there. I'm closer now, almost touching her; one hand is resting on her back and I will her to turn round, but she doesn't. I grip both shoulders and she's resisting me all the way but, a tiny bit at a time, she turns and at last, I can see her, but the face is my own and it's laughing at me, taunting me . . . Then I wake up.

I came back to earth with a jolt as the bus hit a pothole in the road. I was trying to forget the face at the window. I'll always wonder if everything would have been different if only I hadn't looked back that day.

CHAPTER ONE

'Katy? You look like you've seen a ghost.'

I could feel goosebumps breaking out on my flesh. 'It's nothing, Nat. I saw someone . . . a complete stranger . . . and she stared as if she knew me.'

'Maybe you met in one of your past lives?' she joked.

Hannah snorted. 'Or you have a telepathic connection?'

'Everyone has,' I answered seriously. 'But we've forgotten how to tap into them.'

Nat waved her arms above her head and did a really bad ghost impression. 'Katy gets messages from the other side.'

'I do not.'

Her hand prodded me in the ribs. 'Remember Mrs Murphy, the new religion teacher? You were certain she had a bad aura, and she turned out to be a complete and utter cow.'

'I *was* right about her.' I grinned.

'What is it? Some sort of gift?'

'No . . . just intuition.'

Hannah and I were sharing a seat and she nudged closer. 'Does it tell you when Merlin will make a move?'

My stomach lurched as if I was on a roller coaster just before it hurtles downwards. 'I thought we were going nowhere, and then today . . . it's weird . . . something changed.'

'What?' two voices asked in unison.

I wrapped my arms around myself, hugging the memory like a blanket. 'He looked at me in this incredible way. Like I was the only person in the whole world who existed.'

Hannah clapped her hands excitedly. 'You think something will happen between you?'

'Think so,' I answered shyly.

'Soon?'

'Mmm. It feels like when thunder and lightning are moving closer and the air is really charged and . . . electric.'

'Your psychic vibes again?'

I was used to being teased like this and stuck out my tongue. 'I don't need them with Merlin.'

'How's his aura?' Nat asked.

'It's fabulously clear, strong and very pure.'

Hannah gave me a searching glance and wrinkled her nose. 'You should be jumping for joy, Katy, but you look almost . . . depressed.'

I gripped the metal bar as the bus shuddered to a temporary halt. 'What if I said it all seems too good to be true?'

A hand reached over and felt my forehead, but I shook it off. 'It sounds pathetic, but I'm just not the type of girl who gets a guy like Merlin . . . one of the A-list.'

'Who're they?' Nat asked indulgently.

'They have perma-tans, highlighted hair, beach bodies and waxed . . . everywhere.'

Nat and Hannah laughed and I was really grateful for their support. They were always-there-for-each-other best friends, the kind I'd never managed to have, but having me hang around on the sidelines seemed to work for the three of us.

'You *could* be one of the A-list,' Hannah said kindly.

'Not with my corkscrew curls, hips and flaky mother,' I insisted.

I always got in the bit about the flaky mother before anyone else could, and my appearance could never be described as conventionally pretty.

'Why shouldn't someone like Merlin be interested in you?' Nat suddenly demanded.

I looked away into the distance. 'Have you ever dreamed of casting some sort of spell to conjure up the perfect guy? Well . . . I have, and that's Merlin.'

'Life *can* be magical.' Nat sighed. 'You of all people should believe in that.'

I looked at her with affection and ruffled her crazy pink hair. 'But it's all happening so fast. I'm on the brink of something new and amazing and I'm completely . . . terrified.'

Hannah took out a compact and retouched her already perfect make-up. 'This is a new start for *all* of us,' she declared. 'No more school uniforms, no awful Miss Owens with her moustache and polyester blouses full of static, and everyone in their pathetic little groups.'

'You're right,' I agreed. 'College is great. We've got much more freedom and everyone is so friendly.'

I closed my eyes for a second to whisper my own private wish.

And this is the year I'm finally going to find my feet and make a splash. A great life is around the corner waiting for me – I just know it.

I stood up and rang the bell as my stop approached.

'Come back to my house,' Hannah urged. 'We're searching for holidays on the Net.'

'My mum hates me being away even for one night,' I moaned. 'There's no way she'll let me go.'

'She'll have to let you go one day, Katy. You have your own life.'

I shook my head and frowned. 'She completely relies on me. We'll probably end up dressing the same and finishing each other's sentences.'

'Ever seen the movie *Psycho*?' Nat called after me.

I stumbled off the bus, deep in thought, and from nowhere came a surge of unexpected hope. Hannah was right – I *should* be jumping for joy. Everything was coming together for me – college, friendships, Merlin; there was even hope that Mum might improve. I grabbed hold of a lamp post and ran around it until I was dizzy while Nat and Hannah knocked on the window and waved madly. It took a few moments for my vision to clear and I shielded my eyes. There'd been a shower and heat was actually rising from the pavement, making everywhere hazy. I looked again – the girl with the green eyes was standing on the corner of the road. I blinked furiously. She was there, but only in the way that smoke is there for a second before it dissipates. She was a wisp of a memory that evaporated but left me feeling unsettled again. My eyes must have been playing tricks on me.

It was inevitable that I'd have to come down to earth. My heart sank as I opened my front door. The living-room curtains were closed in the middle of the afternoon.

'Hello, Katy.'

Mum always said my name as an apology. The room smelled stale and musty. She was still in her nightdress, eyes screwed up at me in the semi-darkness.

'Headache?'

She winced and lay back on a cushion, nodding. I plonked my bag on the carpet, thinking how nice it would be to disappear upstairs and work on a new design for textiles. It was like a drug to me, the only time I could really lose myself, but Mum had been alone all day and needed company. I tried to sound sympathetic. 'Is there anything I can get you?'

She coughed. 'I haven't eaten and there isn't much in the fridge.'

'I'll raid the cupboards,' I told her, 'rustle something up.'

The kitchen was depressing – dirty washing on the floor, dishes in the sink and my feet glued themselves to the ceramic tiles. Mum had always been unstuck around the edges, but the older I got the worse she seemed to become. I cleaned up, trying to stop the growing stabs of resentment, and microwaved a frozen shepherd's pie for her. Because I'm a vegetarian, the smell of warm mince made me feel queasy. I heated up a can of tomato soup for myself and dunked a stale white crust in it.

'My throat is like glass, and the pains in my head are blinding . . .'

Sick people can be so selfish. Where did I read that?

'It'd be nice if you could make it home earlier. I know you love college, but the day drags so much . . .'

If you tried to help yourself and went to the support group or bothered to talk to anyone about your problems . . .

'You're not thinking of going away in the summer, Katy? I really couldn't cope on my own.'

Home is starting to feel like a prison, without a reduced sentence for good behaviour. And you've never even let me apply for a passport, so how could I go abroad?

'Maybe you could take a year out of college . . . until I'm feeling better?'

I pleaded a ton of homework and escaped to my bedroom, desperate for some space, and stayed there until

Mum shouted me down later in the evening. She sounded unusually excited, and when I reached the bottom stair I noticed that her cheeks were flushed and her face animated.

'You've just missed her, Katy. I had a visitor, a young girl selling jewellery. Look what I bought for you.'

Mum dangled something green and silver in front of my face as if she was trying to hypnotize me. I held out my hand and she placed some kind of pendant in it. The prickles began again and the sensation was so strong it felt as though insects were crawling all over my skin. It was made of emerald glass which was exactly the same colour as the pair of green eyes that had stared at me so intently today. Mum didn't have to describe her caller. Instinct told me who she was.

CHAPTER TWO

Katy - Be the first to see the new studio XXX

In my eagerness to answer I overstretched and knocked my phone off my bedside table. There was a loud thud and a reverberating series of smaller thuds, because I ripped up my bedroom carpet last year and stained the floorboards an amazing shade of indigo, my favourite colour. I hardly dared look in case it was broken, and when I did my hands were shaking. Merlin's text held the promise of something I was too scared to think about, but not going just wasn't an option.

I was ready in less than fifteen minutes but it wasn't cool to appear too eager, so I twitched, bit my nails and changed clothes six times before setting off to his house. Mum watched me leave wearing her abandoned face, but nothing could make me feel guilty today. I quickened my pace, not wanting to talk to Luke, my next-door neighbour, because he always teased me and I couldn't have handled that right now. I was so strung out with anticipation that all my senses were super-alert. It had been a wet summer and the landscape was so lushly green that it almost hurt my eyes. I could hear creatures moving about in the grass, leaves rustling in the breeze and a bird cry from far away. A faint rainbow beginning just behind Merlin's tall Victorian house spurred me on. I never quite wanted to believe that if I ran far enough and fast enough I wouldn't eventually reach it.

'Hello, Katy . . . I'll show you through.'

Merlin's mum smiled as she opened the front door. She was tall and slim, with long glossy hair coiled on top of her head. She wore a kimono-style robe and looked great without a scrap of make-up. I knew she was a sculptor who had commissions from famous people, which made me a little in awe of her. I followed her up to the attic room, which had now been converted into a studio for Merlin. She gave a discreet knock on the door.

'Merlin, it's Katy.'

He hadn't heard us because he was so engrossed in his painting – the tip of his tongue just visible, eyebrows knitted together and deep-set grey eyes focused yet far away at the same time. His features were sharply interesting and full of angles, with razor cheekbones and a deep cleft in his chin. His skin seemed exceptionally pale in contrast to the dark tangled hair that fell into his eyes and was impatiently brushed away with a flick of his wrist. I could have watched him all day, but a hand in the small of my back urged me to go in and a voice whispered, 'I'll leave you two alone.'

I didn't want to shatter the moment because Merlin appeared so self-contained, but after a minute it felt wrong, as if I was spying on him. 'Merlin . . . your mum let me in.'

'Katy? You're here.'

He got up quickly and covered his canvas with a sheet.

'Can I see it?'

'Not until it's finished,' he insisted. 'Well . . . like the space?'

'It's fab,' I said, knowing that even if it was a shed at the bottom of the garden smelling of cats, I'd have said the same thing. 'The windows are huge and the view's amazing.'

We both moved towards the angled roof windows, my shoes echoing on the paint-splattered floor. 'The light is perfect,' Merlin admitted. 'I could stay up here all day.'

This was the closest we'd ever been. Our arms were touching and I didn't dare move in case I ruined the moment. Sometimes when I was with Merlin I found it difficult to breathe. Neither of us spoke. A century ago I'd have probably swooned because my corset was too tight, and Merlin – who had the looks of a brooding romantic hero – would have swept me into his arms as if I was as light as a feather. But girls weren't supposed to pass out any more just because they were close to a member of the opposite sex.

One of his fingers began to stroke the palm of my hand and the other joined in. My heart was beating crazily. My hand moved its way into his, but we both still stared out of the window, frozen.

Why did this always happen? I couldn't stand it any longer and had to say something this time.

'Why don't you kiss me?' I blurted out.

I couldn't believe I'd said it, but it seemed to break the ice. He turned and slowly bent his head, his six foot one inch versus my five foot five, until our lips touched and the room became a kaleidoscope of different colours.

'That was worth the wait, Katy.' His gorgeous face was instantly lit by a smile, as though the sun had burst through a cloud.

'You've been waiting for it to happen?'

Merlin said just one glorious word. 'Desperately.'

I still needed reassurance. 'When did you first think about me like that?'

He sighed. 'The first time you walked by I felt something weird happen. I was pulled towards you like . . . you were a magnet.'

I tried not to grin insanely but failed miserably and, even better, Merlin hadn't yet finished with the compliments.

'You had almost a glow surrounding you. Does that sound stupid?'

'It sounds amazing.' This was an understatement – I could have died of happiness on the spot. I nervously studied my feet. 'Does that mean we're . . . you know . . . together.'

He squeezed my hand and stared directly into my eyes. 'We're together.' He didn't look away for a second and I was drawn into the intensity of his gaze, noticing the perfect arch of his brow and his ridiculously thick lashes. 'There's something I have to tell you.'

'What's that?' I was instantly worried.

His lips curved upwards. 'The painting . . . it's of you.'

I covered my face. 'When can I see it?'

'Not until it's finished . . . I'm painting it from memory.'

The idea that he knew my face well enough to paint was completely mind-blowing. I wanted to savour the moment, but he made a sudden suggestion that sounded more like a command. 'Let's go out.'

With barely enough time to grab my bag, I felt myself being dragged out of his studio and down three flights of stairs. 'Where to?' I panted.

'Anywhere.'

There was a fleeting glimpse of Merlin's mother taking her art class in the conservatory, the living room with its mismatched furniture, brightly coloured canvases and oriental rugs, the dining room with an enormous trestle table and the kitchen with an original range oven, quarry tiles and giant dresser. There were humane mousetraps in a couple of the corners and the weird thought came to me that even the vermin in Merlin's house were hopelessly cool.

We finally stood outside, breathing in the last rays of summer, which seemed more special somehow because it was a last farewell to the sun before winter killed everything off. We dawdled along the canal and then through the railway arch into the town. Merlin stood out from the crowd, and people stared at him and then at me because I was with him. I laughed and moved as close as I could to him. We reached a cafe, La Tasse, a trendy espresso-type place filled with businessmen with their laptops and ladies lunching. We sat in a booth by the window on cream leather seats positioned back to back like in a railway carriage. We were newly together, and I figured we must be generating some kind of energy. Even the waitress did an about-take when she noticed us, and I rested one hand on Merlin's arm as he ordered our drinks.

This was how it felt to be one of those bright girls with the world at their feet, the type who expected to be happy instead of just apologizing for taking up space in the universe. At a party once, something strange had happened to me – I actually sparkled. Everyone laughed at my jokes, girls talked to me like I was someone and boys wanted to dance with me. I knew something magical was in the air and I wasn't really me that night – invisible Katy. This other person was still there inside, but she never came out again. When I was with Merlin I almost dared to dream I could be the other girl – the best of me.

Merlin watched me drink my latte and kissed the froth off my top lip. With flushed faces and excited smiles we sat side by side in the booth and talked about our plans for the future. We imagined his first art exhibition and my first fashion show. We talked about Rome, Venice and Paris as if these amazing cities were there just waiting for us to conquer them. Merlin looked down at the table and fiddled distractedly with a spoon.

'There's something else, Katy.' For a moment he struggled to continue, and his face was so attractive, his eyes wide and beseeching, generous mouth parted slightly, his voice husky. 'I'm not great at relationships . . . girls expect me to phone when I'm painting, and they seem to get so jealous over nothing . . .'

'I don't get jealous,' I interrupted hastily. 'I'm the least jealous person around.'

'I sensed that,' he answered with relief. 'I felt you were different . . . and completely special.'

I was dreamily hanging on his every word, happy that Merlin seemed to be letting his guard down, but something distracted me – a flash of green – except that when I looked properly the green must have been in my mind. Walking past the window next to me was the girl, and she was dressed in blue denim. She swivelled around to stare at me.

'Did you see her?' I asked Merlin. 'That girl with the green eyes.'

He hadn't taken his eyes off me for a second. 'I can see her now. You have beautiful green eyes.'

'Not like these,' I protested. 'They're really . . . impenetrable and creepy.'

He laughed, kissed my hand and went to the counter to pay for our drinks. I shivered, realizing she must have been in the cafe at the same time as us.

'Excuse me,' I asked the waitress. 'My . . . friend was in here, but we must have missed each other. She has straight dark hair and she was wearing jeans and . . .'

'She was sitting over there,' the woman replied, pointing to the end booth. She gave me an odd look and I began to cough to cover my embarrassment.

I felt spooked again, thinking of *her* sitting close to us, although, thankfully, not close enough to hear our conversation. Merlin walked me home and I tried to push her to the back of my mind. It wasn't hard – with him beside me I was almost floating. When we reached my road I pulled Merlin into a small alleyway that ran along the back of my house, the entrance flanked by a two-metre wall, just the right height to keep us concealed from prying eyes. It took us ages to finally say goodbye. Whenever I tried to prise myself away, Merlin would pull me back again. My face and neck burned as if they were on fire. I rubbed my cheeks self-consciously, wondering how to explain away my kissing rash, but when I finally got inside Mum didn't seem to have noticed. She gave a brave smile when I asked how her day had been, but I could detect an undercurrent of reproach.

I hummed around the house, delirious with happiness, reliving every minute of the day and texting Nat and Hannah to tell them about it. Midway through my exclamation marks, Mum called my name. I raced into the living room to find her waving a packet of cigarettes in the air, her face like thunder.

'I'm very disappointed, Katy,' she said, lowering her voice to a hush that was somehow worse than being roared at. 'You've always promised not to take up such a disgusting habit.'

'They're not mine,' I replied incredulously. 'Smoking is horrible.'

'They fell out of your bag,' she continued, her eyes boring into mine. 'I suppose Merlin's convinced you it's fashionable or something and you want to please him.'

'Merlin hates smoking,' I insisted, growing more and more indignant. 'All my friends do . . . I can't think how they got there.'

Mum cut an imaginary line in the air with one hand. 'End of discussion, Katy. If Merlin *is* involved, I won't hesitate to stop you from seeing him. You can count on that.'

There was no point in arguing further. Mum always had the last word. It was a mystery how the cigarettes had got into my bag to make such a sour end to a perfect day, and I felt aggrieved to have been accused so unfairly, but Mum had made it clear that the subject was closed. I had the definite impression that she wasn't happy with me seeing Merlin and this had provided an excuse to express her disapproval.

It took me ages to drop off to sleep and I tossed and turned all night. That dream always came when I was feeling stressed and it had never changed . . . until tonight. This time, when I grabbed the figure sitting at the mirror and forced her to look at me, the face wasn't mine, it belonged to the girl on the bus. This time her eyes were green and fathomless. I stood back, drowning in her hatred.

CHAPTER THREE

No matter how busy I kept myself, a nagging sense of foreboding lurked deep inside, but I tried to suppress it and concentrate on Merlin instead. It was official – we were a couple. There was no need for an announcement at college – word soon spread and my popularity soared. We spent every minute we could together, and Nat and Hannah joked that they were sick of seeing us mooning about and gazing into each other's eyes.

Merlin made arrangements to call at mine on Saturday, which was nerve-wracking because Mum had already judged him. I was on pins all morning, and when I peered out of our front door for the twentieth time to see if he was coming it was impossible to miss the sight of Luke unloading his ancient car of all the stuff he'd brought from his flat. It was filled with boxes, plastic bags, crumpled clothes thrown into a heap and there were plates, cups and a kettle rattling around on the back seat.

'Where's my favourite Kat?' he called over.

I smiled at his usual nickname for me and went over to him. 'No more student life,' I taunted, flinching as a glass smashed on to the pavement. 'Now you're a proper grown-up.'

'Not in a million years,' he scoffed. 'You're talking to the guy who used to put snails down your back and spiders up your nose.'

Luke Cassidy was five years older than me and had spent the last ten years terrorizing me in every way he could. I spent my childhood trailing after him and his friends, but they always managed to shake me off. Then he went away to university and I was surprised how much I missed having him around. But he was back and still teasing me.

'Little Kat's grown up too,' he said, gingerly picking up the broken pieces. 'I saw you with your boyfriend and waved, but you were kind of occupied.'

I blushed, knowing how spaced out I must have looked holding hands with Merlin. I hastily changed the subject. 'So what's it like being a journalist?'

'So far I've covered three church fêtes, a dog show and the story of an old man who sleeps in a tree house with a squirrel.'

'No calls from the nationals?'

Luke gazed skywards. 'Maybe next year.' Out of the corner of one eye he seemed to be peering at me.

'What's wrong? Is my make-up smudged?'

'You look different, that's all,' Luke muttered, and quickly lowered his eyes.

I stretched out one finger to touch his chin and grinned. 'So do you. Luke finally has to shave.'

'I've been shaving for years,' he protested, and I pressed my lips together so as not to laugh. Luke had a smooth baby face and corn-coloured hair which made him look younger than he was. Leaving his car doors open, he marched through our front door, without being invited. I tried to head him off, but he reached the kitchen, pulled up a chair and said lazily, 'Put the kettle on, Kat.'

My hands glued themselves to my hips. 'You can't treat our house like your own any more.'

He shrugged. 'Why not?'

I was trying to come up with a reason when Mum appeared from nowhere and ruined everything. She got out Luke's 'special' mug, which had his name on, and brought over the biscuit tin. I refused to sit down and glanced at the clock.

'You're edgy, Kat.'

'Merlin's calling for me,' I announced, trying to sound aloof and worldly wise. 'Then we're going to his house. He's a talented painter and has his own studio.'

Luke didn't laugh at Merlin's name, but I could tell that he wanted to. 'Where does he live?'

'Over on Victoria Road, by the riding school.'

'He's a posh boy then.'

My mouth opened and closed like a goldfish. 'He is not. Merlin's just ordinary, even if his house is really grand.

And his mum devotes lots of time to penniless students and lets them work in her studio.'

'How noble,' he commented sarcastically.

'Don't be so judgemental, Luke. Mum is already convinced he's encouraged me to smoke, and now you think he's over-privileged.'

Luke leaned back in the chair, taking a long satisfied slurp of coffee. 'You haven't fallen for that tortured-artist thing, have you? This . . . Merlin probably has a whole line of girls whose portrait he's painting.'

I narrowed my eyes dangerously, about to make a sharp retort, when the doorbell rang. Merlin hovered on the doorstep with his usual air of confidence, but I suspected he might have dressed up for the occasion, because his jeans weren't even faded and his shirt had been ironed. I pulled him into the lounge and stammered an introduction to Mum, hoping that Luke would stay in the kitchen, but he chose to come through right then. He and Merlin looked each other up and down. If it wasn't so uncomfortable I might have laughed because they were so different – Luke, stocky, blonde with an open friendly face; Merlin, tall and dark with guarded features. I mumbled something about Luke living next door, grabbed my coat and shot off. Merlin took my hand. His thumbnail dug into my skin and it hurt but I didn't stop him.

'What's so important?' I asked, finally drawing breath as my house faded from view. 'You said I had to come over to yours urgently.'

Merlin hesitated. 'It's the portrait, Katy, I just can't get the colours right.' He leaned over and nuzzled my cheek. 'My concentration's gone. Can't think why.'

'How can I help?'

'You can sit for me. The light is best at this time of day. If you pose, then it might all come together.'

'OK, no problem, Merlin.' We walked the length of his sweeping drive and I kicked myself for sounding so lukewarm. 'I mean, of course I will. It's the least I can do.'

I draped myself across the battered chenille sofa, trying to minimize my hips and not think about Rubens paintings of amply proportioned naked ladies, their flesh soft and dimpled.

'Have to change,' Merlin said.

Without warning, he opened the poppers on his shirt in one swift movement and threw it on the chair. He took an old T-shirt from a hook and pulled it over his head. I averted my eyes, but not before I'd glimpsed his bare chest and the line of black hairs snaking downwards past his navel.

My face burned with embarrassment and I was worried about being immortalized in the painting with giant rosy cheeks. I tried to blame it on the sun. 'It's quite . . . hot in here, isn't it?'

Merlin muttered something about warm air rising and opened one of the roof windows. He made a square with the fingers of his left hand, looked at me and then back at the canvas. He shook his head. 'Your hair is impossible to replicate . . . it's unreal . . . like spun gold crossed with warmed chestnuts, and your complexion is . . . alabaster freckles.'

He smiled and I melted inwardly. Most guys would struggle to come up with the feeblest compliment, but Merlin managed to make one sentence sound like an entire sonnet. I tried not to fidget, but it was torture for me to be under so much scrutiny, and the temperature in his studio was increasing. I had to take off my cardigan, hoping that this didn't look like a bad attempt at striptease. Merlin worked for ages and I stayed silent because he was so wrapped up in what he was doing. Even though Merlin was painting me he seemed distant, almost as if he saw me in an abstract form. My eyes flickered as the sun grew more intense and I could see a drop of sweat shining on his brow.

'Time for a break?' I suggested.

Merlin nodded. He wiped his hands on a piece of cloth and sauntered over.

'Room for one more, Katy?'

I sat up quickly and drew my legs under me. 'How're your . . . colours?'

'Much better.'

I fidgeted and stared at the door.

'There's nowhere to run,' he said softly.

I rubbed my nose, smoothed down my hair and looked about the room while Merlin stayed perfectly still, watching me. I rubbed my arms, shivering now despite the heat.

'I want to look at you, Katy.'

I tried to laugh it off. 'You've been staring at me for ages.'

'Not like this.' He put one hand under my chin and I was forced to look back. His eyes were penetrating, sharp and flinty grey.

Merlin's head inclined towards mine as one hand slipped the strap of my camisole over my shoulder and his lips kissed me all the way up my throat.

'Your mum might walk in,' I muttered, tensing up.

'She won't.'

He made his way to my cheek, my nose, even my eyelids before turning his attention to my mouth when it became impossible to speak. He wrapped his arms around me so tightly that I could barely breathe. It felt so natural and I shocked myself by sneaking one hand under his T-shirt, counting each rib with my fingers. I felt him shudder.

'Cold hands?' I laughed, knowing this wasn't the reason. I felt an unexpected sense of power.

At last I knew what all the fuss about kissing was. We were so tightly pressed together that I didn't know where my limbs began and his ended and we both slid down the sofa until we were horizontal. It felt like I was drowning in him. Then loud voices made me flinch.

'They're coming from the garden,' Merlin reassured me. 'Mum's gathered her collection of stray artists together.'

There was a banging sound and the studio door flew

open, sending papers flying into the air. I extricated myself from his embrace and sat up again.

'It's just the wind. Mum's a fresh air freak.'

'Sorry, I mumbled. 'Don't know what's the matter with me.' I pointed my head down towards the floor. 'I'm . . . not sure I'm ready for something . . . heavy.'

'Heavy?' Merlin ran one hand through his hair and blew out slowly. 'Katy, I'm in so deep already . . . If you just want to see a movie once a month and hold hands, I'm not sure I can do that.'

I bit my lip, shamefaced. He stroked my arm but I held myself rigid. 'Maybe it's just a bit . . . too soon.'

His voice was raw with emotion. 'I knew how I felt about you in seven seconds but if you have to wait to feel the same about me . . .'

The lump in my throat grew bigger. 'I do feel the same, but maybe we just need somewhere more . . . private.'

Merlin smiled knowingly. 'I'm thinking of locking you here in my tower to keep you away from the rest of the world.'

I was about to reply when I noticed the time. The afternoon had vanished and I needed to get back to Mum. Whenever I was with Merlin the hours flew by. I peeked at the painting when he left the room. It was nothing more than a series of fine brushstrokes, but my face had begun to take shape, shining pale and ethereal, the colours muted, completely unlike Merlin's usual bold style. I heard footsteps returning and quickly moved away. Reluctantly we left his house, hand in hand, and walked back through the garden. When we reached the gate I glanced back, squinting, even though the sun had dropped. There was a figure moving through the trees so quickly and lightly that it could have been a sprite, but something about it made me uneasy. I looked at Merlin, but he didn't appear to have noticed anything, and I was beginning to think that the girl had bewitched me. She couldn't be everywhere like this, it wasn't possible. I quickened my pace because it felt as if hundreds of eyes were watching us. When I kissed Merlin goodbye it was with a strange desperation that I couldn't explain.

I dreamed about her again that night. This time she was supine across Merlin's battered sofa, languishing, luxuriating in her own beauty. I couldn't escape her eyes as she gracefully rose to her feet, sashayed across the room and turned the easel towards me, forcing me to watch. The painting wasn't of me, it was of her, her crimson lips curled up with a secret smile of triumph. I woke with a start and sat bolt upright in bed. The green pendant was still on my dressing table and it almost seemed to glow in the dark. I jumped up and stuffed it away in my handbag.

CHAPTER FOUR

'I have my own stalker.'

Hannah stopped yawning long enough to express surprise. 'You have Merlin – best-looking guy in college – and now your own stalker. How unfair is that? Who is he?'

'It isn't funny,' I insisted, wishing Nat's dad would slow down going over the speed humps because my head kept hitting the roof of his car. 'And it isn't a guy . . . it's a girl. I saw her from the bus, in the street, in the cafe, *and* she called at my house selling jewellery.'

I delved into my bag and handed the pendant to Nat.

She turned it over and then held it up to the light. 'It's pretty cool. What's it made of?'

'I think it's sea glass,' I grunted. 'Emerald sea glass . . . just like her eyes. It might be cool, but I think it's a warning.'

'What's sea glass?'

'Ordinary glass, but it's been in the sea for ages until all the edges are smooth and the glass is opaque.'

Hannah glanced at her watch. 'Why would she be

warning you? Sure you're properly awake? It *is* only six thirty a.m.'

I lowered my voice, making sure that Nat's dad couldn't hear. 'I think she's used some sort of . . . magic on me so she always knows where I am.'

The laughter was so loud that I had to cover my ears. 'You're priceless,' Nat chided.

I stared out of the window, biting my lip. 'She's everywhere I go, watching, listening, and she knows where I live.'

'You really believe in this . . . witchcraft then?'

'I wouldn't exactly call it that,' I answered, taken aback. 'But there's something unnatural about her. That day on the bus . . . something passed between us, and I haven't felt the same since.'

They were both looking at me oddly. 'So . . . why did you buy the pendant?' Hannah asked.

'I didn't. Mum got it for me.'

'And what did your mum say about her?'

'That she was nice, talented and very persuasive, but – how weird is this? – when Mum went to fetch her purse, she . . . the girl . . . disappeared and didn't take any money for it.'

Hannah shook her head. 'I just don't get it. An unknown girl calls at your house and leaves a gorgeous pendant, almost like a present?'

'It doesn't feel like a present,' I muttered.

'We're here, girls,' Nat's dad called as he drove through

the huge gates of the country park. A feeling of excitement ran through me when I saw all the cars and vans spread out on the grass and most of the stalls already set up. This was the biggest car-boot sale and craft fair around, and the three of us could wander for hours, searching for bargains. It was definitely worth getting up at five in the morning for. We were in such a rush that we tumbled out of the doors and Nat screeched as she almost landed in a cowpat.

Hannah made a beeline for the table closest to us and immediately picked up a wide pot decorated with a design of blue and white flowers. 'It looks quite old,' she announced importantly, 'probably Edwardian. This would look really pretty with a plant in. I'll buy it for Mum.'

'It's a chamber pot,' Nat giggled in my ear. 'For weeing in. Don't tell her until we get back home.'

My mood lifted as we walked around. The grass was wet with dew and the bottoms of my jeans were soon saturated and heavy, my canvas pumps sodden. Hannah was no better, as she gingerly picked her way across the field in a smock dress with bare legs, the grass chafing her skin. Nat was the only one who had dressed sensibly, in pink and green fluorescent wellies over black tights and denim shorts. Once the early morning mist lifted, the sky was startlingly blue and we all stripped off our jackets and cardigans. None of us had bothered with breakfast, and the smells of coffee, doughnuts and croissants wafted through the air. My feet began walking towards the food stall, but two pairs of hands tugged my arm. 'We can't stop yet – we'll miss all the good stuff.'

They were right – within ten minutes of frantic rummaging I'd spotted a pinstripe trilby that I knew Merlin would love and a 1950s-style dress with a flared skirt decorated with cabbage roses. I knew it wasn't proper vintage and managed to beat the lady down from eight pounds to five. Nat pounced on a stuffed cat because she collected them and a beaded evening bag from the 1920s, which cost her a cool fifteen pounds. Breakfast couldn't wait any longer and all the plastic seats had been taken so we sat on the grass sipping hot coffee and eating sugared doughnuts, so sweet they made our teeth ache.

It felt great being here with Nat and Hannah, taking in the early-morning rays and watching the crowd swell. Far from deterring us, this made it more of a challenge, and we enjoyed people-watching too. Every now and then Nat would sigh about Merlin's friend Adam, with whom she was hopelessly in love since meeting him at a party. Hannah stood up to put her rubbish in a bin and I leaned towards Nat. 'Why don't you use the power of your mind to captivate him?' I whispered.

Nat's eyes widened mischievously. 'So you dabble in magic as well?'

'No . . . not magic,' I tried to explain, 'just positive energy to help something along. Anyone can practise it, but some people have a . . . head start.'

'What sort of people?'

'Well . . . your mind has to be open, but if you want something really, really badly, I think you can kind of . . . manifest it.'

'Sounds like a love spell,' Nat teased. 'Maybe I should try one. Is that how you enticed Merlin?'

I folded my lips together and refused to divulge the answer. Hannah reappeared and looked at us both quizzically, but I tapped the side of my nose and told her it was a private joke. She pulled a wry face but didn't appear bothered. I uprooted a few daisies from the ground and scattered the petals around.

'Hannah? You've known Merlin the longest,' I began casually. 'Has he had lots of girlfriends?'

'Weirdly not,' she replied slowly. 'Although plenty of girls have tried, but he's so . . . intense and wrapped up in his work. I think he's been saving himself for you.'

I stood up, trying to hide my pleasure at her words, and brushed sugar from my jeans. It was then I saw her, cool as anything, arranging a collection of jewellery on a rickety wooden table and smirking at me. The doughnut stuck in my throat and my stomach felt instantly queasy. The cardboard cup fell out of my hand on to the ground.

'She's over there right now,' I growled. 'I've had enough of this, I'm going to confront her.'

Without waiting for Nat or Hannah to reply, I marched towards the stall, keeping my eyes fixed on her. A man rudely pushed past and distracted me. It was only for a second, but in that time she vanished. An older woman was now standing in her place looking peeved.

'Where did the girl go?' I demanded.

'I've never seen her before,' a voice grumbled. 'She asked me to keep an eye on her stall, but I've got my own to worry about.'

Something flickered in my field of vision. It was nothing more than a glimpse of material disappearing into the crowd, but I knew it was her and I had to follow. But there were people everywhere as I tried to push my way through. I was slow and clumsy, whereas she was as light as gossamer, a feather floating and dancing in the air, an escaped balloon, a pirouetting ballerina. Each time I lost her, a fragment of something would resurface, a glimpse of her earring, her hair or just the corners of her mouth as she turned around – I could almost hear laughter around me.

The sensible thing would be to stop and go back to my friends, but I couldn't do that and she knew that I couldn't. It was growing harder to force my way through the people, and I no longer cared if I stood on someone's foot or elbowed them in the ribs. Once I sent a stall flying, and books and dishes tumbled on to the grass. The outraged cries didn't make me stop. There was a clearing where the crowd thinned and I could see patches of tarmac, which signalled the beginning of the car park. I speeded up, and when I reached the edge of the field it was possible to breathe again. For a few seconds I looked up at the clouds and panted, disorientated by the wide open space. A glance to my left and right revealed nothing – it was as if she'd been swallowed up into the atmosphere. She couldn't be real – the way she moved, her speed and the fact that she kept disappearing in front of my eyes.

A noise suddenly made me start. Someone clearing their throat. I turned around slowly and froze. The girl was less than two metres away, filling a jug from an outdoor tap. I was rooted to the spot. She was definitely flesh and blood, not some phantom of my mind. I stared for about thirty seconds and she finally looked up and watched me without blinking.

I came to my senses. With my hand outstretched, the pendant sitting squarely in the middle of my palm, I walked towards her. 'I think this is yours.'

'Is it?' she asked playfully. 'I didn't drop anything.'

'You called at my house, but you didn't wait for the money . . .'

Her oval eyes half closed. 'Did we speak?'

This was stupid. I felt as tongue-tied as if she was an adult and me a child. 'I wasn't . . . no, we didn't speak. My mum answered the door. You talked to her.'

The water overflowed from the jug and splashed her feet, but she didn't turn off the tap. 'Then how do you know it was me?'

'The st . . . stall,' I faltered. 'I recognized the pendant from your jewellery stall.'

Her lips curled in a slight smile. 'I don't have any pieces like that.'

My face turned brick red. 'Well . . . my mum described you, and then I saw you here and put two and two together and . . .'

'Followed me,' she finished.

This was crazy. I was beginning to look like the stalker instead of her. And it was impossible to gauge her tone, whether there was an edge to it or not. 'So it isn't yours then?' I challenged.

'Let me look.'

As she took the pendant her fingers touched mine and it felt as if an electric shock had passed through me. I actually took a step back, my heart racing, but she appeared completely unmoved. She frowned and threw it back at me. 'I'm not sure.'

This was going nowhere, but I refused to crawl back to Nat and Hannah in defeat. I tried to stop my voice from wavering and resolutely faced her.

'Were you in Hillside Street last week?'

She finally turned off the flow of water, kicked off both her ballet pumps and gracefully brushed the grass with her toes. 'I don't remember.'

'You must remember.'

She shrugged her shoulders. 'What's the problem anyway? You should keep the pendant.'

'I don't want to keep it,' I fumed, and tried to pass it to her again, but this time she refused to take it.

I stared at her mutinously, but her expression softened and she began to laugh gently. After another minute of confusion I started to laugh too, suddenly realizing how ridiculous I must appear, charging after her with all kinds of strange accusations.

'Sorry we got off to a bad start,' I apologized. 'I didn't want you to lose out on a sale, that's all.'

'Do you like the pendant?'

'It's lovely,' I admitted.

She tilted her head to one side and looked at me from underneath her lashes. 'You should keep it then, Katy.'

'You know my name?'

She still seemed to be laughing. 'I know lots about you.'

I frowned. 'But I don't know anything about you.'

She was closer now and I could feel her breath on my face. Her lips parted and moved inaudibly. There was no sound, and yet I could hear her. She was saying the same phrase over and over again and I couldn't tear myself away.

A hand on my shoulder made me flinch. 'Katy!' Nat exclaimed. 'We've been looking all over for you.'

Hannah jumped in. 'Why did you disappear?'

I could see them both looking at me and then back at the girl. She smiled, batted her eyelids and gave me a friendly wave.

'Everything OK?' Hannah asked.

I nodded and, linking arms with Hannah and Nat, headed back towards the stalls. I turned around only once, to see the girl looking back at me, strangely transfixed. I shook my head, cross with myself because my imagination must have been running riot. But no matter how hard I tried to forget, I could still hear her voice resounding in my head over and over again: '*I'm your worst nightmare.*'

CHAPTER FIVE

The new cafe in the high street was decorated in Neapolitan colours – vanilla, mocha and strawberry. There were giant photographs of coffee beans on the wall and attractive people with perfect teeth laughing together in leather club chairs, clutching outsize cups. Nat, Hannah and I had decided to try it out before going to college for the first student exhibition of the year. I was nervous about my work, but this anxiety stopped me focusing on the real thing that was troubling me.

Hannah sipped a banana smoothie, her forehead creased with concern. 'We're the three musketeers, remember? All for one and one for all. What's bothering you, Katy?'

Nat guiltily tucked into a slice of carrot cake and spoke with her mouth full. 'Is it Merlin?'

'No, everything's great with him.'

'Your mum?'

'It's not her either,' I answered, tipping the pepper pot and making patterns on the table with my finger.

'You've been quiet all week,' Hannah persisted.

I looked from one face to the other. They were right; I had to get this thing off my chest. 'Look, I know this will sound stupid, but it's . . . the girl we saw at the craft fair.'

'Ah . . . your stalker.' Nat winked.

'Thing is . . . I thought she said something to me, something I can't stop thinking about.'

Two pairs of eyes fixed on me expectantly, but my mouth felt dry and there were butterflies in my stomach. I went back to blowing on my coffee. 'It doesn't matter . . .'

'Spit it out,' Nat urged, and pulled a stupid face which made me smile.

I studied the hexagon shapes on the floor, not wanting to look at them both. I chewed my lip, adjusted my position in my chair and took a deep breath. 'She said, "I'm your worst nightmare."'

The silence seemed to go on forever. Hannah eventually broke it. 'Just like that. She said, "I'm your worst nightmare," just like that.'

I squirmed a little. It felt horrible having to justify myself like this. 'She called me Katy, and I asked how she knew my name, and she told me she knew lots about me and then she said—'

'I'm your worst nightmare,' Nat interrupted. 'You're absolutely certain that's what she said?'

'I *thought* it was my imagination,' I answered defensively, 'but now I'm not so sure. Her lips opened, but she didn't seem to speak . . .'

'She didn't speak?' Hannah echoed.

My fists clenched under the table and I tried to keep my voice measured. 'I'm not sure . . . it's all a bit of a blur.'

There was another uncomfortable silence and I almost began to regret confiding in them.

'Why didn't you tell us at the time?' Nat asked.

'It didn't seem real,' I mumbled.

Hannah's voice was apologetic. 'But you did chase her that day. She didn't come after you.'

'She wanted me to,' I answered, realizing how bizarre this sounded. I didn't even understand it myself. 'I mean . . . I went after her because she'd left that pendant at my house.'

Nat took a sip of her drink and licked her lips. 'It's not something a sane person would say,' she commented archly. 'Did she appear sane?'

'Perfectly.' I groaned, my previous doubt returning in one hot embarrassing wave. 'And you're right, of course. My mind was all over the place that day . . . I was probably a bit . . . wound up.'

Nat yawned. 'It's silly to get upset about this anyway. I mean, how much damage could one girl do?'

I didn't answer and stared down at the floor. A brand-new penny gleamed at me and I remembered the rhyme, 'See a penny pick it up and all day long you'll have good luck.' But I was too ashamed to scramble about on the floor to retrieve it.

'This is the best time of our lives,' Hannah reminded me. 'Nothing should be so serious.'

I managed a watery smile. 'OK, I'll try to lighten up. You're right. How much damage *could* one girl do?'

We finished our drinks and left the cafe, all three of us trying to shelter under a single umbrella. Rain didn't usually bother me, but Hannah was terrified she'd have an attack of the frizzies and huddled further beneath the umbrella, pushing me off the kerb in the process. The sky darkened and thunder sounded in the distance so we quickened our pace.

'She's in my dreams as well,' I announced distractedly, as if there'd never been a break in conversation.

Hannah shrieked as she walked into a puddle. 'Forget all about . . . whatsherface . . . spooky girl with the cat's eyes. She's probably given up on you and decided to stalk a celebrity instead.'

I was about to answer when the rain grew stronger. Within seconds it was bouncing off the pavement, pouring like crazy into the gutters and grilles. We made a run for it and arrived at college out of breath, shaking drops from our clothes and hair.

'Thanks for coming,' I whispered. 'I didn't want to be alone.'

Most students had brought along their parents, who stood by their displays, beaming with pride. I felt a pang of regret thinking about Mum, but Nat and Hannah were here for me. The exhibition was to raise the profile of the art and design department, and the local paper had been invited to do a feature. Neither Nat nor Hannah were the least bit creative and they made a big thing about my designs as if they were the greatest thing on earth. They moved closer to my display and marvelled at my embroidery and appliqué, plus the piece of fabric that I'd printed by hand with a leaf design. I could see Merlin standing head and shoulders above everyone and waited for the chance to go over and talk to him. I felt a surge of pride again, remembering how he kind of belonged to me now.

Events then seemed to happen in slow motion. Merlin's mum walked in through the glass doors, her hand protectively placed on a girl's shoulder. The girl had her back to me but I could see the admiring expression on Merlin's face and my stomach churned with jealousy. I wanted to walk confidently over there and break them up, but something stopped me and I stayed in one spot studying her. She had straight hair, almost the same shade of red as mine, and was wearing a crushed velvet coat similar to my own, a complete original that I'd made myself. They were almost identical in style, even down to the hand-stitched border. I didn't hear a word that was being said to me until someone moved their hand up and down in front of my face.

'Sorry, I was miles away.'

'She's always on another planet when she sees Merlin,' Nat joked.

I tried to act normally. 'I'm not. No guy will ever come between us . . . right?'

'You've had plenty of nice comments,' Hannah assured

me. 'One lady said she hadn't seen embroidery so skilled since she was a girl.'

'Really? I suppose that's a compliment, especially if she's about one hundred.'

'Gels knew how to stitch back then,' Nat mocked. 'And play the pianoforte and walk with books on their heads and rustle their petticoats . . .'

The girl was definitely flirting now. Really moving in for the kill, one hand playing with her glossy hair. Damn. I'd just told Nat and Hannah that they were always more important than any male, but Merlin was practically being eaten alive. I had to do something.

'I should really go over and say hi to Merlin. Thanks so much for giving me some moral support.'

Hannah rolled her eyes. 'Does that mean you're dumping us?'

'No course not. I just kind of promised . . .'

Nat squeezed my arm affectionately. 'We wouldn't stand in the way of true love . . . go to him.'

They pushed me in Merlin's direction and I said an inward prayer that he wouldn't humiliate me. We were still at the awkward stage where we weren't sure how the other would react. My prayer was answered. He saw me before I reached him and actually held out his arms to me. I was enveloped in a suffocating hug, which should have said everything – this is where I belong; Merlin is *my* boyfriend. One hand brushed my cheek, and he kissed me in front of everyone. I even stood on my tiptoes and whispered something in his ear, which was pretty pathetic but I couldn't help it. There was no need to turn around to see the girl's face, I could feel her eyes burning into me and it even felt as if there was a stabbing pain between my shoulder blades.

I kept my back to her as a deliberate snub, at the same time grabbing Merlin's hand and giving him a secret look that said, 'Let's go somewhere alone.' He took the hint and made his excuses. We were just at the door when he smacked his head as though he'd forgotten something and swivelled around on the smooth floor.

'Katy, I'm so rude, I forgot to introduce you. Katy, meet Genevieve Paradis, Mum's new protégé. She's joining the college next week.'

The blood rushed inside my head and it felt as if a train had whooshed past the building. The girl with the green eyes. Her voice echoed all around the hall, bounced off the vaulted ceiling and pierced me in the heart.

CHAPTER SIX

Merlin grabbed me just in time as my legs seemed to buckle beneath me. I took deep breaths, smiled grimly and pretended this was just a joke, annoyed because this girl had such an effect on me.

I extended one hand towards her. 'Hi. I think we've already met.'

She turned to me and her eyes widened. 'Have we?'

'Yes, at the craft fair. The pendant . . . remember?'

'Of course, *that* Katy.'

'You looked . . . a little different then,' I couldn't help but point out.

'Did I?'

Her smile was warm, but for some reason it made me uncomfortable. 'Your hair was a different colour, I'm sure.'

The dark hair had made her skin look unattractively white; now it was fresh and dewy in an annoying country-maid-type way and in contrast mine appeared dull and lifeless. The same went for the coat; hers flattered every line and curve of her body rendering mine frumpy and ill-fitting.

'This is my natural shade,' she answered, and mussed her hair with a modest frown. 'I was sick of colouring it all the time, and I hate to stay the same.'

'Change is good,' I began tetchily, 'but I like to stick to my own style and be original.'

'Nothing's completely original,' she came back. 'Fashion, literature, art . . . it's all been done before. If you look at my display over there I'll tell you which artists and designers influenced me.'

It was impossible to keep the annoyance from my voice. 'There's a difference between influence and complete imitation.'

'But, Katy,' she said sweetly, 'imitation is the sincerest form of flattery.'

This ping-pong backwards and forwards was beginning to wear me out. I really needed to escape from her and took the first opportunity to drag Merlin away.

'Sorry, but Merlin and I are going somewhere. It was nice seeing you again . . . Genevieve.'

I didn't even reply to her parting remark, which sounded almost ominous. 'Hope we'll see a lot more of each other, Katy.'

Merlin and I walked for a while in silence but, without knowing why, it felt slightly awkward between us.

'You're quiet,' he commented.

'I'm just tired.'

He kissed the top of my head. 'Not of me?'

'Course not.'

We sat down inside a little hut in the local park by a perfectly striped bowling green. Merlin's hair looked even better in the driving rain, in a sort of windswept Heathcliff way, but mine had started to resemble a blackberry bush. I tried to tame it with my fingers and failed miserably. His jeans had paint splatters on them and lots of rips, but not in a contrived way. He looked like a Bohemian artist from another century, and every time I closed my eyes I saw the awful nightmare of Genevieve lying on his battered sofa, luxuriating in being painted by him. *He's painting YOU,* I tried to remind myself.

My head rested on Merlin's shoulder as I wondered how to bring up the subject I dreaded. There was no alternative but to jump right in. 'So . . . how does your mum know Genevieve?'

'It's a really tragic story,' he began quietly, and I had to bite my tongue not to say something sarcastic. 'Her parents died in a car crash on Christmas Eve when she was only about seven . . . She didn't get on with her adoptive parents and she's been shunted around children's homes ever since.'

'How terrible,' I murmured, because he paused as if waiting for a reaction.

His voice grew even more concerned. 'She ended up sleeping rough for a while, until one of Mum's friends stepped in and fostered her.'

'Where do they live?'

'In a converted barn, not that far from my house . . . close to the stables.'

'Mmm . . . I think I know it. Isn't Genevieve a little old to be fostered?'

'She's already sixteen,' Merlin replied, 'but it's to help with the transition period.'

'And that's how you met her?'

'Yeah, Mum pulled out all the stops to get her a place at college because she didn't have all the necessary exams.'

I moved position, suffused with sudden anger. 'She helped her get a place at college? But we had to work so hard to earn the grades.'

Merlin's sharp tone took me by surprise. 'It's not Genevieve's fault she was homeless. She couldn't go to school, so Mum encouraged her to put together a portfolio and present it to the college board. They agreed she deserved a place. Did you see her collection?'

My teeth were clenched so tightly together that they hurt. 'No, but I'm sure it's awesome.'

'The weird thing is, she's a real all-rounder . . . fine art, fashion design, textiles, jewellery. Most people can only manage one.'

'Good for her.'

'And her work is completely formed, not just experimental, but . . . she had to sell her designs on the street or she probably wouldn't eat that day.'

I was like a robot. 'Of course.'

'Knowing about Genevieve makes you realize how easy our lives are.'

'Absolutely.'

'Don't repeat any of the things I've told you, Katy. I'm not sure how much she wants broadcast.'

'No, of course not.'

There was a hole in the roof of the hut and the rain plopped on to my head and down my nose. Merlin didn't even notice my abrupt answers because he was still talking rapturously about Genevieve.

He paused for breath and I sniffed. 'You never mentioned her before.'

'Mum only brought her over recently.'

'You mean last week?'

He looked at me oddly. 'Yeah, it was . . . Saturday, I think.'

So, while Merlin was painting me, she was at his house, and it could have been her I saw through the trees.

'Is that important?' he asked.

I waved my hand airily. 'I was curious how long she'd been around.'

'Not long, but you have a lot in common. I think you'll be friends . . . real friends.'

It wasn't Merlin's fault, but he seemed contaminated by her. He'd been mine and only mine for such a short time. Already I could feel him slipping away from me. I looked around. There wasn't another person in sight, not even a lone dog walker brave enough to face the rain. I buried my face in Merlin's neck and ran my tongue upwards to his chin. He tasted like salt with just a touch of sweat. I slid my legs over his until I was sitting on his knee and began kissing him. He gave an involuntary groan.

'Katy . . . you weren't like this the other day.'

I laughed. 'Maybe being outside . . . makes me feel . . . er . . .'

'Wild,' he finished, holding me at arm's length to study my face with amazement. 'I didn't expect to be eaten alive on a park bench.'

Merlin clutched my head as I kissed him some more, trying to erase every last trace of Genevieve. I unfastened the first three buttons of his shirt and rested my cheek against his chest, listening to his heart.

'It's beating like crazy, Katy. Can't you feel it?'

'Mine's going crazy too.'

Merlin's hand tentatively wormed its way under my T-shirt, all the time watching for a reaction, then across my stomach until it pressed against my heart. We didn't move for what seemed like ages.

'Wouldn't it be nice to be completely alone?' he whispered. 'Somewhere miles from here.'

'Where?' I sighed.

'We could pitch a tent on one of the campsites.'

'That'd be great,' I breathed, convinced he didn't mean it.

'It might be cold.'

'I love cold,' I told him, which was true. I always felt happy when the days were growing shorter and summer was nearly over.

'What would you tell your mum?'

I pulled away. 'You're serious then?'

Merlin's smile was broad. 'Why not? You can't relax in my house, and yours is off limits . . .'

I wasn't ready to tell him the full extent of Mum's problems because I wasn't sure that he'd understand. 'Mum's a bit . . . clingy,' I said at last. 'It might be difficult. She doesn't even like me going to sleepovers and you're . . . you're a guy.'

'You've noticed,' he teased. 'Just one night, Katy. I'd love to watch the sunset with you . . . count the stars . . . and wake up together.'

I tried not to shiver at this image and smiled hopefully. 'Nothing's impossible. I'll think about it, try to come up with a plan.'

'But you do want to?' he pressed.

'Of course I do.'

It was totally unlike me to agree to something so risky, but I was determined to get Merlin all to myself to discover his innermost thoughts. Even when we were together, I sometimes felt shut out, and I knew there was a place he went to inside his head that I couldn't share with him. Maybe being alone together, away from everything familiar, would bring us closer. We walked home at a snail's pace, savouring every minute, while I tried to obliterate all memory of Genevieve. We kissed at the same spot by my house, but no matter how much I tried to convince myself that it was exactly the same, it wasn't – Merlin still reeked of her.

CHAPTER SEVEN

Mum was out of bed when I arrived home and there was some colour in her cheeks for once. The house felt different – warmer and almost cosy for a change. I could see she that was trying to make an effort and I should have been pleased, but the news about Genevieve had spoiled everything. Mum looked at me expectantly.

'I'm sorry I couldn't be there, Katy. How did it go?'

'It was fine,' I lied, and made an excuse to go straight upstairs.

I locked myself in the bathroom, determined not to cry, and gazed in the mirror, smoothing down my hair and sucking in my cheeks, trying to look like Genevieve. But I still looked horribly ordinary, as always. In a frenzy I threw open my wardrobe, stripped off my clothes and, indiscriminately, pulled T-shirts, dresses, sweaters and shirts off hangers. One by one I tried them on, mixing and matching, attempting different looks and different poses. It was pathetic, but I was trying to match Genevieve's lazy couldn't-care-less attitude, her languid smile and easy movements, because I'd just realized that my style wasn't remotely offbeat and anti-fashion, it was total bag lady. I closed my eyes in despair, trying to banish her from my mind, but she was still there like a retinal echo. I blew my nose, ran a comb through my hair and went back down to Mum. She had so few good days that I felt guilty about leaving her alone and tried to put on a show that everything was OK.

'So how did it *really* go today?' she asked quietly.

Everything must have been bubbling close to the surface because, without really thinking, it all spilled out. 'The exhibition was great, but this new girl at college . . . she's really got under my skin.'

Mum gave a wry laugh. 'I knew it. I can spot envy from a mile away. You're positively green.'

'I do that as well,' I told her in amazement. 'See a colour when I look at people.'

She leaned over and patted my hand. 'I didn't mean it in the way you do, but I can spot a teenager whose nose is severely out of joint. The green-eyed monster is rearing its ugly head.'

'Green-eyed monster?'

'It's a quote from Shakespeare's tragedy *Othello*. Jealousy is compared to a green-eyed monster.'

Luke was always quoting Shakespeare at me as well, but I wasn't in the mood to even feign interest. I just pulled a face.

'Do you want to talk about her, Katy?'

I took a deep breath. 'This girl, Genevieve, seems to be everywhere, following me and now copying me. Today I found out she's had a terrible life . . . she was in a children's home and then ended up sleeping rough. But I can't find one shred of pity for her – it's like something's taken all my niceness away and turned my heart to stone.'

'That's not like you at all,' Mum frowned. 'Is there something else?'

Of course there was something else – something I didn't want to face. I swallowed, closed my eyes and winced with pain. 'I think she's trying to steal Merlin from me.'

I gulped. That wasn't what I'd intended to say. I meant to mutter something about Genevieve flirting. Admitting to this was my darkest fear, the worst thing I could imagine.

Mum gave a derisory laugh and my heart sank. 'You teenage girls are so dramatic. You both like the same boy, and you think it's the end of the world.'

'It's more than that,' I glowered.

Mum knelt on the carpet at my feet, warming herself in front of the roaring fire because it had begun to get chilly in the evenings. I always loved our real coal fire, but it was usually too much of an effort to light so we'd just plug in an ugly electric heater when the temperature dropped. For the first time in ages I could stare deep into the flames, searching for shapes in the same way I used to do when I was little. But even here I couldn't escape from Genevieve – the flickers reminded me of her glorious red hair.

'If he's that keen on you, Katy, then he won't betray you. But don't drive him away with your jealousy. Jealousy is a poison that will destroy, you not her.'

I was barely listening. 'The weirdest thing is . . . she's everything I could be but I'm not.'

Mum gently shook my arm. 'What does that mean?'

'We're about the same height,' I said, scowling, 'but she looks willowy because she's so slim, and we've got the same colouring but her skin is disgustingly luminous, and our hair is the same shade but hers is silkily gorgeous . . .'

'You have your own beauty, Katy, and people like you for what you are.'

'I just want everything to stay the same,' I replied wistfully.

I didn't want to add that it'd taken me years to feel that I finally belonged somewhere. I was always an outsider who never could make friends, but during my final year at school I'd grown closer to Nat and Hannah and now, unbelievably, there was Merlin in my life as well. Deep down, I had suspected it was too good to be true. Mum hadn't finished with the sermon.

'You'll always meet people you don't see eye to eye with – just think of it as one of life's little lessons.'

'I don't want to,' I said in a sulk. 'I just want her to go as far away from me as possible . . . preferably to the other side of the world.'

Mum finally lost her temper with me. 'Katy,' she scolded, 'you've always had such compassion for people, especially those without the same advantages in life. I really think it's you who has the problem, not this girl Genevieve.'

I sat quietly for a moment digesting this uncomfortable accusation. Was Mum right? Genevieve had done nothing except let me keep an attractive pendant that she could have charged me for. She didn't have any family and had endured things that I couldn't even imagine. Shame washed over me as I realized how jealous and vindictive I must appear.

'This really isn't you,' Mum added, but more gently this time. 'If dating Merlin is going to turn you into the kind of girl who would shun a vulnerable teenager then . . . maybe he isn't the one for you.'

'He *is* the one for me, but . . .' I bit my tongue and didn't whine again about Genevieve flirting with Merlin. This was probably all in my head too. And Mum was right. This lack of feeling *wasn't* me at all, it was totally out of character.

'You have to trust Merlin, Katy. You can't cage someone you love.'

At that moment Mum seemed to crumple before my eyes. I put my arms around her and found tears wet on my neck.

'I'm sorry,' she apologized. 'I don't know what came over me.'

Her grip tightened on me and it felt claustrophobic, as if I couldn't breathe. I pretended not to notice that the skin around her nails was red and angry. Mum had this obsessive-compulsive disorder and could chew her fingers until they bled. Usually it made me feel sad, but today I was oddly annoyed. I wanted her to comfort *me*, not the other way round.

'If I thought I would ever lose you, Katy . . . it would break my heart.'

'Why would you lose me?' I asked, puzzled.

She smiled wanly, trying to collect herself. 'Things happen . . . random things that change everything.'

'It can't change you being my mum.' I laughed.

Mum ran one hand through her limp hair, a pained expression on her face. 'I didn't want things to turn out this way,' she said eventually. 'I wanted to be the best mother ever, to always be there for you and protect you.'

I tried to reassure her. 'You are the best . . . honestly.'

There was a catch in her voice. 'You deserve a beautiful life . . . full of fun and laughter, new experiences and travel. Not burdened with me, a prisoner in this house.'

For a moment I had a glimpse of another woman, one I barely remembered, who was vibrant and lived for the day. I didn't know when it all changed because she seemed to have been this way forever. But I couldn't let this opportunity pass. We so rarely had a heart to heart that it could be the break I'd been waiting for.

'The doctors say only you can change the way you are,' I urged. 'There's help available – you just have to take it.'

Mum spoke so quietly that I had to bend my ear towards her mouth. 'I've tried so hard, but something holds me back . . . a dark cloud hanging over me.'

'What is it?'

She shook her head regretfully. 'Memories, I suppose . . .'

'Maybe . . . if you share them . . . they won't seem so bad.'

Her eyes closed and she slumped in the chair. 'One day I will tell you, and I know you'll understand . . . but not yet.'

I was disappointed but tried not to show it. Every so often a small window would open but then close just as quickly.

'I will make an effort, Katy. I'll go back to the doctor and take his advice . . . promise.'

'That's a start,' I answered flatly.

'Let's toast some muffins,' she suggested, a little too brightly.

I nodded my head and tried to look enthusiastic. Gemma, our marmalade-coloured cat, was asleep in her basket, and I moved over to stroke her. The claws of one of her front paws grazed my hand and then retracted. I knew what this meant – Gemma was letting me know she was the boss and, if it suited her, she'd scratch me without any remorse because she had no conscience. With complete disdain she opened her beautiful liquid eyes, glared at me and closed them again. I swallowed hard, trying not to remember another pair of green eyes that could appear just as unnerving.

Mum came from the kitchen with the packet of muffins,

spearing one with an ancient toasting fork. Soon the smell of burnt bread filled the room. I did feel a little closer to her now, but it was tinged with frustration. She'd hinted at fears, regrets and black clouds oppressing her, but not told me why. Part of me was always afraid that this depression was genetic and I would end up seeing the world through Mum's eyes.

She was right about one thing though – I had to trust Merlin and lighten up over Genevieve. Merlin thought we'd have loads in common, and maybe he was right. Mum chatted as we ate, warm butter running down our chins, while I wondered just what had happened in her past to make her stop living.

The dream still haunted me – parts of it familiar, parts of it changing. Tonight I was forced to climb the interminable stairs, but when I eventually reached the top Genevieve wasn't there and I frantically looked around, wondering where she could be hiding. I edged closer to the dressing table and her face was inside the mirror, her eyes magnified and all-seeing. She beckoned to me and I was unable to resist. As my fingers touched the glass it turned to liquid and circular ripples appeared, spreading outwards. I was being sucked into a deep, dark pool. I screamed at Genevieve to help, but she simply watched in horrible fascination. Only when the last bubble left my mouth did she smile.

CHAPTER EIGHT

Resolution number one: Genevieve deserved to be given a chance and I could afford to be generous. Resolution number two: I would ensure that my jealousy was kept under control. Resolution number three: Merlin was unbelievably special and nothing was going to spoil that.

These were my thoughts as I determinedly walked to college on Monday morning. Jealousy *was* a destructive emotion and I had to rise above it. I quickened my pace as I noticed Nat and Hannah waiting on the corner of the main road by the pelican crossing. The wind was really gusty and Hannah frantically held on to her flared skirt, which made me laugh. I grinned at Nat, waiting for the teasing comments about Merlin, but for no apparent reason she seemed to be studying a concrete bollard and could barely look me in the eye. When she did, her face was sheepish.

'There's something you need to know . . .'

I waited for her to begin, sensing something was amiss.

'W-we didn't do it on purpose,' she stammered. 'When

you left with Merlin she came over and began talking. We ended up showing her around.'

Hannah joined in. 'It was awkward. We couldn't get away, and then she kept saying how horrible it was because she didn't know anyone and would have no one to go to lunch with.'

I didn't have to ask who they were talking about; it was obvious. 'So Genevieve invited herself to lunch, with us?'

They both nodded. We walked up the steps together and went into the ladies'. I was glad because we wouldn't be overheard in here.

'It would've been rude to say no,' Hannah apologized. 'But we know you think she's a bit of a . . . witch.'

I leaned against a washbasin and tried to control myself. Somehow I'd imagined myself being magnanimous and inviting Genevieve to join us now and then, not the other way round. This felt a little underhand. She'd waited until I had gone to move in on Hannah and Nat. The reality of her presence hit me anew – she'd wheedled a place in the same college as me, was taking the same subjects, Merlin's mum adored her, and now my closest friends had been targeted.

'Did she ask you?' I said curiously. 'Did she come up to you and expect to be shown around?'

They nodded again.

'This sounds a bit paranoid,' I admitted, 'but it feels as if she's kind of . . . invading my life.'

Hannah's voice held a definite hint of reproof. 'This is

really uncomfortable for us, Katy. You *are* our friend, and we're stuck in the middle.'

Nat began to fix her hair in the mirror, which was just a distraction because, as usual, it was sticking up everywhere like a bird's nest. 'She knows you don't like her—'

'What?' I exploded. 'I haven't said anything to make her think that.'

Hannah rummaged in her make-up bag and applied even more mascara to her thick lashes. They were both so quiet that I knew this wasn't going well. I bit my lip so hard I could taste blood.

Nat cleared her throat nervously. 'She thought you were a bit . . . hostile and was worried she'd done something wrong. She wants to make amends.'

I felt a pain right between my eyes and placed one hand across my forehead. Genevieve wasn't wrong. I'd done nothing to put her at her ease, and she had undoubtedly picked up on my antagonism.

'What *did* you say to her?' Hannah asked softly.

I paced up and down the tiled floor, my shoes making an eerie hollow sound.

'I was a little . . . annoyed about her appearance,' I finally confessed. 'Did you notice how much it's changed?'

Hannah shrugged her shoulders. 'Kind of. But so what? Everyone changes their look from time to time and . . .'

'She's wearing *my* coat,' I interrupted. 'The one I designed, hand-stitched and embroidered myself.'

'But, Katy,' Nat replied slowly, 'Genevieve only just

arrived. She couldn't have copied your coat in such a short time.'

I was dumbstruck because she was right. That coat had taken me the whole of the summer holidays to painstakingly make. No one could have reproduced it so quickly. I looked from one face to the other feeling mortified. I had to show them that I didn't have a problem with Genevieve. I tried to slow down my breathing and appear unconcerned and reasonable.

'Look, I'll prove I have nothing against Genevieve. Let her come to lunch with us and I'll make her really welcome.'

Hannah's face lit up with relief. 'You'll change your mind when you spend time with her. She really is OK.'

'Considering what she's been through,' Nat put in sympathetically.

So Genevieve had told *them* her life story as well. Far from it being a secret, she wanted everyone to know about her tragic past. I tried to speak normally, but my mouth felt as if it was full of sour lemons. 'I know the heart-rending Orphan Annie story already . . . she's told Merlin, and probably the whole college by now.'

There was an astonished silence. Nat managed to croak, 'Katy . . . you sound so spiteful.'

My face reddened. 'Sorry, I don't mean to be horrible but . . . she seems to bring out the worst in me.'

It was an awful admission to make and I felt thoroughly ashamed – again. I smiled weakly. 'Sorry again. Let's not fall out over Genevieve. We're the three musketeers, remember?'

We all walked to our respective classes and I pretended not to hear Hannah quietly point out, 'Technically there were four musketeers.'

Trying to get away from Genevieve was like trying to run from wildfire. She arrived breathlessly, a whirl of colour and movement, when the lesson was already under way, receiving only a gracious smile from our usually stern English teacher. I was relieved when she sat on the other side of the room, but no matter which way I turned she was in my line of vision. I craved quiet, to soothe the headache which had begun pulsating behind my left eye, but she volunteered to answer nearly every question in an irritatingly nonchalant way that had Mrs Hudson eating out of her hand. Her voice grated on me. The horrible truth filtered through that not only was Genevieve prettier, more outgoing and confident than me, but she was streets ahead of me in all the subjects that I loved. I began to feel physically sick. After twenty minutes my vision blurred and there were flashing lights going off in my head. I stood up shakily, mumbled an apology and headed back to the ladies'.

Afterwards, bending over the sink and splashing my face with cold water made me feel slightly better. When I straightened up I almost screamed with fright because Genevieve was directly behind me, her face reflected in the mirror like in my dreams. My bag fell on to the hard floor and all the contents spilled out, but I didn't feel up to bending down to retrieve them. It was left to Genevieve to crouch on one knee and scoop everything back in.

'Sorry, I didn't mean to frighten you, Katy. Mrs Hudson was worried.'

'I'm OK,' I mumbled. 'It's just a headache and dizziness . . .'

'Feeling sick? Eyes hurting?'

I grunted in agreement.

'It's a migraine. I get them too. The best remedy is to lie down in a dark room with an ice pack.'

Another wave of nausea hit me and I doubled up but there was nothing left in my stomach. I hated being seen like this, but it was out of my control.

'You should go home,' Genevieve said, patting me on the shoulder and picking a few stray hairs off my cardigan. 'I'll tell Mrs Hudson what happened.'

She put one arm around my waist and helped me to the door, asking if I wanted her to call a taxi. I screwed up my eyes, feeling utter remorse because she was being so kind.

'I'll be fine,' I assured her, but my legs had turned to jelly and I needed to sit down.

She helped me to the nearest chair, which was positioned outside the office, and then went inside to arrange for the cab.

'I'll wait with you, in case you pass out,' she told me firmly.

'Thanks for looking after me,' I answered gratefully.

'That's OK.'

I decided to clear the air. 'Sorry if I made you feel unwelcome. Merlin thinks we have lots in common . . .'

She turned to me and I was startled again at the colour of her eyes, which seemed to react to the light, the pupils changing from glowing orbs into tiny slits. Her expression was disarmingly serene, her voice almost soothing. 'That's part of the problem with you and me, Katy . . . being alike.'

'Is it?'

'Of course. There just isn't room.'

'Room for what?'

'There isn't room for both of us – you must realize that. And *I* want to stay.'

This was surreal; Genevieve was saying such horrible stuff to me, but the Cheshire Cat smile never left her face.

I felt sick again. 'I don't know what you mean, and I don't want to play pathetic games. Just tell Nat and Hannah what happened and why I couldn't come to lunch.'

'They're not even proper friends . . . you're just an afterthought . . . you don't get close to people . . . boring, sensible Katy. You could spread your wings and fly, but you don't know how . . .'

'What the . . . ?'

Her tone changed abruptly and I was shocked to hear the malice in it. 'I'm everything you're not, and I'm going to take over your life.'

As a car horn beeped I stood up and lunged towards the

taxi. There was movement behind me and I lashed out, my hand coming into contact with soft flesh. I heard a loud cry of pain and looked back only once, as the taxi pulled away, to see the shocked faces of Nat and Hannah comforting the weeping figure of Genevieve.

CHAPTER NINE

Luke was getting out of his car as the taxi pulled away, but I tried to duck into my house without him seeing me.

'Cat got your tongue?' he shouted across.

My facial muscles refused to arrange themselves into a smile. His expression was so sympathetic that without my knowing it was going to happen, I burst into tears, huge great sobs that made my whole body shake. In no time at all I was in Luke's kitchen, sitting at his large oak table and staring into a cup of hot sweet tea.

'I'm keeping you from work,' I wailed.

He checked his phone. 'I'm due in court in an hour, but I've got time for a chat. Now tell me what's wrong. You look awful.'

'I've just been sent home from college with a migraine. It's nothing.'

'Kat Rivers, you always were a terrible liar. Tell me the truth. If it's that boyfriend of yours, I'll—'

'It's not him,' I insisted, wincing at the sweetness

of the tea. 'I'm just having problems with this girl at college.'

'Shoot.'

Luke was a patient listener. I told him what had happened and he didn't once interrupt or defend Genevieve, as Mum had done, with warnings about the green-eyed monster or my being as much to blame. I could see that he believed me completely and I closed my eyes in gratitude. It meant the world to me.

'Do you think people can make things happen to you?' I asked hesitantly. 'Sort of . . . horrible things.'

Luke twisted his mouth to one side. 'I think if you're susceptible and believe you've been . . . cursed . . . then bad things can occur as a kind of self-fulfilling prophecy. But only because your mind expects them to.'

'The glass pendant she gave me,' I said, 'it's really spooking me. It seems to change colour and . . . glow.'

'Some sort of light catcher?'

'Maybe,' I answered doubtfully.

Luke shook his head with exasperation. 'I'll never cure your obsession with anything vaguely magical, will I? Every Halloween since you were six I've had to take you trick-or-treating . . . the first few years I had to carry your broomstick!'

I laughed and snivelled at the same time and my nose ran horribly. Luke handed me a tissue.

'You don't scare me anyway,' he joked. 'You can put a hex on me and turn the milk sour or get your cat to trip me up.'

'Genevieve's the one with the hexes,' I sniffed. 'Since she appeared, everything in my life's gone wrong. Cigarettes mysteriously appeared in my bag and Mum thinks I'm a secret smoker and Merlin is to blame. Then Merlin and I had our first cross word because I was being unsympathetic about Genevieve's tragic life, and now Hannah and Nat think I'm jealous, spiteful and unforgiving of . . . poor old Genevieve.'

Luke began moving his arm in a circular movement, pretending to stir his cauldron, and attempted a hideous cackle.

I stayed completely straight-faced. 'Very funny. I should have listened to my first instinct. I knew there was something sinister about her.'

'She knows just how to get at you, Kat. She's probably found out you're a sucker for tales of hideous crones with pointy hats and big noses.'

I smiled weakly. 'If she came at me with a knife then I'd know where I stood.'

'Don't say that. You're not going to let her carry on like this?'

'I can't stop her,' I told him in all seriousness. 'She's just too strong.'

Luke refilled his cup from the percolator on the stove, brow furrowed in concentration. I idly glanced around his kitchen, admiring the reflective white surfaces that flooded the space with light and the smart stainless-steel appliances, trying to forget the decor in our own kitchen. Mum had kept our 1970s knotty pine units and an ancient brown cooker that the scrap merchant probably wouldn't even want.

When Luke spoke I could smell the coffee on his breath. 'But that's the point, isn't it?' he said. 'This girl, Genevieve, seems to know all your weaknesses, almost as if . . .'

'We mean something to each other,' I finished. 'Except I never in my life set eyes on her until a few weeks ago.'

There was a shout of greeting as Luke's mum came through the front door. She came over and hugged me, chattering as she put away her shopping. I could see Luke making a gesture behind her back towards the door.

'Mum, I'm helping Kat with . . . an English assignment, so we'll have to go upstairs and use my computer. It's a good job you're not a proper girl,' he joked, taking the stairs two at a time. 'Mum disapproves of me taking Laura to my bedroom.'

I didn't mind the 'proper girl' comment; in my eyes he was still the messy boy with the thatch of blond hair who made model aeroplanes and painted plastic soldiers. Laura had been Luke's girlfriend for almost three years, but his mum still treated them like teenagers who needed a chaperone. I tried to look impressed by his bedroom because the tatty carpet had been replaced by pale laminate flooring and the old pine wardrobe by sleek built-in sliding units. Luke now had a double bed with leather headboard, and smooth white walls, no posters in sight, but there were still dirty socks on the floor and papers strewn all over his desk and it still smelt like it did when he was fourteen.

Luke picked up a marker pen and stood in front of the whiteboard which was hanging on one wall. This felt like being in a detective show and I felt a small shiver running through me. He cleared his throat importantly.

'Look, I did a piece on stalking once and picked up some of the psychological stuff. I'll throw out a few possibilities.'

'OK.'

The first possibility is that you have something she wants, which makes you a threat.'

'She wants everything,' I sighed.

Luke began to write. 'She has an urge to make you suffer as well. An irrational but very focused vendetta.'

'That's for sure,' I agreed darkly.

'What could she possibly have against you?'

'Nothing,' I wailed. 'I've done nothing to her . . . except . . . look back.'

'Look back?'

As I remembered that day, I could still feel the sun burning my face and her eyes boring into me. 'I was on the bus and she was on another bus and she stared at me . . . really hard. It all began then.'

'You don't do all this just because of a face at a window.'

'*She* did.'

Luke scratched his chin. 'Mmm. She's gone out of her way to collect information about you, which is obviously important to her. It gives her the upper hand and makes you vulnerable. It proves her campaign is carefully thought out and has taken time and effort.'

'Obviously she doesn't have much of a social life,' I grunted sarcastically.

'There's an element of power in the stalker. They want to feel in control of you.'

'And manipulation. She plays games.'

'Very good,' Luke praised, and I felt absurdly pleased.

With a series of arrows he connected all his points together in a circle. 'This all comes back to my belief that she – Genevieve – knows you from somewhere and—'

'Impossible,' I interrupted.

'Or,' he continued, 'she's targeted you because of something she *believes* has happened between you, a case of mistaken identity.'

'She can't have confused me with someone else,' I said slowly. 'She knows too much about *me*.'

He sat down beside his desk, picked up a glass paperweight and turned it over in his hand. 'She might be a complete fantasist who's made up the whole thing in her own head and dislikes you for no reason at all.'

'That sounds bad,' I answered. 'Because if it's fixed in her head then no amount of denial will change it and I can't reason with her.'

'Want my advice, Kat?'

'Of course I do.'

'While this is going on, you have to be brave and take

everything she throws at you. Don't show any emotion, because she's looking for maximum impact.'

I screwed up my face. 'So just take it – the insults and everything?'

'Play your own game and be reasonable, calm and polite. It'll annoy her like hell.'

I thought about this for a moment. 'I suppose it will. She wants to get at me. . . but I pretend she doesn't.'

'And promise me you won't dwell on the stupid witch stuff. If she makes you believe she has unexplainable powers, then you'll never try to stop her. She's real – hideous but real – and we'll defeat her with logic and cunning, nothing else.'

'Logic and cunning,' I repeated.

Luke gave me a big thumbs-up. 'And here's the best bit: she knows things about you, but you know nothing about her, so now it's our turn.'

'What have you got planned?'

He tapped the side of his nose. 'A journalist never reveals his sources but I told you I'd always be there for you.'

I gave a rueful smile. When Luke was in Year 11 and I was in Year 7, he stopped me from being bullied with a promise that I could always count on him, a promise he hadn't forgotten.

'The weird thing about all this, Luke . . . I'm not the kind of girl other girls envy. I'm so ordinary.'

'Don't put yourself down,' he answered casually. 'I think you're special.'

I opened my eyes in surprise at this unusual compliment, but he immediately put one finger in his mouth and made a gagging noise.

'Whereas Genevieve,' I went on, 'she could light up a whole room. She's got this way about her . . . charisma, self-assurance, magnetism . . . whatever it is, she's got bucketloads.'

Luke took hold of one of my hands to calm me down. His were warm and reassuring but surprisingly rough.

'Dad's roped me into helping him work on the house,' he explained, examining his palm. 'And he's a real slave-driver.'

I didn't want to leave, but he picked up his car keys and jangled them impatiently. I stood up cautiously and held on to a chair because the room was still slightly tilting.

'What about Laura?' I asked with concern. 'She's just welcomed you home and now you're off on some wild goose chase for me.'

'She'll understand . . . I'm sure she will. Mind how you go, Kat.'

I walked back to my house feeling better and more together. Luke had made me see that there was a way out of this. I was going to fight for what was mine and not fall into the trap of being set up again. I took some tablets for my migraine and went to my room. It was soothing to be alone. I meant to work on some designs, but my head still ached and I sat staring out of the window. My desk was deliberately arranged so that it faced our garden, which was only a small patch of straggly grass dotted with overgrown shrubs, but it still inspired me. The clouds were indistinct and raggedy today, reminding me of flotsam spread on water, but a plane had left a trail in the sky that looked like two crossed spears.

I was busy studying the emerging pattern when the room darkened and a bird appeared from nowhere and sat on the ledge, staring right in at me. It looked distinctly like a crow – jet black with a huge wingspan and beady yellow eyes. It pecked on the glass for a few seconds and then seemed to fall. I raced downstairs in case it was hurt and might become victim to Gemma's sharp claws, but all that was left was a large black tail feather lying on the patio. I picked it up and ran it through my fingers. The oily texture made me shudder so I put it in the bin. On impulse I went upstairs to grab the pendant and threw that away as well, wondering why I hadn't done this sooner.

My mood nosedived again when I delved into my bag only to discover that my key ring was missing. It contained my first photograph of Merlin and was undoubtedly my most prized possession. When everything had spilled out of my bag at college it definitely hadn't been left on the toilet floor, and the unwelcome thought came to me that Genevieve had stolen it for a reason.

Mum and I spent a gloomy evening together watching TV. At bedtime I realized that no one had even rung to see how I was.

CHAPTER TEN

It was lunchtime before I had the chance to confront Hannah and Nat. I slunk over to their table in the cafeteria, my eyes still red and bloodshot from yesterday. My performance was worthy of an Oscar.

'Will you let me explain?' I began, pulling up a chair to sit down. They both seemed embarrassed, confused and a bit standoffish. My voice faltered, which wasn't put on because I really was nervous. 'I . . . I should have told you how bad things were at home. I just haven't been coping and it's making me . . . really bad-tempered and a bit weird.' The first tear rolled down my cheek and on to the ugly plastic table. Several more followed and I wiped my face with one hand.

The reaction was immediate. They both moved over and put their arms around me.

'Why didn't you tell us?' Hannah cried. 'We could have helped.'

'We knew you were stressed,' Nat added. 'You've

coped with so much; it was bound to get to you eventually.'

The group hug lasted for minutes until I broke free. 'Mum's going to get some help – talk to people and try some counselling.'

Nat pummelled my arm until it hurt. 'That's great. I'm going to buy you a double latte with chocolate sprinkles to celebrate.'

'I don't deserve you two.' I sniffed some more. 'Thanks for being so understanding.'

'That's what friends are for,' Hannah declared, just as Genevieve walked through the door. Our eyes met and time stood still. She tried to compose her expression at the sight of our three happy shiny faces, but she failed miserably. I saw rage and disbelief fighting one other. She moved forward, attempting to smile, but it looked more like a grimace.

And now for the real scene-stealer. I stood up, dried my tears and walked towards her. My arms enveloped her slim body and she immediately recoiled, but I held on grimly, enjoying her discomfort. We were locked together in a weird symbiotic embrace and I could almost believe that some of her blood was now coursing through my veins.

My voice was deliberately raised so that everyone could hear. 'Sorry if I made you feel unwelcome. That's not like me at all. I've had some problems at home.'

'It's OK,' she muttered ungraciously. 'I really wasn't bothered.'

'No. It was awful of me. You do forgive me?'

'Yes. Of course,' she replied woodenly.

'And we're friends?'

I let go of her and she flinched as though she'd been struck. Nat had turned away for a minute, her purse open, asking Hannah for change. Genevieve took advantage of their distraction.

'Over my dead body,' she whispered malevolently.

I threw back my head and laughed like a drain. 'Genevieve! You've got a wicked sense of humour.'

She wasn't expecting this reaction and the flush that spread across her face gave me a thrill of power. I'd seen a chink in her armour and I was determined not to let up. For the next hour I laughed, swivelled on my chair and kept up a stream of bright brittle chatter to show everyone how completely at ease I was. I made sure to include Genevieve in every conversation and continually used her name, even shortening it to Gen. Her green eyes grew larger with disgust. The bad vibes between us were so strong I thought everyone must be able to feel them, but when I glanced at Nat and Hannah there was no recognition.

After a while, the strangest thing started to happen – Genevieve began to droop before my very eyes, like a wilting flower. The more I acted, and the more I talked, and the more I pretended that she didn't get under my skin, the weaker she became, as though we were in a tug of war and I was winning. I blinked, wondering if my eyes were playing tricks on me. Her eyes went dull, her speech dried up until she spoke only in monosyllables and even her hair seemed to lose its lustre. She was the invisible one now, while I glowed.

After lunch Nat and Hannah went to classes, which left Genevieve and me alone together. Part of me actually relished this as I tried to stop my own Cheshire Cat grin from filling my face.

'Think you're clever?' she said.

'No, I don't.'

'Whatever you're up to, it won't work . . .'

'You're the one playing games.'

She moved closer, her eyes almost hypnotizing me. 'Don't underestimate me. It really isn't a game.'

I squared up to her, straightening my back and lifting my chin. 'It's obvious you crave attention and don't care how you get it.'

She spoke with real menace. 'Don't practise your amateur psychology on me. You don't know what you're dealing with.'

I gave a mock shiver. 'Ooh, you're terrifying me.' She didn't move a muscle and could stare for ages without blinking. Eventually I had to look away. 'I don't dislike you, Genevieve, and I don't hold grudges.'

'Obviously, Katy, I'm not trying hard enough. When this is over you'll detest me so much you'll want to . . .'

She left the rest unsaid. I gave my best benevolent smile, remembering Luke's advice to stay calm. 'We're not the same. I don't feel that way. If you must know,

I feel sorry for you . . . all that hatred must eat you up inside.'

She studied me with contempt and moved away, slinging her bag over one shoulder. 'You're wrong,' she said easily. 'It's what keeps me alive and makes me strong.'

On my way out I bumped right into Merlin. He did an about-turn, taking a few steps backwards and looking me up and down.

'There's something different about you.'

'Is there?' I teased. I didn't have to look in a mirror, I could feel my skin shining and my hair bouncing with victory.

'You look so amazing . . . no . . . I mean, you always look amazing, but today you look especially amazing. Your eyes are so . . . luminous.'

He leaned forward and ran his fingers through my curls. 'When the painting's finished, I want it to reflect your face right now, this very second.'

I grabbed his hand and pulled him into a door recess, not even caring if the college principal walked by and suspended us for inappropriate behaviour. My cheeks burned with his long hot kisses. How could I have even thought about Genevieve taking him away from me?

'Katy, we're leaving right now,' he croaked. 'We'll sneak away together . . . go somewhere, anywhere . . .'

'I can't. I've already been seen by Miss Clegg.'

'Tell her you're ill.'

'I can't afford to miss any work.'

'After college then.'

'I promised Mum I'd come straight home.'

He sighed with disappointment. 'You always seem to be rushing somewhere or fretting about your mum.'

I stood on tiptoe and and held his face between my hands. 'We *will* be together . . . soon.'

He closed his eyes. 'Is that a promise?'

'It's a promise.'

'Katy Rivers . . . you're absolutely amazing,' Merlin said, gluing his lips to mine.

'You wouldn't believe anything horrible about me?' I panted, as we finally pulled apart.

'Never. Why would I?'

A sudden feeling of dread swept over me. 'Someone might do or say things that'll make me look really . . . bad.'

'It wouldn't alter what I think of you.'

'Honest?' I grinned.

'Honest.' He grinned back, kissing my nose.

I sheepishly crept into my next class late, jealously guarding the memory of every touch and every word that had passed between us. He saw the real Katy. Nat and Hannah might waver, but Genevieve could never succeed in poisoning Merlin's mind against me. I drifted off, replaying everything in my head, delicious prickles of excitement running through me. It didn't last for long. I came down to earth with sudden terror, remembering my promise and realizing just what I'd agreed to. I needed some advice, and quickly.

CHAPTER ELEVEN

Hannah pushed open her bedroom door with one foot, her arms full, and threw everything on to the bed.

'Chick-flick DVDs, popcorn, muffins, mags, smoothies, marshmallows, chocolate spread, nail varnish, hair tongs, make-up box . . . This is a great idea of yours, Katy.'

Nat lay against the pillow reading. She burst open the packet of popcorn and crunched madly. 'We haven't had a girlie night in for ages.'

Hannah picked up her hula hoop and began gyrating her hips wildly. Even just hanging around the house in a slouchy tracksuit without make-up, her hair scraped off her face, she still looked great. 'What's first, Katy? Movie or hairstyle? Who fancies a beehive?'

'Just wanted a chat really,' I mumbled. 'About . . . things.'

Nat immediately closed her magazine and shuffled towards me. 'This is serious.'

'No, no, it isn't,' I protested feebly. 'But some things are a bit . . . personal and need more . . . privacy.'

Hannah's eyes looked huge in her delicate face. She dropped the hoop and joined us on the bed and now I was sandwiched between them both. I flopped backwards, keeping my feet on the floor, and stared at the pink chandelier, unsure if I was ready to open up. Her room was so cool, decorated in a French shabby chic style with duck-egg-blue walls, a canopy over her bed, and a series of blown-up prints from her last visit to Paris, all showing Hannah next to famous landmarks.

'What've you done?' Nat asked bluntly.

I breathed in deeply. 'Mmm . . . something a bit out of character.'

Hannah reached over and covered Nat's ears. 'She shouldn't listen to this – she's wanted to be a nun since she was seven.'

Nat blew a raspberry. 'I have not.'

'You saw *The Sound of Music* stage show and started to wear a veil and call yourself Sister Natalie.'

Nat threw her shoe at Hannah, missing by miles. 'Shut up and let Katy get on with it.'

I'd started to giggle and it was ages before I could speak. 'Well . . . it's like this . . . Merlin has asked me to go camping with him . . . just for one night . . . and I've agreed.'

Hannah's hands flew up to her face. 'Oh wow, that's awesome.'

'It's soon,' Nat commented in a completely different tone.

'I know it's soon,' I answered defensively. 'I mean, we haven't been together long, but it feels like I've known Merlin forever and he admitted he wanted to be with me the first time he saw me but he was slow getting started . . .'

'He did take his time,' Hannah agreed.

'But he's making up for it now.' I blushed.

'Katy's in *luuurve*,' Nat gently mocked.

Hannah sat up on her knees, her face glowing. 'Are you?'

I held out my hands. 'Think so . . . but it's never happened before so I'm not sure.'

She peered at me inquisitively. 'Symptoms?'

'Well . . . I've got permanent butterflies . . . palpitations, insomnia, weird dreams, fever, inability to think . . . it feels as if I'm ill.'

Being in love *is* an illness,' Hannah answered knowledgeably. 'I read somewhere that a scientist analysed all the physical symptoms and it was the same as being temporarily insane.'

'That's helpful.' I grinned.

Nat turned her mathematical brain to the problem. 'Statistically the chance of meeting your soulmate is 720,000,000 to one against.'

'That's so unfair,' Hannah cried. 'How can you improve the odds?'

'You can't. It's completely random.'

'This makes it all the more amazing,' I said dreamily. 'Merlin and I being in the right place and the right time to meet like this. It was meant to be.'

'You must be sure about how he feels,' Nat commented.

'Of course,' I answered quickly, but then had to backtrack slightly. 'Well, almost sure. Merlin is amazing, but sometimes . . . it's like I'm fighting for his full attention because he can be so . . . deep and . . . preoccupied.'

'Sure he's not just playing hard to get?' Nat joked. She stirred a smoothie with a straw and made a loud sucking noise as she drank. 'We want all the gory details.'

I looked from one face to the other. 'Well . . . it's like a railway station in Merlin's house with all those *artists* milling about, and we want to be alone . . . that's all.'

'That's all?'

'Yes, just a chance to watch the sun going down and wake up in each other's arms.'

Nat began to play on an imaginary violin while Hannah tickled my neck. 'Are you really that stupid? To wake up together you have to sleep together first.'

'It's a tent . . . we'll be in sleeping bags.'

She gripped my shoulders and spoke to me in an exaggeratedly slow voice as if I was a child or really stupid. 'You do know what you've agreed to, Katy? It won't be like camping with the Girl Guides. He'll have *other* ideas.'

Nat rolled over and kicked her legs in the air, convulsed with laughter. Soon I joined her, feeling all the tension of the past few weeks draining away from me. The banter continued for another hour or so, interspersed with marshmallows dipped in chocolate spread. We talked about every boy we'd ever dated, and *exactly* what we'd done – which didn't take long in my case: a few gross kisses with lots of saliva.

'There's something else I have to confess,' I began, chocolate smeared across my chin. 'I can't do this alone, I need an alibi. Maybe I could say I was staying here?'

Hannah looked slightly crestfallen. 'Mum and Dad are cool, but they hate me lying to them. If they found out . . .'

'It's only one night, so they won't find out. I've already set the scene at home and said your parents are going away and you don't want to be alone.'

'What if your mum meets them by chance?'

'No chance of that. She hardly goes out, and she'd ring my mobile if she wanted to speak to me.'

'Merlin isn't pressuring you, Katy?' Nat asked, sounding a note of caution.

'No, he's not like that.'

'You might not even realize he's doing it.'

I smiled with contentment and didn't care how nauseating I looked. 'No, this feels just right somehow.'

Nat opened Hannah's laptop. 'Let's put it on Facebook then. Katy's in luurve and she's ready to . . .'

She stopped and stared at the screen. With each second that passed her face slowly blanched. She opened her mouth, but no words came out and her bottom lip began to judder. I'd never seen Nat like this and it was awful to watch, like witnessing a car crash in slow motion and being unable to help. She momentarily raised her eyes and they rested on me. I didn't have a clue why, but there was something in her gaze that made me feel immediately guilty. I looked to Hannah for an explanation, but she just shook her head in bewilderment. Nat eventually gave a strangled sob and fled from the room with Hannah in pursuit. I heard the bathroom door lock and the handle rattle several times as Hannah tried to talk to her through the door. I was left sitting alone on the bed, totally confused.

It felt like prying, but curiosity got the better of me and I turned the laptop round to see what she'd accessed. As I began to read I physically shrank into myself. On Nat's Facebook page was humiliation on a scale never before seen. There were numerous comments posted from people at college about Nat being in love with Adam, but worst were the love spells. It looked as if everyone had got together and written their own – some just cringe-making, some completely brutal. No, this was beyond humiliation, and of course it would spread – no wonder Nat was so upset. I distractedly munched my way through the rest of the popcorn, trying to imagine how I'd feel if this was me and unable to come up with anything to console her.

A wan figure with pink swollen eyes eventually emerged from the bathroom. She walked towards me, stopped, and said just four words: 'Who did you tell?'

I hadn't seen this coming at all. 'No one,' I cried.

'Of course I didn't. It definitely wasn't me. I wouldn't tell anyone.'

'Only you and I knew about the love spell, Katy. You suggested it at the craft fair.'

I put one hand on my heart. 'I haven't mentioned it to another soul, I swear, and I didn't call it a love spell . . . you did. I just don't understand. Adam isn't even in our college, and not that many people know him.'

Both of them now looked at me and a shadow seemed to pass between us. I knew straight away what this meant – they doubted me.

Nat attempted a watery smile. 'If you swear you didn't say anything, then I believe you.'

Even now she refused to get angry and was trying to trust me. It was just like Nat to be so forgiving, and that made it so much worse. I hadn't done anything wrong, but I *felt* completely guilty. After this the atmosphere was ruined and I had to get away. I gave Nat a hug and made my way home. It was only 8 p.m. and I texted Luke as I walked, hoping to offload some of my angst on to him.

He texted me straight back. `Operation Genevieve - might have something to interest you X`

'You look like one of those cartoon characters with a rain cloud over their head,' he joked, noticing my glum expression as soon as he opened the door.

I trudged upstairs after him, my whole body drooping and my feet leaden. I sprawled across his bed and told him what had happened.

'I'm sure Genevieve is involved,' I complained, 'but I've no proof. Targeting me is one thing, but hurting Nat just tears me to pieces. At this rate I won't have any friends left.'

Luke nodded understandingly. 'I know . . . which is why you have to fight back.' He took a piece of paper from his bag and handed it to me. 'Don't get too excited. It might be something, or it might turn out to be nothing . . .'

My eyes quickly scanned the page. It was a copy of a newspaper article about a fire that had killed a married couple. I gave a tired sigh.

'Look at the date it happened,' he urged. 'Christmas Eve, 2001. You said Genevieve's parents died on Christmas Eve when she was seven, so . . . do the math,' he twanged.

'But she told people her parents died in a car accident,' I pointed out. 'And what about the name? These people are called Jane and Paul Morton, Genevieve's surname is Paradis.'

Luke blew out several times and joined his hands together in an arch, resting his chin on his fingertips. 'I checked and cross-checked all the fatal accidents and incidents over a two-year period across the entire country. This is the only one on a Christmas Eve where an only child, a daughter, was left orphaned.'

'What was the daughter's name?'

'Grace.'

I jumped off the bed and clutched my head, trying to think straight. 'That would mean Genevieve had changed her name. And lied about the crash.'

'Anything's possible.'

'Then . . . she could have lied about the date as well.'

'Of course,' Luke acknowledged, 'but in my experience, when people lie there's usually a grain of truth . . . and that date is so specific.'

I moved to the whiteboard, hoping for inspiration. 'She *is* a complete mystery because she has no past. She could pretend to be anyone and tell people any story about her life.'

Luke's eyebrows did something alarming and almost reached his hairline. 'But . . . is it worth checking out?'

I nodded eagerly. 'No one who's ever met Genevieve would forget her easily.'

'The fire was in a small country village, outside York, called . . . hang on . . . Lower Croxton. We'll drive over there tomorrow and talk to the locals. Do a bit of digging around.'

I winced slightly. 'Tomorrow I'm supposed to be seeing Merlin . . . but . . . he wouldn't mind this once. I'll think up an excuse.'

Luke seemed surprised. 'You'll not tell him the truth?'

No . . . it's just a small fib, and this is so important. I'll phone him later. When it's all over he'll understand.'

'We can set off early,' Luke suggested.

I closed my eyes in excitement. 'Shall we go undercover?'

'You can wear the fake beard and glasses, Kat, and I'll . . . just go as I am.'

I began hitting him with one of his pillows and didn't stop until he promised to stop taking the mickey out of me.

CHAPTER TWELVE

The thrill of being able to retaliate at last somehow cushioned the awful memory of Nat's hurt face looking at me in accusation. I barely slept and woke up before seven, tense and hyper as if I'd downed a double espresso before breakfast. I threw open my wardrobe and surveyed the contents. The weather had turned cooler, which meant I needed something warm, and we were heading for the sticks, so I needed practical shoes in case we had to trek across fields or dodge a herd of cows or do whatever people did in the countryside. I settled on combats and a waterproof jacket that Mum had bought for my geography field trip, along with sensible boots I normally wouldn't be seen dead in. It might be an advantage to look older, so I slapped on some make-up and tried sweeping my hair up, attempting sophistication, but it made me look even more of a schoolgirl so I left it down. I couldn't face breakfast but filled a small bag with crisps, biscuits, chocolate and bottled water.

Luke looked decidedly dishevelled in old jeans and a thick sweater, sporting just-rolled-out-of-bed hair and stubble. I couldn't help feeling how nice it was to be heading somewhere different. Our town seemed so much more claustrophobic now that Genevieve was everywhere.

'Doesn't Laura mind you giving up your day like this?'

He gave a lopsided smile. 'Laura likes to hit the shops on a Saturday. You've actually saved me from a fate worse than death.'

I was relieved. I had been worried in case our trip was a source of friction between them.

'What about Merlin?'

'I told him Mum wasn't well . . . it's only a tiny lie. I want to see him of course, but this is too important to put off.'

'Doesn't he think this thing with Genevieve is weird?'

'Can't really explain it to him,' I admitted. 'His mum thinks she's great and talented and she just fools everyone.'

'Poor Kat. She's got everyone caught in her web, hasn't she?'

'Kind of.' I turned my face towards the window and watched the landscape fly by, wondering when life had got so complicated.

'Ever been to Yorkshire?' he asked with a yawn.

I shook my head.

'We spent a few holidays here when I was a kid,' Luke began. 'It has loads of atmosphere – windswept moors, rolling hills and fells, potholes, forests, waterfalls, valleys, not to mention all the historic spooky buildings. In fact, York is the most haunted city in Britain.'

'You sound like an advert for the tourist board.' I laughed.

He gave me a sly wink. 'I didn't mention all the famous witches who lived there.'

'I'm off witches now . . . remember?'

Luke seemed to liven up as we hit the motorway and spent the next two hours telling me funny stories about his job and his boss. For the first time in weeks I felt myself again. It was almost as if Genevieve's hold on me relaxed the further we travelled.

'Phew . . . we're definitely in the country now.' I hastily closed my window as the smell of manure wafted in.

Luke consulted his satnav. 'Almost there. Only five more miles to go.'

He pulled over into a lay-by to let a tractor go the other way as the road had become single-lane traffic only. As far as the eye could see there were patchwork fields planted with row after row of cabbages and bright yellow rapeseed. The wind cut through the open landscape, shaking the newly bare trees and stirring up the fallen leaves. I could feel its force even though we were safely protected in the car.

'This is it,' Luke announced, and pulled over on to a grass verge.

The village was no more than fifty or so properties dotted around a green. Most of the buildings looked like former workers' cottages, with small paned windows and low door frames. A few new-build houses contrasted harshly with the old worn bricks and slate roofs. A farmhouse sat proudly on a hill with several barns around. It took me a moment to work out what was odd about Lower Croxton – the silence. I'd imagined jolly farmers riding tractors, sun-kissed children dashing through the corn and women in bonnets carrying baskets of newly laid eggs and warm milk, but there wasn't a person in sight.

'Everyone must be inside,' Luke said.

'We'll never be inconspicuous here,' I complained, noticing the twitching of a net curtain. 'This isn't the kind of place where anyone simply passes through.'

Luke stretched as he got out of the car and looked around. 'We should find the local inn or pub – anywhere the locals hang out.'

I pulled a face at the word 'locals', and Luke pulled my hood over my eyes. 'It isn't the *Village of the Damned*, Kat.'

I frowned. 'Doesn't seem to be a pub around.'

Luke pointed straight ahead. 'What about that building? There's a notice outside.'

'It used to be the dairy,' I said without thinking, and he stared at me in amazement.

'You know that for certain?'

'No.' I laughed in embarrassment, not wanting to explain the déjà-vu feeling. 'I mean, it looks like it was once a dairy.'

We walked towards the sign which advertised fresh

farm produce, and Luke took my arm in a strangely old-fashioned way.

'I'm too young to act like an old married woman,' I complained.

He stopped and gave me an appraising glance. 'When I went away to uni you were still a brat with braces on your goofy teeth.'

'You visited plenty of times in three years, Luke,' I said. 'You were just too busy enjoying yourself to notice me.'

'I'm noticing you now,' he said, and for some reason my stomach felt peculiar. 'And you're still a brat, Kat.'

I managed to kick the back of his calf as we walked. He chased me to the green and wrestled me to the ground with a rugby tackle while I screamed at him to get off, wondering what the villagers would make of us.

'We'll start with the farmer's wife,' Luke said, brushing grass from his jeans. 'She'll be fifteen stone with ruddy cheeks and arms like a wrestler. She's bound to have lived here for fifty years and know every birth and death for miles around. Her daughters will look like milkmaids and her sons will wear dungarees and chew pieces of straw.'

I didn't even smile because panic began to rise. 'We can't just blunder in there. We have to work out a story first.' Luke completely ignored me and kept on walking. 'Luke? We have to get our stories straight . . .

He waved one hand dismissively. 'Just leave it to me. I'm a journalist. This is what we do best.'

The girl sitting on a high stool had raven hair, a white face, purple lips and kohled eyes. The leather miniskirt, fishnet tights and Doc Martens didn't quite go with the milkmaid image, nor did the piercings in her nose, eyebrow or cheek. I had to bite my lip to stop myself from laughing out loud as Luke's jaw dropped. She didn't seem remotely interested in why we were here or make comments about 'strangers' and 'not being from these parts'. She looked us up and down with a sulky expression, then went back to reading a book. Luke was dumbstruck, despite my attempts to elbow him in the ribs. I noticed a small round table and two chairs in one corner.

'Do you sell sandwiches or drinks?' I asked hopefully.

'I can do a ham or cheese roll with a hot drink,' she said, turning a page.

'Two ham rolls with tea, please. We've had quite a long drive.'

No reaction. She disappeared into the back while Luke and I stared at each other.

'Milkmaid!' I hissed, and Luke kicked me under the table.

'She looks like something from a zombie movie,' he whispered.

Luke didn't share my love of old properties so I didn't bother enthusing about the thick crumbly walls or the beauty of the ancient crossbeams. Everything had been left original and exposed down to the tiny recessed windows. We heard a rustle of material and I put one finger on my lips to warn Luke not to speak. A woman bustled in, carrying two plates, and I deliberately refused to catch his eye. She was a caricature of a farmer's wife, even more exaggerated than his description – huge dimpled red face framed with grey hair, and an apple-shaped body under a large apron.

'Well, well,' she began, setting the plates in front of us. 'What brings you to our neck of the woods?'

I suppressed a smile. 'We're . . . just passing through. We wanted to take the scenic route, see some countryside. We're from the city . . . smoke, smog and all that.'

'We have seen cows before,' Luke joked at my expense.

I pulled a stupid face at him behind her back. 'Have you lived here long?'

'All my married life,' she answered stoutly. 'The farm has been in my husband's family for three generations. You're sitting in what used to be the dairy.'

Luke made a noise of surprise but I ignored him. 'So you'd know everyone from the village?'

Her eyes darted suspiciously between us. 'I would.'

Luke opened his mouth to speak, but I jumped in first. 'It's just that . . . I'm trying to organize a family reunion, and there're people who live in this village who might be . . . sort of relatives of mine.'

'So you haven't really come to admire the countryside,' the farmer's wife commented, vigorously stirring a pot of tea. I was parched, but she made no effort to bring it to our table. 'And what's their name?'

'They're called Morton, Jane and Paul Morton.'

A definite shadow crossed her face. 'Are they close relatives?'

I felt a familiar flush starting at my neck and spreading to my cheeks. 'Noo . . . just a second cousin, once removed, on my mother's side. They lost touch ages ago.'

The shrewd eyes bored into mine. 'But you're sure they live here, in Lower Croxton?'

I squirmed because she didn't seem keen to give us any information. 'My mum has an old Christmas card,' I squeaked, 'and this is the last known address.'

The farmer's wife folded her meaty arms and shook her head with regret. 'Well, I'm sorry to be the bearer of bad news. Jane and Paul did live here, but they perished in a house fire years ago.'

I covered my face with both hands. 'How awful!'

She made a tutting noise. 'Everyone in the village was shocked – such a terrible thing to happen. It was on Christmas Eve. I shall never forget . . . no one here could.'

'Is the house . . . ? I mean, is it still standing?'

'It was razed to the ground,' she answered bluntly.

Luke's voice was suitably subdued. 'Were there any survivors? Anyone who escaped the fire?'

The woman moved away from our table and busied herself behind the counter. 'No. Now I must get on. Just leave two pounds in the jar by the door, and good day to you both.'

I was shocked at her sudden departure and called after her, 'But what about . . . ?'

Luke leaned over and clamped one hand across my mouth. I shook it off angrily. 'She hasn't told us about their daughter. She must have known her.'

Luke refused to speak until we were outside. We both sat in silence while I watched him finish his sandwich, take a final slurp of tea, count out some change and put his jacket back on. I angrily trailed after him with my head down, trying to escape the wind.

'Sorry about that,' he apologized. 'I didn't want her to hear us.'

'But why would she lie? We read all about Grace Morton in the article. It's impossible she wouldn't have known her . . . it's such a small village.'

'We can't bully her into telling us,' Luke answered resignedly.

'Let's ask someone else,' I announced, and before Luke could stop me I waved my hand at a man working on one of the cottages. He noticed me but carried on sanding a window frame and didn't react as I approached.

'We're looking for some information on the Morton family who used to live here. I wonder if you knew them.'

His answer was curt to the point of rudeness. 'No, I didn't.'

'Maybe someone else? Someone from the cottage might remember them.'

'I'm certain they wouldn't,' he grunted.

Luke pulled me by my hood in the direction of his car. 'There's one thing I've learned doing my job.'

'What's that?'

'You can tell as much from someone's silence as you can from their words.'

I was glad to be back in the car but annoyed that our journey seemed to have been for nothing and now Luke was talking in riddles. 'You mean, it's important . . . the fact that no one wants to talk to us? How?'

'I don't know yet, but I'll be glad to get out of here. This place really is starting to give me the creeps.'

He put his foot on the accelerator and the tyres locked and spun on the gravel. With a screech he finally took off.

'I know what you mean,' I muttered, more to myself than to Luke.

I took one final, defeated look out of the window and my hand flew to my mouth in horror. A cyclist was approaching from the left and there was no time to shout a warning. There was a sickening thud as she rode straight into the car.

CHAPTER THIRTEEN

Luke's face was ashen as he threw open the car door and leaped out. I followed closely behind and tried to stop an elderly lady from standing up, terrified she'd broken something. We were both amazed when she bounced to her feet and dusted herself down amid a flurry of underskirts, thick tights, a long tweed skirt and mac. She probably only weighed seven stone and was lost inside the various layers.

'It was my fault entirely,' she insisted. 'I suffer from cataracts, and you can see the unfortunate result.'

'Are you sure you're OK?' Luke whispered. I pretended not to notice that he had leaned against a tree to steady himself.

'I'm fine, my shopping broke the fall.'

Her many clothes would probably have protected her anyway, but she'd landed on several canvas bags that looked decidedly squashed.

'We'll pay for anything that's damaged,' I told her.

'Of course,' Luke echoed. 'It's the least we can do.'

'No, it'll be fine, really.' She sighed stoically. 'I've nothing breakable, just a slab of cheese, some leeks, potatoes and a few rashers of bacon . . .'

Now that he was certain the old lady was unhurt, Luke gazed longingly at his warm car, but I pinched him on the arm to let him know we couldn't abandon her like this.

'We'll see you home,' I suggested, 'make sure you're not a bit . . . wobbly.'

The old lady gestured at Luke and clucked mischievously, 'Your friend looks in a worse condition than me.'

She didn't stop me from supporting her arm though, as we walked. Reluctantly Luke locked the car and followed us. Little more than a hundred metres on she stopped outside a thatched cottage with a wooden sign announcing 'Snuff-in-the-Wind', and rifled in her bag for a key.

'Now, will you stay for a cup of tea?'

Luke politely declined. 'Sorry, but we've got a long drive ahead. We need to get back.'

I apologized again to the old lady as a hand attached itself to my hood and pulled me away for the second time that day. We'd probably taken no more than ten steps when a voice called after us, 'So you don't want to know about the Morton family?'

We stopped. 'Who told you that?' I asked with surprise.

She smiled knowingly. 'News travels fast around here.'

The inside of the cottage was like stepping back in time – low ceiling beams stained dark chocolate, ancient furniture and an uneven tiled floor covered by a large rug. A black cat lay curled into a ball, warming itself in front of a crackling cast-iron stove. The old lady was nowhere in sight, but there was the sound of water being run in the adjoining room.

Luke's eyes narrowed, trying to adjust to the dim light. He scowled. 'She looks really sinister . . . thin face, big nose, luring us in here. She'll be boiling a pot to cook us in, you wait and see.'

'Shh . . . she's coming back.'

'And I'm not drinking nettle tea laced with frogspawn.'

The old lady emerged from a narrow corridor carrying two cups that rattled in their saucers. I jumped up and took them off her.

'Tea always tastes better in a china cup. Don't you agree, dear?'

Luke grimaced as he took a cup from me.

'So . . . let me see what I can tell you about Jane and Paul Morton.'

I nodded. 'If you would . . . anything you can remember.'

The old lady rubbed her hands together in front of the stove and adjusted her position in a worn armchair which had been patched with squares of different-coloured fabric. She looked as though she enjoyed having an audience and moistened her lips to speak. 'They kept themselves to themselves, that's for sure. I think they moved here to do just that . . . shun the world. They were deeply religious people but . . . a bit too fire and brimstone for me. Not much joy, I'm afraid. They were more concerned with finding sin everywhere.'

I tried not to appear too eager. 'How long before the fire did they move here?'

'I think . . . no, I'm certain . . . it was four years. We don't have many new families and it sticks in the mind.'

I cleared my throat nervously. 'Were you . . . I mean . . . did you see the fire that night?'

She nodded gravely. 'It was stormy, and the flames were twenty feet high . . . the wind fanned them wildly . . . bits of debris, soot and ash were flying around as the whole village tried to stop it from spreading . . . It was then we saw her . . .'

'Who?' I demanded, but the old lady seemed far away, as if she'd forgotten we were there. It was another minute before she spoke again.

'Walking out of the house through the flames . . . strolling almost, as if she didn't need to hurry.'

'Who walked out of the house?' I repeated.

'Grace did,' she breathed. 'Grace Morton gazed around with those unnerving green eyes of hers. It sent a shiver down my spine.'

'Was Grace their daughter?' Luke asked.

'Yes. She was only seven, but she had a way about her that made you think she was years older.'

The handle of the white china cup was so small that I had to pinch my thumb and forefinger together to pick it up. I wondered how Luke was coping and realized that he had his big hands wrapped around the cup itself, ignoring the handle entirely.

'So Grace survived that night?' I commented. 'It's just that the lady in the farm shop said no one did.'

The old lady sniffed. 'People don't like to talk. That night is something we've tried to forget around here, and you should do the same.'

I was unsure what she meant. 'We should forget about Grace? Why?'

There was a noncommittal grunt and she raised her bony shoulders. 'Maybe it's not my place to say, but I think you should leave the past where it is. Grace always made us all a little . . . uncomfortable. Her stare could turn a person to stone.'

Luke gave a sceptical cough. 'She was just a child.'

The old lady folded her arms and her tone became more defensive. 'She didn't speak like a child, and certainly the other children in the village were wary of her. I think that suited her parents – they didn't believe in school anyway and taught her at home.'

We all lapsed into silence except for a contented purring from the cat, but I was worried that we were wasting time. 'And you don't know how Grace escaped the fire?'

The old lady's face darkened. 'No. It was unearthly the way she glided into the cold night air.'

Luke clenched his fists. 'So . . . this small girl managed to walk through twenty-foot flames like it was some kind of . . . miracle.'

'I wouldn't call it that,' was the sharp reply. 'I've lived long enough to know there're things in this world that can't be explained and things I wouldn't want to confront. Grace is one of them, and I don't need a smarmy young man telling me otherwise.'

Luke leaned back in his chair, surprised by this attack. The heat from the stove was so great that I was having trouble breathing. 'And where is she now?'

'She has an aunt and an uncle who live just outside York. He's a vicar at St John's church. They took her in, and that's the last we heard.'

Luke was growing impatient. His foot tapped on the rug and he seemed to want to twitch all over. I drank the last of my tea and got up to leave, thanking the old lady. As we reached the door she became more animated. 'Our village might be tiny, but we have a claim to fame.'

'What's that?' I smiled.

'The witch trial, dear. It took place in the city, naturally, but the accused was from this very village.'

'Really?' I felt Luke close by, prodding me in the back and quietly snorting.

'And the case was all the more chilling because the woman who was hanged was condemned by her own daughter . . . who was only a child herself at the time.'

I deliberately refused to look at Luke. 'So . . . she had her own mother put to death?'

'Yes, and the rumour was that *she* was really the witch but was far too clever to get caught. Her disguise was perfect, you see – she inhabited the body of a beautiful child, but evil always comes through in the end.'

It was impossible to think of a suitable reply. 'Er . . . OK. Thanks again . . . for the tea and everything.'

Luke strode on ahead as an arm suddenly reached out and pulled me closer. The skin that touched mine was the colour and texture of parchment and a pair of lips whispered into my ear, 'You have the gift, but you don't realize it yet. You must find her flaw.'

I pulled away with fright and caught up with Luke, who finally gave vent to his anger. 'What's she doing riding a bike if she can't see? And she is clearly nuts. You know what she's getting at, don't you? Making out that Grace was some sort of reincarnated witch.'

'I didn't see that connection,' I fibbed. 'Besides, it's just a story.'

'They thought anyone was a witch back then. I mean, look at you, Katy – red hair, green eyes, and you have a cat . . . you'd have been first on the bonfire.'

'Thanks for that vote of confidence,' I drawled.

'And what about the other stuff?' he complained. 'A seven-year-old couldn't walk through flames unharmed.'

'She kept talking about her eyes,' I said softly. 'No one who'd ever met Genevieve would forget those eyes.'

'So you think it's her?'

'I just don't know.'

'She said the girl had family outside the city. If Genevieve used to be Grace, then she wouldn't end up on the streets if she had relatives to look after her.'

'Maybe she spooked them as well.

'Does she have any scars you've noticed?'

'No,' I answered bitterly. 'She has gorgeous peachy skin.'

Luke's mouth set in a determined line that I recognized. 'I think it's a false lead . . . much too far-fetched.'

As we got into the car I bit the inside of my cheek, resolving not to tell him about the old lady's final words to me.

'There's still something odd about all this, Luke. She warned us to stay away from Grace as if she's frightened or there's something she's not telling us.'

'She's probably lonely and eccentric and just wanted someone to talk to.'

I felt crushed and couldn't hide it. 'You don't believe it's Genevieve?'

Luke smiled sadly. 'No, it's too fantastical . . . the suspicious villagers and the fire that didn't burn her and that strange old woman and her superstitious warnings.'

I reached out one hand to stop him from driving off and impulsively flung open the car door. 'I've left my scarf behind . . . won't be a second.'

I ran back to the cottage, my heart thumping, overcome by a compelling urge to question the old lady about her strange advice. I banged on the door, but no one answered and I peered in through the tiny windows, figuring that she must be hard of hearing. I looked again, rubbed my eyes and looked for a third time, but I wasn't imagining it – the warm cosy room we'd just left looked cold and bare; no crackling stove or lazy cat warming itself. I banged again and then gave up as Luke tooted his horn. I made sure that my face gave nothing away as I got back into the car.

Luke started the engine. 'Ready to go?'

I nodded and we moved off, both of us relieved to be on the only road out of here.

CHAPTER FOURTEEN

She was the most beautiful child that I'd ever seen – hair like spun gold and skin like porcelain, radiating innocence. She glided up the winding staircase without her feet touching the wood and floated along the corridor into the room with the set of mirrors. I followed her, for the first time without any apprehension or fear. This was Genevieve, uncorrupted and pure. She beckoned me to sit next to her and reached out her hand to hold mine. Our fingers threaded together. But something wasn't quite right: her tiny, perfectly round pink nails were stinging my palm and I tried to loosen my grip, but I couldn't and the pain was growing steadily worse. I looked down and her nails were now curled yellow claws boring into my hand, droplets of scarlet blood staining the floor. She wouldn't let go; she'd never let go. I didn't want to lift my head, but I had to look into the mirror, and Genevieve's reflection was that of a wizened old crone with a hooked nose, black teeth and gimlet eyes. She was mocking me, rocking backwards and forwards, her laugh high-pitched and hysterical. I woke with a violent shudder.

Once the horrors of the dream fell away, my first thought was that I had to see Nat. It couldn't wait until college tomorrow. I had to look her in the eye and see if she still believed me now she'd had time to think things over. It might prove painful, but it was something that had to be done for my own sanity. I pulled back the duvet and pointed my toes, searching for my slippers, aware how cold the floorboards suddenly felt. I made a gap in the curtains and noticed small pools of condensation on the window ledges. It seemed like ages since this had happened. In winter it was so cold in my bedroom that my breath was sometimes visible, and once there was actually a layer of ice on the inside of the glass. I pulled my thin robe tight around myself, wondering if it was time to dig out my favourite woolly striped dressing gown and thick pyjamas.

It was only 8 a.m., too early to call Nat, and I felt twitchy thinking about the hours ahead and how I could fill them before finding out whether I had any friends left. My previous insecurity seemed to be returning. Before Nat and Hannah, I was always fearful that girls didn't really want to be my friend and I tried much too hard to be liked. It felt the same now, as though I had to prove myself all over again. I padded down to the kitchen and noticed there were only a couple of spoonfuls of coffee left in the jar, so I made myself a weak cup, waiting for Mum to wake. The kitchen was north facing and never received any light until late afternoon, which made it particularly depressing. I went and sat in the dining room, which had French windows on to the garden, and drank my coffee, deep in thought. My phone beeped and my heart jumped, hoping it might be Nat, but it was only Luke. He must have noticed that my curtains were open.

Don't bother searching for the witch of Lower Croxton. I already have and there's nothing on the Net, not even the hint of an urban legend. Told you that old lady was a fruitcake ha ha X

Luke could be such an unbelievable know-it-all. I was annoyed that even without being aware of all that had happened he had correctly anticipated that I would be fixated by the old lady's words. I sat for a few minutes longer, now consumed by a sinking feeling that the day was going to drag. Merlin was busy with last-minute coursework and Mum was still sleeping so I retreated back upstairs and turned on my computer. Luke thought that he was the only person who was able to do any research and I had the strongest urge to prove him wrong. You didn't have to be a journalist, I told myself with stubborn optimism.

It seemed sensible to dive right in, and my fingers began to type as if they had a life of their own. 'Witch of Lower Croxton' produced nothing specific, as I'd already been warned, so I broadened my search to 'Witches', which was short and to the point. Thousands of websites for modern-day witches and pagans popped up and I clicked on a few of them for some light relief, but then told myself not to get sidetracked. I narrowed it down again to 'Medieval Witches in Britain' and it was impossible to avoid the grisly descriptions of torture, drowning, hanging, beheading and burning. If a witch confessed to something especially evil then a slow-burning wood might be used to make her suffer even more. After death, iron rivets would be driven into her knees and elbows to stop her from rising from her grave. I drained the dregs from my cup with a strange feeling in my stomach.

Mum had gone downstairs and I tore myself away to join her, feeling completely famished. Breakfast was only two slices of cardboard bread and scrambled eggs, but it was more than welcome.

'Do you know anything about witch hunting?' I asked brightly.

She raised her eyebrows and then moved her head from side to side noncommittally. 'I seem to remember the witch finders used to look for devil's marks,' she said slowly, 'which could be anything – freckles, moles, warts or any unusual blemishes.'

I was still hungry and decided to have some cereal. Luke and I hadn't eaten since the sandwiches in the village cafe, which was why I felt so empty inside. I cleared my throat importantly, armed with my newfound knowledge. 'Lots of experts thought the hysteria over witches was the result of a hatred and fear of women . . . by men.'

Mum nodded enthusiastically. 'Most of those put to

death were female. We were considered more devious and cunning.'

'Mmm,' I agreed, 'but . . . women pointed the finger at other women too. Your chances of being persecuted were higher if you were old, ugly, poor or lived alone, and lots of accusations of sorcery began as village disputes. Even children would give testimony in court and be treated as credible witnesses.' I suddenly thought of the old woman's words and shivered.

'That's very interesting, Katy.' Mum smiled. 'Is this college work?'

'Kind of,' I lied.

'If you need any help, just ask. I'm fascinated by your research.'

'Really?'

'Yes, really.'

I went back to my bedroom feeling newly buoyant and sent Nat a text, but she didn't reply immediately, which somehow felt ominous. I went back to my search and trawled through all the documented witch trials around York, but Luke was right, none of the Yorkshire witches fitted the profile of a mother who had been accused by her own daughter. When I next glanced at the clock I'd been on and off my computer for almost three hours and my eyes were beginning to blur.

I got up, stretched, yawned, paced up and down and racked my brains, still intent on proving something to Luke. The old lady had cryptically told me to look for Grace/

Genevieve's flaw, and I was sure she was hinting at finding ways to ward her off. I flexed my fingers as if about to play a piano concerto and went back to Google.

'How to repel a witch.'

As I read my eyes lit up. This was fascinating because the methods were so varied. They ranged from using holly, hawthorn and oak to protect the exterior of a house to burying a cat in your foundations or putting a broomstick or iron sword across the threshold. I heard Mum shouting for me to come down, but something else had caught my eye. It was a short piece about a respected historian who had discovered many strange artefacts in a Grade I listed house that he had rescued from dilapidation. What really drew my attention was that the house was in Appleby, the next village along from Lower Croxton. Luke and I had passed through it on our way home. It was just as quaint but much larger, with its own pub, ancient church and village school. For some reason my fingers trembled as I scrolled down the page.

> Thomas Winter unearthed several unusual artefacts during his renovation of 'Martinwood' and told local reporters that, centuries ago, superstitious items would have been strategically placed with the sole purpose of repelling evil spirits. Thomas himself was of the opinion that the house was haunted by a malevolent presence. However, he later issued an apology and admitted that his report was fabricated to increase interest in the history of the village and boost local tourism.

I traipsed downstairs, my mind whirring. Mum was looking quite smug. She must have sneaked out when I was engrossed and splashed out on some real coffee and gooey chocolate eclairs. She pressed the plunger on the cafetière and poured me a cup. I inhaled the lovely aroma and took a large gulp before posing the question on my mind.

'Mum, why would a respected historian make up a story about his ancient house being haunted and finding all this spooky stuff in it?'

She stroked her chin in deliberation. 'People do all kinds of strange things, Katy.'

'It seems so bizarre,' I persisted, 'despite his explanation.'

'He might have wanted publicity,' Mum suggested, 'or just got really carried away and wanted to find things that weren't there . . . or . . . he might have been really obsessed with witches, like us.' She laughed. 'Isn't it odd we have that in common, Katy?'

I looked at her scathingly. 'Not really, Mum. It's a little thing called genetics.'

'Of course,' she answered breezily, and began blowing on her drink. 'What sort of things did he make up?'

'Dunno.' I shrugged. 'It was a few years ago. Apparently he wrote a column in the local paper because of the interest in his house, but nothing else came up on Google.'

'Have you tried the archives? Most newspapers have them.'

I sat up in my chair with renewed interest, glad that the trail wasn't yet cold. The day wasn't turning out so badly after all. Mum seemed more animated than she had been for a while and I couldn't deny that I was enjoying every minute of my search. I just wished that Nat would contact me to put my mind at rest. I polished off the chocolate eclair, licked my fingers and told Mum I was going to try the archives. My robe flapped open. It was 3 p.m. and I still wasn't dressed.

I sat poised at my desk. I needed to be systematic about this. Thomas Winter's apology had been issued at the beginning of 2007, so his column must have been published earlier than that. I clicked on the archives section, amazed how easy it was to access. There was a small calendar for every month of every year. The paper was only issued weekly, which cut down the search even more. And then I found it, an account of Thomas Winter's journey to restore 'Martinwood', and his discoveries about seventeenth-century life. I skimmed through the boring parts about replicating medieval building techniques, stopping halfway down the page when it grew interesting.

> . . . I began to take apart the fabric of the house and uncovered several items that led me to believe that the residents of 'Martinwood' had felt the need to protect themselves and their dwelling from a malign influence. These included a child's shoe – believed to be a symbol of good luck and protection – and crosses carved into ancient beams together with horseshoes, which legend told would prevent the Devil from entering a property. The

> disturbance of the main fireplace and chimney revealed a ledge or niche concealed about two metres from the hearth. A small block of wood was discovered there, bearing a name – Greta Alice Edwards – together with a crude carving of an eye. In medieval times the chimney was considered important because it was an opening through which malevolent spirits could enter a dwelling. The wood was undoubtedly intended for the flames and this would have been part of a ritual to ward off a person of evil intent. It's impossible to guess why the wood was never burnt.

I read with bated breath because this would mean that the woodblock contained the name of . . . the actual real-life witch from the seventeenth century. If only it hadn't all been a hoax. My eyes were out on stalks as I immersed myself in the story. There was an appendix to the effect that Thomas Winter had checked a local parish register and the named person did exist. She was born in 1675, died in 1691 and was interred in the twelfth-century church of St Mary. I tried to forget that this strange man had used his knowledge to deceive people.

I glanced out of my window. Luke, dressed in a pair of overalls and covered in white dust, was looking up at his roof. He'd mentioned something about helping his dad with work on their house, and normally I'd be interested, but not today. I kept my head down in case he spotted me and dashed stones at my window.

A quick search for 'Martinwood' produced only a small photograph of a black and white timber building so old that it appeared to lean out from its foundations. There wasn't much text, but it seemed to have had a chequered history over the centuries. It had been owned by the local council from the 1960s until 2007, when it had been auctioned to a private bidder. I drummed my fingers on my desk. It was time for another break.

'You look as if you've seen a ghost, Katy . . . or a witch.' Mum laughed raucously at her own joke when she saw my pensive expression.

'I've just read about one,' I sighed, 'but she isn't real. I mean the person is real but she wasn't a witch.'

'Is this the historian? The one who made it all up?'

I nodded glumly.

'Well, never mind,' she replied cheerfully. 'There was a grain of truth in it, and lots of history is blurred with legend.'

'But this was different,' I grumbled. 'He made it all seem so . . . compelling.'

'He's just a good storyteller,' she chuckled. 'Maybe he should abandon history and become a novelist instead.'

I couldn't let it go and didn't want Mum to either. 'But . . . it feels like watching a good movie and never knowing the end.'

'Sometimes,' Mum warned, 'you're a little too inquisitive and fanciful for your own good.'

'Am I?'

'When you were small,' she recalled with a fond smile, 'you were always saying funny things about recognizing places you'd never been before . . . and those terrible nightmares you had.'

'You never said. What were they about?'

'I don't know, Katy, but you used to cry and flail about . . . even in winter you refused to be covered, as if you had a temperature and were . . . burning up.' She swallowed hard. 'But you grew out of it, thankfully.'

'Wow. I don't remember. Guess I must have had a vivid imagination.'

I went back to my room, worried that Nat still hadn't called. When I drifted off to sleep that night my head was full of Mum's words. I couldn't help but wonder why all these strange feelings of recognition and déjà vu had suddenly resurfaced after lying dormant for so many years.

CHAPTER FIFTEEN

Genevieve was a chameleon. She had changed again over the weekend. Her face was now framed with curls, not wiry untamed ones like mine, but soft tumbling ones that bounced and danced in the October sun, golden like the autumn leaves. Her features appeared even more delicate than usual and she wore an ethnic smock over leggings that made her look like a beautiful waif. Whenever I tried to pull off this look I managed to resemble a heifer in a sack. I tried to ignore her, focusing on Nat, who had her back to me. I tugged her sleeve, my heart missing a beat in case I detected hostility in her eyes. But she turned to me and looked as open and friendly as ever.

'Everything OK?' I asked nervously.

She nodded ruefully and whispered. 'Sorry about yesterday. I had to endure quality time with my family . . . no texting allowed. It was torture.'

'What about the . . . you know . . . Facebook thing?'

'I'm just going to brazen it out,' she answered bravely.

'They'll soon be picking on someone else and I'll be yesterday's news.'

My eyes felt moist with relief that she was so cool about everything. It was such a weight off my mind, although I was still livid with Genevieve, who simply refused to be ignored. She came right up to me, vainly fingering her gorgeous curls. Hannah and Nat must have sensed something was going on because I could feel their nervous sidelong glances.

'Love your hair,' I trilled, trying to reassure them.

'Do you?' Genevieve answered casually. 'My straighteners broke and this is the result.'

I stretched out one finger and wound it around a tendril, feeling her cringe at my touch.

'How was your weekend?' she asked pointedly, and something about her knowing smile made my blood run cold. She was probably hoping that Nat would have cut me dead and I was so glad that things seemed the same between us.

'It was fine, thanks.'

We walked into class together. 'Did you do much work on your project, Katy?'

So that was why she was extra smug. It was the final session before our first semester's project was due, and Genevieve's submission was bound to be fabulous. Despite starting college later than the rest of us, she was still streets ahead. I couldn't compete and she knew it.

'I didn't do anything at the weekend,' I admitted. 'But I'd already finished.'

'Good luck then.' She smirked. 'I really hope you do well.'

Her moods were a complete mystery and I was glad to move to my own desk away from her. When she was close by, this battle of wills wore me out and drained all my energy. I slowly unzipped my art folder. Time seemed to stop as I stared, uncomprehendingly, at what was inside. Dazed, I took out each piece and studied it, thinking I was hallucinating or they must belong to someone else. There was a roaring sound in my ears as if I'd been submerged in water, and warm terror engulfed me. My hand-drawn designs were almost obliterated with navy-blue dye and my fabric samples were unrecognizable. Weeks of work ruined. Miss Clegg must have noticed the horror on my face and made her way over. She peered over my shoulder and gave a deep sigh.

'I'm sorry, Katy. You mustn't have used a colourfast solution . . . this can sometimes happen. What a shame it spoiled your other designs.'

My voice was unnaturally high-pitched and panicky. 'But it wasn't like this on Friday. Everything was dry and crisp. I wouldn't have been so stupid . . .'

She smiled sympathetically. 'It could happen to anyone. There's still a week to redo them.'

'It's six weeks' work,' I said, tears filling my eyes. 'I'll never manage to finish, and if I hurry it'll be rubbish and I'll fail and . . .'

She raised her hand to stop me mid-flow and her voice

was kind but firm. 'See how you get on. If you can't finish in time, we can work something out. I know you've put in a lot of effort.' She turned and walked away from me as fast as she could.

I tried to stop my lip from trembling, terrified of breaking down completely. Miss Clegg, my favourite teacher, had witnessed me acting like a drama queen and completely put me in my place. This was almost as bad as having my work ruined. I should have kept my dignity. When I lifted my head from the desk, everyone seemed to be looking my way. It was like the dream I sometimes have when I'm walking the street without any clothes, trying to get home. I felt so naked I actually hugged myself and tried to disappear.

After a few minutes I plucked up the courage to look up again. People were still staring and throwing embarrassed smiles my way. Everyone except one person – Genevieve. She was perfectly focused and engrossed in her own work, appearing oblivious to anything else. The hairs on the back of my neck began to rise again one by one and the first beginnings of suspicion filtered through. She surely couldn't have got to my folder, could she? I always kept it close to me, although on Friday I did leave class for five minutes to go to the office and hand in my sheet of contact numbers. There were plenty of materials lying around, and if she was really clever no one would have noticed.

Why was I so shocked? It was so completely like her to be this underhand and vindictive. She'd already declared war and made it clear that she wanted to destroy my life. But Luke was right. I had to resist the urge to retaliate because it would only rebound on me.

It wasn't that easy. I was so incensed by the injustice of it all that my hands shook and I could barely hold a pencil. I tried to work, but no matter how much I warned myself to stay calm, the anger inside me bubbled away until it reached boiling point. My hair was sticky and I pushed it off my face and used my book as a fan. It felt as if I was suffocating from within, my breathing growing shallower and my throat constricting.

I could stand it no more. I stood up and moved forward like a sleepwalker, my vision cloudy and the room no longer familiar. Genevieve knew what was happening and she was feeding my anger. It felt as if she was inside my mind, fanning this blaze within me, all the time goading me to make a scene. Suddenly I was determined to resist. But I couldn't completely contain my rage. With a tiny cry I ran outside to the corridor and banged my head against the cold of the white and blue wall tiles.

At lunchtime my mouth was so dry that I couldn't swallow. My tuna-melt sandwich had turned to sawdust and even a moist, gooey muffin stuck in my throat. I took huge gulps of scalding coffee, which only made my heart race more. Genevieve arrived in the cafeteria with Nat and Hannah.

'We heard what's happened,' Nat began. 'It's awful.'

'Is there anything we can do to help?' Hannah offered.

I wrinkled my nose and blinked, terrified of blubbing again. 'No, but thanks anyway. I'll just muddle through.'

'I can help you finish on time,' Genevieve announced, and I was forced to look directly at her. There was no emotion in her cold green eyes.

'I'll just be accused of copying then,' I told her bluntly, wondering if this was another one of her ploys. 'That would be worse than handing in nothing.'

She shrugged regretfully. 'Suppose.'

'Thanks so much for the offer, Genevieve,' I made a point of saying through gritted teeth. 'It's so thoughtful of you and really appreciated.'

When lessons ended I took the long way home, away from the main roads, even though Mum would disapprove. The weather came out in sympathy with me – a persistent drizzle fuelled by low-lying grey and black clouds. I didn't even lift my feet going through the puddles and my shoes squelched horribly. My route took me down a narrow road that ran beside a row of Georgian terraces with long gardens, each painted a different period colour, from palest pink to dove grey. It was peaceful here, away from the noise of the cars and the traffic fumes. The road wasn't even properly surfaced, just a track which was formerly used for coaches and horses.

My mind went over and over what had happened. I even resorted to talking to myself because there was no one around, except for an annoying crow which followed me, squawking loudly and bobbing up and down. I looked at it suspiciously, trying to work out if it had a tail feather missing and then laughed because this was so ridiculous. I didn't hear any footsteps, but a vague feeling of unease made me spin around quickly and catch my breath. Without any indicator of where she'd come from, I was confronted by Genevieve, who must have moved as softly as a panther. She didn't even have the grace to look guilty at creeping up on me like this.

'You live in the opposite direction,' I told her rudely.

'Yes, but I wanted to commiserate with you.'

'How nice. Why's that?'

'I know how it feels for your life to be ruined.' She took one step closer and her nose nearly touched mine. 'Don't imagine your little game with Luke will work. You both think you're so clever . . .'

My body began to tremble. 'I don't know what you're talking about . . . Luke's my oldest friend . . .'

'I'll always be one step ahead of you . . . just remember that, Katy.'

My eyes closed with frustration, and when I opened them, she had disappeared as silently as she arrived.

When I got home I paced around my bedroom, unable to rest until I'd spoken to Luke. As soon as his car turned into our street I was outside on the pavement shouting through his open window.

'Genevieve must have my house bugged – she says she knows about us and what we're up to.'

Luke calmly closed his windows and got out of the car.

'How would she organize something like that, Kat? Is she an electronics expert as well?'

He took me inside and sat me down in his kitchen. He was completely unfazed by my hysterical tone. 'There has to be an explanation. She didn't follow us and she doesn't have psychic powers. So think, Katy.'

'I can't. My head's all fuzzy.'

'Who knew we were going out together on Saturday?'

'No one,' I answered quickly.

'Your mum?'

'Well, *she* did, of course.'

'Phone her,' Luke instructed in all seriousness.

I did as he said, and, after less than two minutes, put away my mobile, completely shamefaced. I could hardly look him in the eyes.

'Nat and Hannah didn't ring, but a very friendly girl called Genevieve did. She and Mum had a chat together about all sorts of things, including you. Mum forgot to mention it.'

Luke's voice was gentle. 'I told you there'd be an explanation . . . a really boring, simple explanation.' He sat down beside me and mussed up my hair, which he knew annoyed me. 'You've given this girl supernatural powers and made her into something you can't defeat. She's just ordinary and everything she does is ordinary. Don't build her up into something out of this world.'

I rested my head on his shoulder for a few seconds, wondering what I'd do if Luke wasn't there to keep me sane.

CHAPTER SIXTEEN

Merlin texted me to meet somewhere away from the college and suggested La Tasse, which seemed like a good omen – to meet in the cafe where we had our first proper date. I couldn't wait to see him. The weekend had flown by with hardly any contact between us, and yesterday was so eventful I barely noticed he wasn't around. The problem was, if I had to devote every minute of my spare time to my extra coursework then our time together would be even more restricted, and I wondered if this was Genevieve's intention.

For once I'd dressed to look alluring and had to admit that my super-skinny jeans and fitted white shirt were quite sexy, with no hint of the bag lady about them. I swung open the cafe door looking eagerly for Merlin, but he was nowhere to be seen. He arrived late, with a downcast face, and his half-hearted kiss landed on my chin instead of my lips. Instead of sliding into the same bench as me, he sat opposite. After a couple of awkward minutes I turned around, almost expecting to see Genevieve watching me. That's when I realized that this place was tainted by her as well.

'Sorry I couldn't come over on Saturday,' I gushed.

Merlin seemed distracted as if he hadn't heard me. The waitress approached and I ordered a jacket potato, salad and milkshake, but Merlin settled for a large cappuccino.

'How was your weekend?'

He exhaled loudly. 'Pretty boring.'

'Did you go anywhere?'

'Not really . . . I did some painting, and helped Mum with her class.'

I tried to keep my face composed. Merlin's mum's class meant just one thing to me: Genevieve. 'Is everything OK?'

'Fine.' Merlin didn't lift his head as he spoke but traced the knots on the table with his long fingers. There it was again, the feeling that he was a million miles from me.

'Tell me what's wrong.'

Now he looked at me and his dark eyes were distant, like rain clouds overhead. 'There's no easy way to say this . . .'

He stopped and so did my heart. I waited to hear the words I dreaded.

I've fallen for someone else. Don't know how it happened. We didn't plan it and I'm sorry to hurt you . . . it's Genevieve . . . but it isn't her fault, I'm the one to blame. I hope we can still be friends.'

'Just tell me,' I demanded mutinously.

'Is there . . . I mean . . . is anything going on between you and Luke?'

I laid my head on the table and broke into relieved laughter. When I finally looked up I had to wipe the corners of my eyes with my sleeve. I reached over to touch his hand.

'Don't be silly. He's like a big brother. I've known him forever, and he has a girlfriend . . . fiancée almost.' Merlin's face stayed immobile and I had to keep on gabbling. 'He doesn't even think of me as a proper girl, and he's seen me at my absolute worst. Once I sneezed on him when I had a bad cold and . . . you can imagine what went all over his T-shirt. He still teases me about it.'

Merlin still didn't smile. He reached into his pocket and deliberately laid a photograph on the table as if he was setting up a card trick. Even upside down I could make out the identities of the two figures. Something inside my chest seemed to expand and fill me with trepidation.

'What is it?'

'Look,' he urged.

I reached across and pulled the photograph towards me. It wasn't quite in focus, but it was clear enough to see Luke and me, locked in an embrace. It did take me by surprise – not the fact that we were hugging, but how intimate we looked.

I immediately tried to defend myself. 'It's not what it looks . . . I hug Luke all the time. Where did you get it?'

'It was posted on the college noticeboard this morning. Lucky I was one of the first in.'

My mind was whirring and jumbled, trying to keep pace with Genevieve. On Friday she'd played the trick on Nat, on Monday my art folder was ruined and now Merlin thought I was two-timing him, plus the news of my deceit would be around the college. Genevieve told me yesterday that she hadn't even started yet, and it looked as if her threat was sincere. How could she wield such power over me?

'There's something else, Katy,' Merlin continued gravely. 'You and Luke were together all day Saturday, but you said you had to stay in with your mum.'

To play for time I tucked into my jacket potato, but I hadn't realized how hot it was and had to drink the milkshake all at once to cool my mouth. I hadn't mentioned my day with Luke, and there was only one way he could have found out. I licked the strawberry cream from my lips, wishing we could go back a few weeks when everything was so bright and new.

'You know when I said people might . . . imply things about me, things that aren't true. Well, that's the sort of stuff I meant.'

Merlin nodded, but without approval. 'What's so secret?' he asked. 'Why didn't you talk about it?'

I couldn't tell him the truth. Being evasive was the only solution, a sort of damage-limitation exercise.

'I'm helping Luke with something and that's why I didn't tell you. You know he's a journalist . . . well . . . he's investigating someone. It's not exactly undercover work, but it's not something to shout about.'

'Maybe someone's investigating you,' he commented drily.

I grimaced. 'Can't imagine who.'

Merlin didn't know about my ruined art folder, so I filled him in on the details and how it couldn't have been an accident. He sat chewing this over, making sympathetic noises, but he still hadn't touched me. I knew how awful it would feel if he had spent a whole day with another girl and lied to me, so I couldn't blame him for being like this, and in a way his jealousy was flattering. I stood up, leaned across the table and kissed him full on the lips, breathing in paint and something unique that was indefinably Merlin.

'I would never do anything to hurt you, and I'd never be unfaithful . . . that's despicable.'

Merlin leaned back on the leather bench and the tension visibly drained from him. 'Sorry for the interrogation, but it's been eating me up.' He placed one hand in the middle of the table, fingers apart, and I placed mine on top.

The ice was broken between us and I plucked up the courage to ask, 'Who told you about Luke and me going out for the day?'

For just a couple of seconds guilt crossed Merlin's face and he rubbed his nose awkwardly. In the end he had to come clean.

'It was just an innocent remark,' he murmured. 'No harm intended. Genevieve wanted to go shopping to buy Nat's present, but she couldn't reach you. Your mum must've mentioned where you were.'

No harm intended! Genevieve had malice coursing through every vein in her body, but I was the only one who could see it. I couldn't blame Mum either. The only solution was to lead the double life and turn into a kind of split personality. I forced myself to talk and act normally with Merlin.

We walked back via the canal. There were a couple of brightly coloured barges passing and I thought how great it would be to travel all year long, never in the same place, sleeping above deck when the weather was hot. Merlin must have seen the wistful look on my face and put both arms tightly around me.

'We could live like that . . . be gypsies.'

For a minute I blocked Genevieve and everything else out, imagining Merlin and me alone, with no one to cause any misunderstandings.

'We wouldn't need much money,' I agreed. 'You could paint and I could make clothes or do alterations or . . . anything really. No one would bother us.'

He pulled me down on to the nearest bench and pressed his face to mine, our noses touching, like Eskimos. He squeezed my arm so hard I knew there'd be bruises tomorrow, but I didn't care. Neither of us spoke for ages. I wanted time to stop, right then, and keep this moment. But it was tinged with sadness because I was treasuring time with Merlin as if it had already ended.

'I see you everywhere,' he whispered. 'In the street, around every corner, when you aren't really there. You've bewitched me, Katy. I've never felt this way about any girl before.'

For a second his words conjured a horrible image in my mind – Genevieve with her beguiling beauty and strange ability to be everywhere. I screwed up my eyes, eager to banish it from my thoughts. *I've never felt this way about any girl before.* This was *me* Merlin was talking about. He wasn't comparing me to Genevieve at all.

'Me neither,' I answered shyly, and then realized what I'd said. 'I mean, I've never felt this way about any guy.'

'You know I said you had a glow when I first met you – I think it was love at first sight.'

I wound my arms around his neck. 'I felt it too.'

'Say it then,' he pressed.

'You say it first,' I squealed, overcome with nerves.

He blew out slowly, looked around and swallowed hard. 'Katy . . . I love you.'

I was too shy to look at his face. My head burrowed somewhere into his armpit as I whispered, 'I love you too.'

Merlin moved his lips to my ear. 'But will you love me forever?'

'Of course,' I answered straight away.

'Even when I'm as old as Luke?'

I tickled his ribs. 'He's only twenty-one.'

'That's ancient,' he mocked, unfastening his jacket and enfolding me inside.

Merlin loves me, Merlin loves me, Merlin loves me.

A voice inside my head chanted with insane happiness

and then I pinched myself to make sure this was real. I was suddenly consumed by the realization that it could have been so different and how close I'd come to losing him.

I took a deep breath. 'Merlin, we should plan our night away and not put it off any more.'

'What about this Friday?' he said immediately. 'Maybe . . . you could arrange an alibi for then.'

My stomach lurched. 'This weekend? But . . . my coursework needs attention.'

I felt rather than saw his disappointment and could have kicked myself. My arms circled his waist as my heart beat faster. 'Maybe . . . if I can . . . I mean yes . . . yes, I will.'

'Really?'

'Really.'

'You can arrange it?'

'Sure,' I answered impulsively. 'We should live for the day and just . . . go for it.'

'Live for the day,' he repeated, and almost crushed the life out of me.

'I've already set the scene with Mum . . . told her Hannah's parents are going away soon and she doesn't want to be alone.'

'I'll arrange the booking,' Merlin replied eagerly. 'I'll have to pretend to be eighteen, but that's no problem. Are you OK, Katy? You're trembling.'

He reached for my hand, and our fingers threaded together. 'Promise me you won't stop believing in me,' I whispered, so faintly that he didn't even hear.

*

Genevieve was the first thing I saw in class that afternoon, sitting with her self-satisfied smile and rearranging her curls. I strode over, unable to stop myself from taunting her.

'Sorry I wasn't home when you called,' I announced with feigned regret. 'You wanted to go into town with me to look for Nat's present. What about after college today?'

I wanted Genevieve to know that I was on to her and force her to invent reasons why she couldn't go, but incredibly she turned her iridescent eyes on me and said lazily, 'OK Why not?'

This was awful. I opened my mouth to retract the offer, but Hannah was already behind us and had heard my suggestion. I quickly asked if she was free to come with us, but she had to pick her little brother up from school. What had I done? After spending every moment trying to avoid Genevieve, I'd invited her to go shopping with me. For once I couldn't blame her; I'd walked right into this one.

CHAPTER SEVENTEEN

The bus driver did an about-turn. 'Hello, girls. Thought I was seeing double for a minute.'

This was downright annoying – even strangers noticed how alike we'd grown. Close up, I could see even more similarities. We had similar coats, of course, and Genevieve had changed her hair to a side parting like mine and copied my make-up. I didn't wear much eyeshadow and I liked dark shades of lipstick because they suited my pale complexion. I must have lost weight over the last few weeks because my jeans now rested somewhere around my hips, which made us look even more alike. Genevieve didn't seem bothered, but I was and toyed with the idea of taking off my coat, except that it was cold and a fog had descended. It was wet, choking, and so thick that it was in my mouth, the same taste left by fireworks after they've fizzled out.

'So what sort of stuff does Nat like?' Genevieve asked when we got off the bus. People stared at her. I was conscious of that, and knew there was something that made her stand out from the crowd, just like Merlin.

I decided to make my own mischief. 'What about a scarf and hat?'

Nat hated hats of any kind because her hair was so wild, and she always said that scarves made her think of scarecrows and old people.

Genevieve fixed me with her cool unblinking stare. 'You think she'd like that?'

'Love it,' I lied.

'Suppose I could manage that. Why isn't she having a party?'

I grinned to myself, thinking back to last year, dancing until dawn and then jumping into the town fountain on our way home. I caught a terrible cold and was off school for a week, but it was well worth it.

'Her mum forbade it after her sixteenth. It got a bit . . . er . . . wild, so this year's is just a civilized lunch.'

'Can't imagine wild around here,' Genevieve grunted sourly.

It was only late October and the shops were already full of Christmas things, their windows decorated with fake trees and even faker snow – boxes tied with string, cardboard cut-out roaring fires and all the tinsel and baubles you could ever want. It was cheesy, but still made me feel as excited as if I was seven years old. I followed Genevieve into a craft shop, shivering at the thought of my first Christmas with Merlin.

She chose some wool in an awful bottle-green colour, which I knew Nat would hate. She was a hippy, dippy sunshine kind of girl. I'd already made an oversized cushion embroidered with yellow and orange cats because she was mad about them. It was mean of me, but I couldn't stop grinning to myself imagining Nat trying to look thrilled when she unwrapped Genevieve's present and then having to wear the scarf and hat so as not to offend her.

'OK . . . that's that,' I muttered as we left the shop. 'There's nothing else I want so . . . I'll just make my way home.'

Genevieve spluttered with disbelief. 'Don't pretend like this, Katy. You really can't tear yourself away from me.'

'I'm only here for Nat . . . I don't choose to be near you.'

Her voice was as smooth as silk. 'Admit it. You engineered this. You might not know it, but your subconscious wants to get close to me.'

I was beginning to learn that Genevieve inverted the natural order of things; she could make out that white was black and vice versa. I had to stop a red mist from taking hold so I regulated my breathing and tried to picture Luke's face telling me not to let her rattle me.

'Be careful what you wish for,' Genevieve breathed, looking up at the sky. 'You wished for the perfect boyfriend and you got Merlin . . . and you wished for a special person in your life. Here I am, Katy. Someone who understands you . . . perfectly.'

This was way too close to the truth. I *had* wished for a boyfriend, and for the best friend I'd never had.

She slowed down and studied her reflection in a window. 'Have you had enough yet?'

'Of what?'

She didn't answer and continued to stare in the glass, but this time at me. 'How does it feel, Katy, to watch your life trickling away? Scarcely a ripple and you'll be gone. Hardly anyone will notice.'

'Merlin knows the photograph means nothing,' I told her. 'So that little scheme of yours failed.'

She tapped the side of her head. 'He says he knows . . . but he'll see it in his mind's eye and never quite escape, no matter how hard he tries. Images are so powerful, we see them even when we don't want to.'

'He trusts me completely.'

Her voice was hypnotically assured. 'It only takes one small seed of doubt to grow and spread until the whole thing is rotten. All trust eroded.'

I wondered if she was referring to Nat and those awful love spells. Nat, who would always suspect that I had gossiped about her. I clenched my fists, trying to block out the pain.

'You're growing weaker all the time, Katy.'

I extended my arm. 'Just get away from me, Genevieve.'

'It doesn't matter where you go or how far you run, Katy . . . you're marked.'

This girl was mad. Her pronouncements were getting more and more intense.

'I walk this way,' I growled, trying to shake her off.

'I go this way too.'

She stuck to me like glue and I figured that I wouldn't be able to dump her until we reached the bus stop, where we took different routes home. We passed a charity shop and, it was totally weird, we both stopped dead at the same spot staring at the window display. There was a sign advertising evening wear for all occasions. A male dummy had been kitted out in a black dinner suit and the female dummy in a cream backless long dress. In that split second I knew exactly what Genevieve was thinking because I was thinking exactly the same thing – the college Christmas ball. The theme was Hollywood, which was great because it meant Merlin in a tux and me looking like a film star in something gorgeous.

'It might be worth a look in,' Genevieve suggested, her voice suddenly normal, as if nothing unusual had just occurred.

I stared at her suspiciously, wary of her motive, and then tried to put her off because I wanted to go in alone.

'It's pretty lame this year,' I complained. 'Hollywood is a terrible idea.'

Genevieve gave a superior sniff. 'Well, if you don't want to. . .'

She swung open the glass door but, instead of taking this opportunity to escape, I kept pace with her. Her head swivelled around like an owl's as she scanned the place but my eye was already focused on the most fabulous dress ever, which was hanging at the far end of the shop. The train caught my eye first because it was greyish green in a two-tone material that reminded me of a mermaid's tail. I made a beeline for it and tried to grab the hanger, only to discover that someone had hold of it from the other side.

'I saw it first,' a familiar voice cried, but I stubbornly held on tight.

Genevieve poked her head through the rail of dresses, her face flushed and angry. 'You'll rip it if you don't let go.'

'You let go,' I said childishly.

'It wouldn't fit you anyway.'

A volunteer must have heard the commotion and came running over to stand between us. She had immovable hair, pink lipstick and a chiffon scarf tied around her neck.

'Now, girls, that's enough.'

Reluctantly we both gave up our claim to the dress and the woman held it aloft. It was even more beautiful than I had thought and shimmered like the sea on a rough day. It was glamorous but not in a starlet way, and the £20 price tag was unbelievable.

'This is the damaged rail,' the voice lectured. 'This evening gown has an obvious tear, and it isn't on a seam. It will be almost impossible to repair so you both may wish to reconsider . . .'

I was sure that Genevieve could do an amazing invisible mend, better than I could, but I still wanted the dress. If she stole it from under my nose then the ball would be ruined because nothing would come close to this amazing find. The volunteer decided to act as relationship counsellor.

'Maybe it's better if neither of you takes it, dears – it isn't worth damaging a friendship over one dress.'

Friendship! I tried not to smirk and punched Genevieve playfully on the arm. 'We wouldn't let that happen, would we?'

Genevieve stubbornly thrust out her chin. 'Whoever the dress fits shall go to the ball . . . and I'll try it first.' She might as well have added that Prince Charming was going to be hers and the glass slipper would be a perfect fit too.

Pitying looks were being thrown my way, and it was obvious why – Genevieve would look a million times better than me; in fact, I'd probably rip the dress even more trying to squeeze into it.

It didn't take her long. A confidently smug figure emerged from the changing room, which was just a curtain hooked around one dark corner of the shop. The mermaid dress could have been made for her, and the familiar knife twisted in my stomach with stabbing jealousy. Genevieve sashayed up and down the shop preening in the full-length mirror. Even the other shoppers stopped to admire her. My face was set in some kind of gruesome sickly smile, watching as a woman moved forward to pick up the train.

If I'd looked away at that moment, I'd have completely missed what happened, but I was horribly mesmerized and kept on staring, almost to torture myself. A pair of hands swept Genevieve's hair up from the nape of her neck to see the effect. I expected her to turn her face this way and that, revelling in the attention, but her reaction was completely unexpected. Angrily she pulled away, shaking her head from side to side so that her curls again covered her shoulders. Then she stomped back into the changing room and yanked the curtain shut.

But not before I'd seen the scar tissue running down her back, a distinct puckering of the skin that looked, for all the world, as if she'd been burned in a fire.

CHAPTER EIGHTEEN

It was unforgivable of me, especially after all his support, but I didn't immediately tell Luke what I'd seen because I needed to concentrate on the most momentous event of my life. In a moment of madness I *had* agreed to go away with Merlin on Friday. The rest of the week passed in a state of nervous frenzy. I had to tackle my coursework, as well as ensuring all the arrangements were perfect. Merlin had booked a campsite about twenty-five miles away – only an hour's journey, but far enough not to worry about being seen by anyone. Mum had given me the green light to stay over at Hannah's and have my tea there, which meant I wouldn't have to go home after college. I'd already packed a small bag to take, and Merlin was responsible for the rucksack containing our tent and all the equipment. We were going to pick it up together from his house and make our way straight to the station.

It was impossible to sleep on Thursday night. Every few minutes I checked my digital clock, but time had come to a standstill and I resorted to counting to sixty waiting for the numbers to change. Eventually I must have dozed.

In the morning my nerves were shredded. A cereal bowl slipped out of my hand and I knocked a cup of coffee over, all within the space of five minutes. Mum didn't even seem to notice. I couldn't look her in the eye as we said goodbye, convinced she would detect some treachery, but she just straightened my collar and kissed me on the cheek. The fact that she was almost cheerful made the deceit worse. Crossly I argued with myself on the way to college.

Why should she notice anything out of the ordinary, Katy? You're not doing anything that unusual, just staying over at a friend's house. The whole point of all the arrangements was that she wouldn't suspect anything. You've covered every eventuality. Stop feeling guilty; it's only a small lie.

I gave the best performance of my life, outwardly cool and collected, but inside my stomach was churning, doing somersaults, cartwheels and backflips. As we left, Nat and Hannah gave me extra hugs for luck and a kind of wistful wave. When I turned around they were still watching us, and this made me feel weirdly sad. We'd reached the bottom of the college steps when my phone beeped.

`Katy could you please stop off at home before you go to Hannah's - Mum x`

My face fell. We were booked on the four thirty train, with only an hour to pick up the gear and board our train.

I began babbling to Merlin. 'I'll rush home, find out

what Mum wants and meet you at the station. It'll be nothing.' I kissed him hastily. 'Wild horses won't stop me from getting on that train, and this might be safer in case . . . certain people are watching.'

I did one of those speeded-up walks that are almost a run and always look completely lame, but I didn't care. Mum was forever summoning me over trivial stuff, but if she saw me now she was less likely to hassle me later. I opened the front door and practically fell through it. There was no premonition that anything was amiss and I shouted my usual greeting as a figure stepped out from the shadows, her face oddly waxy and somehow knotted with fury. My bag slipped out of my hand and thumped on to the hall floor. Neither of us spoke for what seemed like an eternity. In the end I had to whisper, 'Whatever's wrong?'

'This . . . arrived this morning,' Mum croaked, and tears must have been close to the surface. 'More lies, Katy, more deception, more . . . Merlin.'

The letter in her hand was so crumpled I wondered if she'd been clutching it all day. I had no choice but to take it off her. The first thing I noticed was Merlin's name on the envelope but my address underneath. I slid one finger inside and took out a single sheet of paper with shaking hands. It was a receipt from the campsite and a confirmation of our booking. The date was today. It was weird, but shock made me freeze, unable to move a single muscle. I must have stared at it for ages, trying to keep the guilt from my features, but eventually I was forced to look at Mum. She didn't blink once and it was like staring into an abyss. I felt physically sick as my mind fast-forwarded to the cataclysmic fallout.

'You set up the sleepover with Hannah as a cover?'

'N-no,' I insisted. 'We talked about it for . . . laughs, but we weren't going to really do it.'

She stroked her chin like a villain in a pantomime. 'Now, why would Merlin make the booking and why would you arrange a sleepover at Hannah's on the same night, if it was all just . . . imaginary?'

'It's a mistake,' I cried out, 'or someone being malicious. You don't know the horrible stuff that's been happening to me . . . my coursework was deliberately ruined and that's not the worst—'

Mum ignored this outburst. 'So, Katy? You really were going to a sleepover at Hannah's tonight because her parents are away?'

'Ye-es.'

'Don't dig yourself in any deeper,' she growled. 'I've already phoned Hannah's mum, who confirmed she isn't going away and knows nothing about you sleeping there. So . . . what have you to say?'

'It's not how it looks,' I mumbled feebly.

Mum folded her arms in a way that meant business. 'Since you met this boy, Katy, you've been caught smoking, your college work is a disaster and now you've lied and schemed to spend the night with him. Your only defence is to blame everything on another girl. I feel like I don't know my own daughter any more. I'm disgusted with you.'

She turned on her heel and walked away, leaving me standing in the hallway in the semi-darkness too stunned to move. But this wasn't the end of it. She reappeared a few seconds later. 'You'll be grounded for the foreseeable future, and I'd like you to hand over your phone right away.'

My hand covered my mouth in horror. Merlin! He'd be waiting for me at the station. Without my phone I couldn't get a message to him.

It was a long shot but there was nothing to lose. 'Even prisoners are allowed one call.'

Mum pursed her lips, narrowed her eyes and said, 'You have exactly one minute and I'm timing you.'

My hands were still shaking so much that I dropped the phone, then missed all the buttons because my fingers were useless, as if I was wearing mittens. It would have torn me apart to hear Merlin's voice and then be cut off so I sent a text instead.

`Mum knows everything. I'm sorry Merlin. I'm grounded and have to give up my phone right away. PS I love you X`

I ran upstairs and threw myself on to my bed, wallowing in self-pity and misery. Hot tears scorched my cheeks and saturated my pillow until I had to flip it over because it was making my face even blotchier. There was a strange tortured pleasure in imagining, second by second, Merlin trudging home and every emotion he must be feeling, every expression on his face. I hoped he was just as miserable as me, thinking of what might have been. After about an hour I realized how selfish this was. It wasn't just Merlin and I who were involved – Hannah would be in trouble for providing my alibi. I hoped she'd have the good sense to blame it all on me and say she knew nothing about my plan. I covered my face with shame at the thought of what Hannah's mum would think of me now.

Mum never even came near me all evening or asked if I was hungry. So, drained from crying, I fell into a fitful sleep at about eight o'clock, one minute freezing, the next boiling hot and tossing aside the duvet. My dreams were feverishly fragmented. It felt as if I spent hours just running from something or someone, but there was nowhere to hide; every building, every wall, fell flat when I reached it, like a house of cards, and every corner was illuminated by a giant searchlight. I stumbled into some sort of theatre and found myself onstage. The auditorium was gradually lit up, row by row, and all the seats were occupied, but every person had the same strangely blank face and their green glass eyes threw beams of light at me. They stung like tiny swords and I curled into a ball trying to escape the cuts, but soon my whole body was a weeping bloodied mess as Genevieve's laughter resounded in my ears.

Every awful minute detail of the previous day came rushing back the second I awoke. The morning light hurt my eyes and it was tempting to roll over and stay in bed, but I was determined to face Mum and get it over with. I tiptoed downstairs to the kitchen with swollen eyes and hamster cheeks. She was calmly buttering a piece of toast and the smell made me realize how famished I was. No food or drink had passed my lips for almost twenty-four hours. I cleared my throat. She didn't speak or look at me so I turned dejectedly away but never made it past the kitchen door. Everywhere dimmed as if a total eclipse had struck; stars appeared in front of my eyes, multiplying until they joined together to make a fuzzy darkness, and my feet slipped from under me. I remembered nothing until my lids fluttered open to find my head cradled in Mum's lap, her eyes wide with alarm.

'Sorry. Everywhere just went black.'

'How long is it since you've eaten?' she asked gruffly.

'Dunno. Can't remember.'

Mum helped me to a chair, hovering in case I slipped off it. My vision was still a little blurred, but the feeling of faintness had passed. She put two pieces of roughly cut bread in the toaster, waited until they popped and then smeared them with jam. The plate was set in front of me with a cup of strong tea.

'No boy is worth passing out over,' she barked, and when I had the courage to look there was almost a twinkle in her eye. She sat down beside me. 'You think I don't remember what it's like to be sixteen?'

I wasn't sure if this was a rhetorical question so I carried on greedily eating.

'Well, I do, and that's why I don't want you making a huge mistake. Your hormones are crazy, common sense has gone out of the window and you think it's love.'

'It *is* love,' I replied quietly, waiting for her to jump down my throat.

'Katy.' She sighed. 'It's always true love at sixteen . . . but I can't expect you to believe me. You have to find out for yourself.' She was definitely thawing, but determined to assert her authority over me. 'The punishment still stands. I can't be lied to, and you have to realize it's for your own good. You can go to Nat's lunch next week, but you're grounded till then.'

I nodded sheepishly.

'And by the way, look what I found.' Mum uncurled her hand and the pendant was resting in it. 'Gemma was playing with this on the patio . . . can't think how she dragged it all the way downstairs.'

I was forced to take it from her, figuring that Gemma must have ripped open one of our bin bags looking for titbits and now I'd have to get rid of it all over again. It was a relief to have got off so lightly with Mum, but my heart was so heavy it felt like I was dragging a ball and chain behind me. I went back to my bedroom and stared at my computer. Mum hadn't mentioned it being out of bounds, but I resisted the urge to log on. If she found me talking to anyone she might extend the grounding for another week and I'd miss Nat's birthday. There was now no excuse not to get on with redoing my coursework– I was cut off from the outside world in some sort of weird limbo with nothing to do and no one to talk to.

Luke must have been texting me. He called round after

tea. I saw him coming up the path and rushed to the door, mouthing at him that I was grounded. But he wouldn't give up that easily and refused to leave, whispering in my ear that he had a plan. I shook my head and told him that it wouldn't work, but he pushed me inside just as Mum came to the door.

'Kat's English assignment is ready,' he said, turning on his most winning smile. 'There're a few things I need to go over with her.'

'Bring it in,' Mum replied suspiciously, but she smoothed down Luke's annoying lock of hair as if he was a child.

'Thing is . . . it's on my computer.'

Mum looked from one face to the other and said resignedly, 'You can go, Katy, but don't be more than half an hour.'

'You're a genius,' I gushed, falling over myself to speak and quickly bringing him up to date with Genevieve's campaign against me. He must have realized how distressed I was because he was more sympathetic than usual, giving up his chair for me and making concerned noises in all the right places.

The only note of criticism he sounded was, 'Why didn't you tell me before?'

'I . . . I've been so bogged down with my coursework there just wasn't time, and it all happened kind of together.' My face darkened. 'Genevieve's been incredibly busy this week.'

'Obviously.'

'Now, Luke, tell me how she managed to engineer all these horrible things?'

He put on his most solemn thinking face. 'You said she was at the craft fair, so . . . she overheard you joking about spells or manifestations and waited to use it against you. She destroyed your folder when you left it unguarded, she took the photo of us . . . sometime . . . We didn't see her because we're not looking for some crazy girl with a camera, and she came into your college early and put it on the noticeboard . . . simple.'

'But that's not all,' I fumed. 'Look at this letter . . . sent to my house but with Merlin's address on it. It isn't even franked. Genevieve must have hand-delivered it on Friday morning after I left for college.'

I handed it to Luke and let him read it. His reaction totally took me by surprise. He opened his mouth in astonishment and disgust. 'That is beyond anything she's done so far, Kat. This takes it all to a different level.'

'Well . . . yeah, it's definite dirty tricks.'

'To set you up like that and make your mum think you were going away with Merlin . . . when you hardly know each other.'

I gulped. There was something about all this I hadn't quite explained, which was also the reason I'd been too preoccupied to talk to him. 'Thing is . . . we did . . . I mean we were . . . just . . . er . . . going camping for one night.' I didn't expect to feel so flustered and almost added, 'in separate tents' but my high colouring always gave me away, and Luke had known me for so long it was hard to lie to him.

He simply put his head down and spent an unusual amount of time studying the envelope as if he was Sherlock Holmes. 'OK . . . that's easily solved then. Genevieve hung around Merlin's house doing her arty stuff . . . she searched his room and scanned the receipt.'

'You're probably right,' I muttered.

'Where's that photo of us?' he suddenly asked.

There was no way I wanted him to see that. It was stuffed in the back of one of my drawers. 'I . . . haven't got it. Merlin probably threw it away.'

'How did we look?'

I scrunched my features. 'Just like a couple of old friends . . .'

'How come Merlin was so jealous then?'

'He's a little . . . insecure.'

I watched Luke plot the latest developments on the whiteboard. 'She really *is* clever, Kat. I've probably underestimated her, and the trouble is . . . we've got no other leads. I don't know where to go from here.'

My whole face slowly lit up. 'That's the thing, Luke. There's something else I haven't told you. I saved the best till last.'

CHAPTER NINETEEN

Monday morning back in college was strange – it felt as though I'd been let out of prison. I was nervous about seeing Hannah but she seemed quite chilled about everything and told me she'd persuaded her mum it was all a big misunderstanding – Katy Rivers would *never* do anything so risky. Merlin and I sneaked away the first moment we could and he took all the blame for the mix-up with the letters, convinced he'd messed things up on his computer. I didn't even bother arguing with him to point out how unlikely this was.

We had to be extra careful about being seen together because I was wary about being watched in case anything could be used against me. We stole kisses wherever we could and discovered a small doorway at the back of the college where we could hide. It had views of the railway and recycle bins, the smell of rubbish filling our nostrils, the wind cutting through us and the screeching of trains echoing in our ears. I began to stealthily watch Genevieve in the same way that she watched me. It was surprising how satisfying it felt, as if I'd absorbed parts of her predatory and vengeful personality. I counted each day and bided my time until the weekend arrived. There was a lot to look forward to – on Saturday night my grounding was lifted and I was allowed to see Merlin, plus Luke and I had something important of our own to do.

We were going to go back to the outskirts of York, to the vicarage where Grace/Genevieve was sent to live after the fire. Whatever she was hiding, we were going to discover her secret and expose her as the twisted liar she really was. I'd finally faced the uncomfortable truth that she would never willingly stop this campaign against me. I had to stop it for her.

On Saturday morning, we hit the road before 7 a.m.

'How's the magician?' Luke asked slyly as he took a sharp corner and I was flung against the passenger door.

'He's . . . er . . . OK.'

'He doesn't mind you spending another day with me?'

'Course not,' I answered firmly. 'I'm seeing him tonight. We've had to stay apart for most of the week . . . but at least my coursework was finished on time. Miss Clegg gave me a top grade.'

'That's great, Kat.'

'So . . . some good came out of me being grounded.'

Luke didn't comment. Things had been a bit strained between us since he found out about the camping trip, which was puzzling because I'd always assumed I could tell him anything. 'Are you annoyed about something?' He started fiddling with the CD player and I made him put his hand back on the wheel. 'Come on . . . spit it out.'

'No . . . it's just . . . I don't want to see you hurt, that's all.'

'Merlin wouldn't hurt me.'

Luke still looked moody so I pressed him. 'There's something else, isn't there?'

'No . . . well . . . kind of. I thought I knew you so well, Kat.'

I was so hurt at Luke's unexpected criticism that I slid down my seat, completely crushed. After another minute I grew angry and had to defend myself. My voice was cold and flat. 'You *knew* me, Luke. I'm a big girl now.'

He began to nod manically. 'You're right, this has got nothing to do with me.'

'No,' I corrected in a softer tone, 'it does have something to do with you because you're my friend, and if you hadn't supported me like this I'd be completely crazy by now.'

Luke seemed to brighten up at my words. He held out his hand and waited for me to give him a lame high five. 'To friends, Kat.'

'To friends,' I repeated.

He couldn't stop himself from having the last word though. 'Just don't let the first boy you meet break your heart.'

I closed my eyes and concentrated on the movement of

the car, thinking back to Genevieve and the evening dress, the reason we were on the road again. Once she'd seen the look of shock on the volunteer's face, she immediately took it off with a declaration that it was 'horrible'. I pretended to have my head buried in a knitting book and looked up innocently as if to ask if there was a problem. Genevieve's face was like thunder and she couldn't wait to get out of the charity shop. I was enjoying her discomfort so much that I left with her. She barely uttered another word to me and we parted company at the bus stop.

This was the evidence I needed, something concrete that provided proof of Genevieve's past. She thought she could reinvent herself and erase everything, but this was a permanent indelible reminder of her former life.

Luke brought me out of my reverie. 'Maybe we should have phoned the vicarage first? The number should be listed.'

'We don't want to put anyone on their guard,' I yawned. 'And it's harder to read people when you're not face to face.'

'Don't build up your hopes,' Luke warned. 'The vicar might have moved parish or died or something . . .'

'He'll still be there,' I insisted. 'That old lady in Lower Croxton would have said if he'd moved.'

'He could be on holiday or a retreat or whatever vicars do.'

'He'll be there, looking after his flock,' I said laughing.

'He doesn't have to talk to us, and we can't lie to a . . .'

'Man of God,' I finished. 'Why wouldn't he talk to us?'

Luke tapped his fingers on the steering wheel. 'People don't always do what you want them to, Kat. He might think it's a private matter.'

'It's his job to help people,' I insisted petulantly. 'Grace or Genevieve, she's still his family. He's no right to just let her loose on other people . . . stalking and being horrible and trying to ruin their life or take it over or whatever she's doing . . .'

'I agree,' he soothed, and added with a crafty wink, 'Have you finally got over your obsession with her having supernatural powers?'

'Suppose,' I muttered.

'You see, Kat,' he lectured, 'all that hocus-pocus is a product of a gullible mind. If you don't believe then it can't hurt—'

I screamed suddenly and covered my face as something hit the windscreen. Through my fingers I absorbed the fact that Luke was frantically turning the steering wheel, trying to keep control of the car, and we were weaving all over the road. He managed to come to a stop with a huge jolt that threw us both forward. I instinctively cradled my head and heard a shocked voice say, 'It's just a bird, Kat . . . don't look if you don't want to.'

It was perverse but, as soon as he said that, I just had to look and was confronted with the body of a crow splattered across the glass, its dead eyes staring right at me.

'Good job we weren't on the motorway,' he said with

feigned brightness. 'And good job it hit your side or it would have been a lot worse.'

My body felt as though it'd been through a washing machine. I tried not to look as Luke used a plastic bag to scrape the blood, feathers and mangled carcass off the windscreen. He got back in the car again and turned on his washers to clean away any remnants.

'Probably shot by a farmer,' he added, whistling, and I took deep breaths to stave off the nauseous feeling. I opened the window, trying not to think about winged harbingers of doom who wanted to stop us from reaching the church. We didn't say another word to each other until we reached St John's Place.

I expected the church to be tiny and quaint with lots of stained glass and a canopy over the gate, but this was fairly modern and plain, more my idea of a function hall than a church. Lots of cars were parked outside and there was a sign on the noticeboard advertising a jumble sale in aid of a local charity.

'At least we can go in with everyone else and not look out of place,' Luke said, stretching his legs as he got out of the car. His hair looked as if a comb had actually been dragged through it, and his combats weren't that crumpled. I took a minute to glance at him with affection, wondering why he would so gladly give up another day just to help me out. 'Come on, let's see if we can grab a bargain,' he urged, 'and do some detective work.'

I usually loved jumble sales because it was a chance to

buy second-hand clothes which I could alter or just unpick to make into something else, but this was serious Women's Institute country. The only clothes available were tweed skirts, check trousers and paisley shirts with matching scarves. Jars of jam, marmalade, pickled onions and beetroot lined the tables, together with giant cream sponges and fruitcakes. There was also a selection of plants, awful china figurines and gloomy-looking books. I was glad I'd opted for my respectable bootleg jeans instead of my low-rise ones.

'Keep looking for the vicar,' Luke reminded me, smiling and nodding at the ladies on the stalls.

He was pressured into buying a fruit loaf and some apricot jam for his mum while I settled for a limp houseplant that was supposed to need very little attention. Luke seemed to be the only male under sixty in the room and rushed to help as one of the tables collapsed. Before long he'd been roped into lifting several boxes of books and manning the tombola. I stood by drinking awful instant coffee in a plastic cup and listening to an old lady complaining about her bunions.

The man wearing a dog collar and dark suit was noticeable as soon as he entered the church hall because everyone immediately rushed to greet him. I tried to signal to Luke, but he was obscured from view by five or more blue-rinsed perms. The vicar looked about fifty, with grey hair, a beard and gold-rimmed glasses. His frame was tall and spare.

So much for blending in with the crowd. Luke stood out like a beacon and the vicar made a beeline for him. I watched them shake hands and stood up, right in the middle of a story about gall-bladder removal, to go over in case he needed me for support.

'I'm just here for the day,' I heard him say, 'with a friend.'

'We need more young people to get involved in our community. What a shame you're only visiting.'

Luke paused. 'Actually, another friend of mine used to live around here . . . I wonder if you'd remember her?'

The vicar smiled encouragingly. 'Her name?'

Luke's resolve seemed to waver, but he cleared his throat and said confidently, 'It's Grace . . . Grace Morton.'

The reaction was brutal. The vicar tensed up and his features became hard and ugly. The change was so swift that it was scary, like seeing your favourite Disney character turn into Freddy Krueger. 'Sorry, I've no recollection of anyone by that name.'

I flinched with discomfort and then held out my hands to indicate there was nothing we could do, but Luke wasn't deterred so easily. He followed the fast-moving figure outside, with me trying to keep pace.

'Excuse me, but I think you must remember her. It'd be difficult to forget a member of your family.'

The vicar swivelled around, eyes on fire. 'She is *not* a member of my family.'

Luke couldn't help but smile. 'So you do remember

her. We need to ask you some questions. It's very important.'

The vicar would not be swayed. 'I have no wish to answer your questions and I would be grateful if you would leave me alone and not contact me or anyone close to me again.'

We watched him go back into the hall. I sat down on a small brick wall nearby, playing with the zip on my jacket and rubbing my arms. Nervousness or the biting cold had chilled me to the bone. I tried to make light of it. 'That seemed to go well.'

Luke was obviously angry but hid it well. 'Pompous, wasn't he? But I could hardly twist his arm.'

I sighed. 'There's nothing else we can do. But one thing is odd . . . no one wants to talk about Genevieve . . . Grace. It's like she never existed.'

He sat beside me, kicking his heels against the bricks. 'You mean they *wish* she never existed.'

'I guess that's it then? I mean there's nowhere else to go with this.'

Luke pushed his tongue to one side of his mouth and gave a hollow laugh. 'Call yourself a journalist? This is just the start . . .'

'But he'll only get angrier.'

'*He* might . . . but what about the others?'

'What others?'

Luke's eyes were as hard as steel as he stared straight ahead. '"Don't contact anyone close to me," he said . . . so . . . that's just what we will do. He isn't the only one who knew her, and if he doesn't want to talk about her, then we'll wait until we find someone who will talk.'

'How long should we wait?'

'As long as it takes,' he replied with determination.

CHAPTER TWENTY

'I'm freezing.'

'If I put the heater on without running the engine, it will flatten the battery.'

My breath condensed in front of me. 'Could we get out of the car? Move around a bit?'

'We have to watch the vicarage,' Luke reminded me for the third time, 'and not draw attention to ourselves.'

'Are there any more sandwiches left?'

'No.'

'Water?'

'No.'

Luke was only here to help me, and I was acting like a spoilt brat, but I thought that journalists led exciting lives, not sitting in a cold car for three hours watching the same house.

He looked at his watch. 'I know you're fed up. I am too. We'll give it another thirty minutes and call it a day.'

'Sorry for moaning,' I said sheepishly, but then moaned

some more. 'Why isn't life like it is on the TV? Everything solved in a day, all the loose ends tied up and the good guys coming out on top.'

'Because they squeeze months of filming into half an hour and make it all look so easy, which . . .'

I gripped his arm as the front door opened. 'Someone's coming out. It's him . . . and he's alone.'

We watched the lean figure stride down the path and then disappear out of sight as the road curved away. I knew what Luke was planning next and my heart missed a beat. 'He . . . He could come back at any minute.'

Luke took his keys out of the ignition and opened the car door. 'I think he'll be out for a while, Kat. He was muffled up this time – overcoat, scarf and hat.'

I stayed in the passenger seat, looking down, my hands clamped between my knees. 'Don't think I can do this . . .'

Luke came around to my side and gently pulled me out, feet first. 'What's the worst that could happen? We get the door shut in our faces or the vicar returns and has a hissy fit. We're not doing anything illegal, and you'll kick yourself if you give up now.'

He was right, as always. I'd hate myself if I went away without knowing what we might have discovered. 'You're right . . . of course you are . . . I'll come.'

A comforting hand tucked itself under my arm. 'Coping with Genevieve takes a lot more courage than this.'

I smiled gratefully because Luke always managed to say the right thing. Taking a deep breath, I made it past the gate, but the path to the vicarage seemed to have doubled in length and my shoes crunched loudly on the gravel. I gazed up at the sky for distraction. Night was approaching, a purple and black bruise moving in to obliterate the pink, white and touches of powder blue. Now we were at the red front door, with its peeling paintwork and coloured glass, and we couldn't turn back. There was a choice between a brass door knocker and an old-fashioned bell with a rope pull. Luke hesitated and I knew this would be the scariest part, those few moments on the doorstep not knowing who would answer and what we would say. But we didn't have to do either because the door suddenly flew open.

'I-I kn-know why you're here,' a woman stammered. 'M-my husband described you and I saw you from the window.'

The woman was small and birdlike with untidy mouse-coloured hair and scared eyes that darted from Luke to me and back again.

Luke took one step forward. 'We've come a long way. I'm sorry to be so insistent, but it's important.'

The woman retreated further into the porch, holding on to the door frame. 'I can't tell you anything . . . please leave me . . . leave us alone.'

'Let me try,' I whispered. I wasn't frightened any more. Luke was right, the only thing to fear was having no idea why Genevieve hated me and wanted to destroy my life. I looked the woman in the eye and tried to keep my voice steady. 'I don't know what I've done, but since . . . Grace came to our town she's gone out of her way to make my life miserable. I can't carry on like this without knowing why. Please help me.'

The vicar's wife interlaced her hands as if in prayer, and conflicting emotions crossed her face. Finally she peered out into the garden and said quickly, 'Follow me. If my husband comes back, you must leave through the kitchen . . . immediately. The back gate is locked but there's a hole in the fence; it's easy to slip through.'

She led the way through the large hall tiled in geometric blue and terracotta. A grandfather clock stood opposite the porch door. To the left were a set of winding oak stairs with a gnarled wooden banister and scrolled spindles. Everywhere smelt damp and musty, mixed with beeswax. My flesh felt cold and prickly and I rubbed my arms.

'What's wrong?' Luke asked.

'Nothing. Just a creepy feeling . . . like I've been here before.'

'Don't mention I'm a journalist,' he whispered.

We stood in a large country kitchen with a freestanding dresser, butcher's trolley and shelving unit filled with pots and pans, jars and dishes. The vicar's wife motioned us to sit down at an old table with deep grooves in its worn surface. With quivering lips she took a sip of water from a glass. 'How did you trace Grace to us? We haven't heard her name for a long time.'

'Luke's great with computers,' I explained, hoping that she wasn't. 'I told him about Grace and he managed to track you down.'

She twisted a handkerchief between her fingers. 'What do you need to know?'

After coming so far my mind suddenly went blank and Luke had to step in.

'What about Grace's life when she left here? What can you tell us?'

'Not that much,' the woman replied flatly. 'She was taken to a children's home nearby. I tried to keep in touch and would have visited, but she didn't want to see me. She was very hostile . . . to both of us.'

'How old was she then?'

'Probably eight.'

I let out a gasp. 'So she didn't live with you for long? I mean she was only seven when the fire . . .'

I stopped abruptly and in a small voice she commented, 'You know about that then.'

We both nodded. There was a sharp intake of breath. 'No, she didn't stay for long.'

She trailed off without further explanation as I pondered on the missing years of Genevieve's/Grace's life. I still had trouble switching between her two names.

'It wasn't a happy time?' Luke asked sympathetically, and for a moment her eyes looked glassy, but she collected herself and pulled her grey cardigan tightly around her small frame.

'No, it wasn't. We didn't know there were . . . problems before Grace came, but afterwards . . .'

The rest was left unsaid. She jumped at a noise in the garden and I could see how tense she was in case her husband came back.

'Have you any photographs of her?' I asked.

'No. They were all destroyed in the fire, and my own were . . . mislaid.'

'Did you tell anyone about these . . . *problems*?' Luke asked tentatively.

'I-I can't go into details. Grace was placed under supervision and it was taken out of my hands. It wasn't an *ordinary* children's home, you see . . .'

Both Luke and I digested this fact for a minute. 'What did Grace do when she was here?' I asked.

It looked as if she wasn't going to answer but eventually she did in a voice that was barely audible. 'She sat upstairs . . . gazing into the mirror on the dressing table. Day after day . . . those eyes of hers, just watching. Sometimes she would say the strangest things . . .'

'Like what?'

'That they'd taken away her reflection . . . and cut her heart in two.'

The wind blew down the fireplace and a chill ran through me – like someone walking over your grave, Mum would say. 'Did she have any interests?'

The vicar's wife nodded in remembrance. 'She loved the sea. Always on at us to take her there, and whenever we went she'd collect shells, pebbles, bits of glass, and make them into trinkets. My husband didn't approve – he thought they were too pagan.'

Luke tried not to show it, but I could tell from his expression that he was seething inside. 'It must have been hard to lose touch with your niece,' he commented. 'Your sister's child?'

The reaction was as extreme as her husband's had been. 'Grace wasn't my sister's child! She took my sister's married name to have a fresh start.'

My foot accidentally kicked Luke under the table. 'Sorry? She wasn't your sister's child?'

'Not flesh and blood,' was the defensive answer. 'My sister adopted Grace when she was a small baby.'

I looked at Luke, stunned, but he stayed quietly controlled. 'Do you know anything about her real mother?'

'Not really . . . only that she wasn't very stable. My sister never wanted to talk about what had happened to Grace, although the adoption agency might have told her.'

Was she from this area?' I asked, still trying to get my head around this latest piece of information.

The vicar's wife nodded. There was a moment's silence and she burst out, 'One thing I do know, adopting Grace was the worst thing my sister could have done.'

'She was just a child,' Luke commented.

'No ordinary child.' There was a self-conscious cough. 'My husband believes that no one is born wicked. He believes we learn to be wicked from the evil in the world . . .'

'But you're not so sure,' I finished.

She stared into space. 'I still feel her presence here . . . I know that's impossible but it's as if . . . something of her remains.' She glanced at the clock on the fireplace and stood up hastily. 'You have to go, through the back door.'

I stood my ground. 'You still haven't told us the real reason why Grace had to leave.'

'I've told you everything I can.'

I gripped her tiny wrist and it felt brittle as though it would snap in two. 'She blames me for something. Says she's going to ruin my life.'

She put one hand across her heart as though checking that it still had a beat. 'Then you should be wary. She's capable of things most of us couldn't dream of.'

'You can't just say that,' I pleaded, 'and not tell me what you mean.'

The vicar's wife was so white I was convinced she was going to faint and stood close by just in case. From the rise and fall of her chest she was struggling with something and I was sick with anticipation. Her mouth opened and closed until she rasped, 'If you repeat this to anyone, I shall only deny it. Grace told me she killed my sister because she was to blame – for everything – and she said she wouldn't stop there.'

Luke kept his voice level. 'She was angry and probably hurt. They're just words. Children lash out.'

'She was seven years old with a face like an angel, but

she burned them alive because she believed they told lies about her real mother and . . . she wasn't alone – she had help.'

I frowned. 'What sort of help?'

'The sort that cannot reside in a sacred place.'

The interview was at an end. We were practically pushed out of the back door into the cold night air, but something had stuck in my mind. I took a step back and managed to wedge my foot in the door frame to stop it closing.

'The children's home,' I whispered. 'Did it have a name?'

The eyes that gazed into mine were dull and lifeless. The lips barely moved and I heard just one word that was almost a sigh: 'Martinwood.'

Luke and I made our way to the bottom of the long garden and scrambled through a hole in the fence in the darkness. My shirt ripped and twigs buried themselves in my hair but I pressed on, desperate to be back in Luke's car. The minute he opened the door I jumped inside and curled into a ball with each hand inside the opposite sleeve of my jacket to keep warm.

As we both stared straight ahead I scrunched my face up with regret. 'We should have asked Genevieve's real surname.'

'Want to go back?' Luke laughed.

I shook my head. 'Not likely.'

His voice was wearily scornful. 'These people are so

superstitious and ignorant. She might as well have said that Grace was in league with the Devil. Did you get what you came for, Kat?'

'Kind of . . . but we've still got no proof . . . The vicar's wife won't repeat anything she told us.'

'Probably not,' Luke replied.

My teeth began to chatter gently. 'What did you think of the house?'

He shrugged. 'It's a typical vicarage – big, draughty, ancient and full of damp. Why? Did you see a ghost?'

'I've . . . been there before,' I answered hesitantly.

'When you were little, Kat?'

I was suddenly glad of the dark to hide behind. 'No . . . only in my dreams.'

Luke laughed. 'We all have nightmares about spooky places.'

I shook my head and turned my face towards him. 'Not like this. I've been climbing that staircase my whole life.'

CHAPTER TWENTY-ONE

We were so late already that I figured another half an hour wouldn't make much difference to our journey. I asked Luke if he could make a small detour to the village of Appleby because it seemed too good an opportunity to miss. He didn't even seem surprised or ask me why. I think we were both shell-shocked at the way the day had unfolded, and we had closed down, each lost in our own thoughts. It was no more than ten minutes away, but I made a mental note to offer Luke extra petrol money, though he was sure to refuse it. The roads were narrow and the traffic scarce although it was only 9 p.m. I wondered what everyone here did on a Saturday night, apart from stay indoors and watch TV.

Luke headed for the main street, which ran alongside the market square. I could see benches positioned around a small fountain and a war memorial with several wreaths laid at its base. There were only two other stationary cars so he was able to park easily. I noticed a light on in the pub, but everywhere else was deserted and in darkness. Luke switched off his headlights, sat quietly and waited for my instruction. He seemed content to be part of a magical mystery tour. I opened my door without speaking and he followed me out of the car with only a small nod of acknowledgement. It felt good having him as *my* captive audience for a change.

With a sly smile I led him towards the church of St Mary, walking slightly in front with an affected little wave of my hand. There was a hawthorn tree guarding the entrance, twisted and bare without its leaves. It reminded me of a gnarled hand reaching up to the sky in some kind of entreaty. There was a padlock on the gate and I gestured to Luke that we'd have to climb over the wall. He waited for me to go first and gave me a leg-up. I heaved myself on to the parapet without realizing how sharp the decorative stone was and managed to become stuck, rocking forwards and backwards like a stranded porpoise. Luke had to vault over and gently help me down, catching me as I fell. I rubbed my stomach in pain, annoyed at my own clumsiness.

It was lucky that the church was tucked away out of sight because I didn't think the local residents would be pleased with us mooching around the grounds after dark. I quickly left the pathway and began walking among the graves. The ground was springy with bracken interspersed with hard acorns that felt like small pebbles underfoot. Spiky green cases were strewn around, empty of their shiny russet conkers, and rotting crab apples stuck to my shoes. A small light positioned above a buttress of the church helped to guide our way.

'There's a full moon,' Luke said, craning his neck upward. 'And we're in the middle of a very old graveyard miles from home. Should I be worried?'

'I need to find Greta Alice Edwards,' I told him simply.

I could just make out Luke's expression and he seemed vaguely bemused but not annoyed. 'I assume she's dead. What date did she die?'

'Er . . . 1691. Born in 1675.'

He laughed gently. 'You won't find her here, Kat. Look around you.'

I looked from one headstone to other, my brow furrowed, but still I didn't understand. It was only when Luke used his finger as a marker to draw a line under the births and deaths that his meaning filtered through. The earliest dated from 1820.

'But . . . she *was* here,' I told him. 'At one time.'

'She might still be,' Luke replied gently, 'but after so many years they run out of space and have to . . . well . . . reuse the plot.'

'So they . . . bury someone else there,' I asked incredulously, 'and take away the headstone?'

He nodded apologetically, as if he was somehow personally responsible. 'Or worse, Kat. The graves are cleared and the remains stacked in a charnel house to allow for more burials.'

'What's a charnel house?'

'A place to store dug-up bones,' he answered bluntly.

The idea seemed incredible, but there was no reason to disbelieve Luke, and he was a mine of surprising information. 'I had no idea.'

'Why would you know? It's not the kind of topic people discuss.'

'So . . . another dead end,' I groaned. 'I was hoping for some sort of sign . . . I don't know what . . . but something significant.'

'Are you going to tell me who she is, Kat, or do I have to guess?'

I looked far away into the distance, breathing in the woody smell of pine cones mixed with moist earth. I didn't know whether it was the beautiful moonlit night or because Luke seemed more approachable than usual, but I didn't even attempt to modify my supernatural tale. Laying myself open to complete ridicule, I filled him in on the background to the story of Thomas Winter, my voice barely above a whisper because every sound seemed magnified here.

'You did that all on your own?' He sounded genuinely impressed.

'Well . . . Mum gave me some ideas,' I admitted.

'And this guy made up the spooky tale to enthral everyone?'

My cheeks filled with air like a gargoyle's until I blew out again. 'Seems so.'

'But . . . *you* can't think so, otherwise we wouldn't be here.'

Luke could read me so well that it was impossible to hide things from him.

'When I read his account . . . I was certain he was telling the truth.'

'Because you felt it in your bones,' he teased.

I studied his face in the velvet darkness as I prepared to drop the latest bombshell. 'There's something else . . . a link I only just discovered tonight. The vicar's wife said that Genevieve's children's home was actually "Martinwood", the same haunted house Thomas Winter wrote about.'

Luke cracked his knuckles, which sounded like someone stepping on twigs and always made me cringe. 'OK, then. Tell me your theory,' he encouraged.

The moon disappeared behind a cloud as I began speaking, and it helped that I could no longer see Luke's face. 'I think that everything in Thomas Winter's column was true,' I began earnestly, 'and he retracted his story because something . . . well . . . happened.'

'Something or someone,' Luke hissed, and blew on the back of my neck, making me jump into the air.

'OK . . . someone,' I agreed. 'Martinwood is the link between Greta the witch and Genevieve.'

Luke began to splutter as he realized what I meant. 'You don't mean that Genevieve and Greta . . . they're the same?'

'Maybe,' I muttered defensively. 'And after Thomas disturbed all the . . . er . . . devices to protect the house, the evil was kind of . . . unleashed, and she came for him . . .'

'And held him prisoner until he retracted his story,' Luke chortled.

I moved my eyebrows up and down, and put on a spooky voice. 'Mysterious and destructive happenings follow in Genevieve's wake . . .'

'It has to come back to Genevieve, doesn't it?' Luke commented sadly. 'You just can't shake her off.'

I paused for a moment. 'Maybe . . . she really does know me from somewhere.'

'You never met her until she joined your college, Kat.'

I put on a low, portentous voice. 'Maybe not in this life.'

Luke made a noise somewhere between a groan and a guffaw.

'OK then,' I challenged, 'how is it I recognize places I've never been and have this weird déjà-vu feeling around Genevieve?'

'I don't know,' he replied. 'But . . . if history is repeating itself and the witch has returned to continue her 300-year-old search, or vendetta . . . then you don't have long to worry.'

'Why?'

'Because she died at the age of sixteen.'

This hadn't occurred to me before. I clammed up and chewed my lip thoughtfully.

'Kat Rivers,' Luke said with mock exasperation, 'you're so infuriating, maddeningly wilful and . . . completely bonkers.'

I wasn't offended and laughed softly. I scrunched up my face and sucked in some more of the outdoor aroma. I could detect lingering woodsmoke and noticed a pile of leaves and brush in one corner with a rake still beside them.

'It feels like we're the only two people in the world tonight,' I said with wonder. 'Isn't this the strangest place? I know there's a wall, but if you look into the distance the graveyard seems to extend forever . . . right into the wood.'

'Just an optical illusion,' Luke murmured.

'And this church has been here since the twelfth century. Imagine what it's seen.'

He grinned. 'Not sure I want to.'

The hairs on the back of my neck suddenly stood up. 'Luke, what was that? I heard voices.'

He grabbed my hand and we ducked down and made our way towards the far wall of the graveyard, which was covered in climbing ivy and other creepers. There definitely were voices, sounding loud and strident, which indicated that we'd been spotted. I thought I heard the gate opening and footsteps coming our way. My heart was thumping so loudly it must surely have been audible.

Luke will sort it out, I told myself. It's not as if we're doing any damage. He can talk his way out of anything. There was a definite rustling now and it seemed to be coming from all sides, which meant we would soon be surrounded. The moment when we'd have to explain ourselves was getting closer, and I gave Luke a jittery, worried glance. He closed his eyes and tensed up as if he was about to jump into action. The last thing I expected was for him to lunge forward, put both arms tightly around me and sucker his lips to mine.

'Pretend to enjoy it,' I think he whispered.

It wasn't just a peck, but a long, lingering, searching kiss that I couldn't help but respond to. My lips automatically parted, my head tilted to one side and my hands reached for his neck. One of us was even moaning slightly, and I was horrified that it might be me. Kissing Luke felt so normal that this was scary in itself. We stayed this way for at least five minutes until I heard a deep voice laugh. 'Just love-struck kids. Leave them be.' Footsteps moved away and then there was silence.

I finally summoned the strength to push Luke away and sank to the ground to get my breath back and stop my knees trembling.

'Sorry about that, Kat,' he announced breezily. 'It's what they always do in the movies when they're trying to escape attention, and it seemed to work this time.'

'Good idea,' I panted, unable to look at him.

'You look so freaked,' he laughed. 'I was a bit jumpy myself, but we got away with it.'

I stayed on the ground, still trying to compose myself, unsure which had affected me more – the threat of irate villagers or Luke's kiss. For support, I rested my hand on a piece of stone about a metre from the wall. It was only when I rose that I noticed worn lettering among lichen spores and overgrown foliage. It must be an old gravestone that had sunk into the soft earth at an angle, leaving a wedge shape sticking up.

'Wow, look at this.'

I sank on to my haunches and Luke did the same.

'Can you decipher the name?' I asked him.

He shook his head and looked at me pointedly. 'Only the letter G is visible, Kat, but don't read anything into that.'

'There's a number though,' I said triumphantly, tracing my finger across the worn sandstone. 'A number one and . . . a six. This grave dates from the sixteen hundreds. This is one person who *wasn't* dug up.'

'You might be right,' Luke responded, 'but I've found something more interesting. Look at this.'

He moved aside one of the trailing plants and I could see the shape of a hand clearly chiselled into the stone.

'What is it? I mean, it's obviously a hand, but what does that mean?'

Luke stood up and cupped his hands around his face with a pained expression. 'I've seen it before. I'm trying to remember.'

I stayed silent as he paced about, kicking his heels against the bricks. He eventually punched his fist in the air triumphantly.

'I never forget a story. It was Halloween when I read about it – all the crazy ghost tales surface then – and this was about a cemetery somewhere in the Midlands that showed carvings of hands and feet. The locals say they're the mark of a witch, and the belief is that whoever can fit their own hand or foot into the imprint will come to serious misfortune.'

'And you believe that?' I asked with an involuntary shiver, quickly moving my hand away in case it followed the same lines as the carving.

'Of course not, but . . . it could explain why Thomas retracted his story. If the grave was discovered, together with his findings, hordes of ghost and witch hunters would descend on the village.'

'Suppose,' I answered doubtfully.

Luke gazed skywards and I had the strongest urge to wrap my arms around him again. It's only Luke, I told myself, but tonight it was as if someone else had taken his place. It was utterly bewildering.

'Is that the North Star, Kat?'

I looked at him askance. 'I don't have a clue.'

'Something else that might spook you.' He smiled. 'If this part of the graveyard is north-facing, then it's called the Devil's side.'

'You're not serious?' I burst out. 'Why?'

'It's where the unbaptised, suicides and the excommunicated used to be buried in unmarked graves.'

This seemed so horribly sad and I didn't want to stay any longer. It was time to put some distance between the two of us. My voice was clipped. 'We really should go. I shouldn't have brought you here tonight – it was just a stupid whim.'

'Kat, look at me.' Luke's voice made me stop in my tracks and turn slowly around. His face displayed none of the usual jokiness. 'Tonight was kind of . . . different . . . but it has to stop here. I'm worried about you.'

'I don't really believe in all this,' I fibbed. 'It was just a good yarn to impress my favourite journalist.'

He wasn't fooled. 'Come on, Kat. Promise me you'll let all this go,' he begged. 'Thomas Winter and his decrepit house and all the other supernatural past-life stuff?'

'I promise,' I answered solemnly, and meant it. Luke was right, this was all much too crazy to dwell on any longer and there was nowhere left to go with it. I had to give it up.

As we got back into Luke's car and left the village I looked back only once, and noticed a black and white timber-framed building on a small incline, encased in scaffolding. Warning notices were attached to the metal gates that blocked access, and it looked like a building site. I remembered the photograph and had no doubts as to its name – 'Martinwood', abandoned again.

CHAPTER TWENTY-TWO

Sleep was heavy and dreamless that night, so heavy it felt as if I'd never be dragged back to consciousness. Light filtering through my thin bedroom curtains eventually woke me at about ten and I lay under the warmth of my duvet thinking things through. I now knew more about Genevieve. She had a background and a history, which meant that I had more ammunition to fight her. In the cold light of day I wasn't completely convinced she was capable of murder, but Luke and I had confirmation that she was disturbed and needed help.

'You look bright this morning,' Mum trilled as I came downstairs. She studied me critically. 'But you've lost weight . . . You must try to eat more.'

She insisted on cooking me a proper breakfast, and it felt nice to relax and be waited on. Mum definitely seemed to be making an effort since we'd had our talk. She hadn't complained nearly as much and had already been to see the doctor to try a new form of therapy. I was optimistic that things were going to improve.

'Everyone was looking for you yesterday,' she beamed, setting a plate of scrambled eggs, tomatoes, mushrooms and toast in front of me.

'Everyone?'

'Nat, Hannah . . . Merlin. They couldn't get hold of you on your mobile and sounded quite frantic.'

My hands flew to my face, remembering my date with Merlin. I hadn't even contacted him to let him know it was off, but . . . there would be plenty of time to make it up to him at Nat's.

'The reception was awful, Mum, then I lost signal completely and switched off. I was worried about not letting you know how late we'd be.'

'I don't fret when you're out with *Luke*,' she answered. 'How was your trip?'

I waved my hand impatiently. 'It was great, but what did everyone want?'

'Oh, something about a party.'

I was relieved it wasn't anything else. 'Nat's birthday thing is today. They've probably changed the time or something. I'll ring her later.'

When I turned on my mobile there were eight or nine missed calls and as many texts. One voicemail was from Hannah, high-pitched and excited with lots of background noise. It sounded like, 'Katy, can't believe you're not here, ring me urgently.' Hannah had always been a bit of a drama queen. I tried her phone, but it was switched off. Merlin and Nat were unavailable as well so it seemed best to stick to the plan and wander over to Nat's house at about midday. I noticed Mum in the garden burning the last of the fallen leaves in a small incinerator. It seemed like the perfect opportunity to get rid of the pendant once and for all. When she wasn't looking I popped it into the funnel to smoulder into dust. Today felt like a definite new beginning for me.

The sky was blindingly blue with whipped-cream clouds and a first frost that lingered, making everywhere look crisply beautiful. I took my time and walked through the park, even stopping to watch ducks foraging for food in the lake and smiling at a little girl throwing bread into the water. Because of Genevieve I'd abandoned my coat and stuffed it at the back of my wardrobe. I wore a thick knitted jumper over a shirt that was tucked into my jeans. My wardrobe wasn't extensive like Hannah's, but since my weight loss all my clothes fitted me differently, and I could feel myself gliding along instead of my usual untidy shuffle. It was a heady feeling to be happy in my own skin. On the way I looked for faces in the clouds, which was one of my hobbies, although I'd never tell anyone because it was so weird.

Nat's house had a strange deserted look about it and the downstairs curtains were still closed. I was left on the doorstep for ages until her mum answered the door.

'Katy? Goodness. Nat's still in bed, exhausted. You must be too. I'm surprised you're up so early.'

I stared at her blankly. It was already after midday. Nat's cat cushion, wrapped in three sheets of foil paper, was in one hand, and my contribution to the lunch, an enormous strawberry cheesecake, in the other. Nat's mum seemed to realize that I didn't know what she was talking about. There was embarrassment on her face as she ushered me in, making soothing noises about waking her daughter to explain. She disappeared upstairs.

Explain what? I was already late. Merlin and Hannah should be here, but the house was deathly quiet: no balloons, no presents strewn about and no cooking smells from the kitchen. A voice called down to me.

'You can come up now, Katy.'

I climbed the stairs and opened the door a few centimetres. Nat's bedroom was just like her – messy, colourful and warm; lots of different styles going on that should have clashed but seemed to work well together. The blind was pulled down and I could just about make out a figure lying in the bed. The thought suddenly occurred to me that she must be ill but no one had been able to reach me to let me know. I moved nearer now, taking in her pallor and the dark-circled eyes that could barely focus.

'You look awful,' I said sympathetically. 'Is it flu?'

She put one hand across her forehead and croaked something inaudible.

I rested the present gently on the bed. 'I should leave you to get some sleep. Sorry about your birthday lunch. We can always do it next weekend.'

'Katy . . . don't go.'

Nat tried to sit up in bed and I peered closely at her. I noticed that her dark eyes were the result of smudged mascara and her paleness was thick make-up, which was also smeared across her pillow. Her hair was a tangled mess and there were bits of coloured streamers nestled inside.

'I'm so sorry,' she muttered, taking a large gulp from a glass of water on her bedside cabinet. 'We tried to contact you loads of times. I knew nothing about it . . . the party was all a surprise, and Merlin said you were due back in the evening.'

'Party?' I questioned. 'Here?'

'No . . . it was at Merlin's house.'

'Merlin's house?' I repeated, almost falling off the bed in shock.

Nat's voice returned in a torrent. 'His mum had a marquee in the garden, some social evening for her students, and Genevieve persuaded her to throw a surprise party for me. Wasn't that sweet of her? It was all last-minute, and most of the food was leftovers, but . . .'

She stopped because she must have noticed my reaction. I felt sick with disappointment, envy, hurt, anger and just about every bad emotion I'd ever felt in my whole life. Merlin's house was amazing, like a stately home, and even more so with him in it. The thought of everyone partying there without me was unbearable – like someone had punched me in the stomach.

'Where did you go, Katy? We spent, like, forever trying to reach you.'

Something weird had happened to my face. It was tight, as though I was wearing a face pack and couldn't smile or frown in case it cracked. I could barely open my mouth to speak.

'I got held up . . . it couldn't be helped. Luke and I had to wait around to talk to someone.' Nat watched me intently and I tried desperately to sound normal and save some little pride. 'What was the party like then?'

She rubbed her eyes and stretched, a dreamy smile playing around her lips. 'It was incredible. Merlin's mum didn't mind how many people came, and once the word spread the list grew and almost everyone turned up. The night was cold but they had patio heaters and Christmas lights and a live band who could play anything from classical to rock. It was great being outdoors under the moon and stars and dancing on the lawn until four this morning, when I collapsed and had to be carried home . . . by Adam.'

'I'm thrilled for you,' I mumbled, torn between wanting to be genuinely happy for Nat and my own misery.

Her eyes lighted on my badly wrapped present and her face fell. 'Katy, I'm so sorry. I didn't know about the party until I got to Merlin's, and we tried ringing you until late. . .'

'It's fine,' I replied unconvincingly. 'It was a lovely surprise and you deserved it.'

'It would've been better with you there.'

I tried to make a noise of gratitude but sounded like a strangled cat.

'Merlin was in a terrible dilemma – you should know that. He was miserable the whole night.'

'Was he?' This made me feel slightly better. It was the thought of Merlin enjoying himself without me that hurt more than anything.

Nat's phone beeped and she reached over and checked her messages.

'Sorry I didn't hear your call,' she apologized. 'And here's a text from Gen.'

I grimaced but she was too busy reading it to notice.

'Mmm . . . says she's put her photos on Facebook already.'

I must be a masochist because when Nat stumbled out of bed to access her computer I didn't leave but stood behind her, a rictus smile plastered across my face. Grudgingly I had to admit that the photos were great. They weren't the usual cheesy poses of everyone grinning for the camera or making stupid gestures. Genevieve must have moved, virtually unseen, to capture the atmosphere and mood of the party. My favourites were of Nat, with her eyes closed, blowing out the candles on her birthday cake and one of the marquee at night, surrounded by huge oaks lit up by fairy lights. With relief I realized that none were of Genevieve because she had stayed behind the lens.

'Wow . . . they're so good,' Nat breathed.

'They're OK,' I admitted, giving her a hug. 'I'm glad you enjoyed the party, I really am, and don't feel the least bit guilty. I'll make sure not to miss your next one.'

Nat moved her mouse to exit, just as the next batch of photos came through. She hesitated and seemed to freeze. My eyes followed hers as she stared at the prominent centrepiece and I couldn't look away even though I was desperate to. '*I'm your worst nightmare*,' Genevieve had told me the first time we spoke, and that nightmare was right in front of me now, forever imprinted in my mind – Genevieve and Merlin having a slow dance, her arms wound around his neck while he gazed down on her with complete adoration. The worst thing was – it was a look I recognized; it was the way he used to look at me.

CHAPTER TWENTY-THREE

'It was nice of someone to take that photograph,' I said reproachfully. 'I'm really glad Merlin missed me so much.'

Nat's laugh was nervously shrill. 'That was nothing, Katy. Just a joke right at the end of the night, everyone dancing cheek to cheek like in the old days. We all did the same and swapped partners. Don't read anything into the photo . . . Merlin was really pining for *you*.'

But no matter what she said or how she tried to explain, the camera never lied. Genevieve had pointed this out to me and she was completely right. The moment might have lasted only a second, but it was now frozen in time, and when I looked at Merlin it would be all that I'd see. I paced up and down Nat's bedroom trying to think straight, unable to stop venting my frustration.

'I know she's liked Merlin from the start. She couldn't wait until I was out of the picture to arrange a party and make a move on him.'

'That didn't happen,' Nat replied patiently. She was out of bed now, sitting at her dressing table trying to remove last night's make-up and tame her hair. 'The party wasn't planned without you. We expected you back, remember? You told Merlin you'd see him on Saturday night.'

This was true, but it didn't make me feel any better. 'I know I did, Nat, but I was held up and *she* knew that would happen.'

Nat turned and faced me with her calm grey eyes. 'How? A premonition or just telepathy?'

'I'm not sure,' I sulked, 'but she knew. She's really manipulative, sneaky and just plain . . .'

I managed to stop myself in time and the word 'evil' stayed on my lips. Once again, I'd fallen into the trap of criticizing Genevieve and looking jealous and vindictive. So much for staying cool and playing her at her own game, but she'd hit me right where it hurt most – Merlin. Nat patted her cushioned stool, making room for me to sit beside her. I felt like a five-year-old about to be told off.

'Look, I know how you feel,' she began. 'Genevieve is funny, smart and really pretty and you both seem to like the same things but . . . she isn't what you think.'

'You can't see the bad in anyone,' I answered with fondness. 'That's your problem. Imagine if it was Adam, how would *you* feel then?'

'You've changed since she came along,' Nat said, ignoring my comment about Adam. She gave my hair a tug. 'Remember how much fun we used to have?'

'We still have fun . . . don't we?'

She put her head down, playing with the button on her pyjamas top.

This was awful. If Nat felt that being with me was a drag, then what must everyone else think?

'I know the past few months have been difficult for you, Katy – and I know you rub each other up the wrong way – but I think you're too hard on Genevieve.'

'Thanks for telling me what you really think,' I muttered moodily.

She ran one hand through her mussed-up tresses. 'It doesn't matter what she does – you see the bad in it, and when you talk about her it's like she's a different person, a person no one else sees.'

'I know that,' I admitted, ferociously chewing my lip.

'Last night wasn't her fault, but you immediately blame her without any evidence. And it isn't the first time.'

'I don't need evidence . . . I just know.'

Nat pointed to one corner of her bedroom. 'Look at that. Genevieve made it for my birthday. It's amazing and must have taken her forever to paint.'

It was a panelled screen, almost as tall as me, made up of three different sections hinged together, and each panel was hand-painted with a different flower in the softest colours: pink, lavender, pale blue and ivory. It was utterly gorgeous and I hated Genevieve all the more for it, especially after the lies she'd told me about having no idea for a present. My cushion paled into insignificance beside it. I saw my future stretching out in front of me and it was frightening. Genevieve would never stop, and every week would bring some new torment to exclude me or make me look bad. I'd thought that I was strong enough to withstand her taunts, but I wasn't, and if I had to make my friends choose between us, then maybe that was a chance I had to take . . .

I licked my dry, cracked lips and could feel my heart thumping like a drum inside my chest. 'There's something you should know about Genevieve. I didn't want to tell everyone, but I think it's time.'

Nat immediately came back with, 'There's something *you* should know, Katy. She told Hannah, Merlin and me a secret last night, and it's really big.'

I was desperate to discover what new lies she'd been telling so I urged Nat to go first, but she jumped up and announced, 'I'll get us both a drink. Wait here for me.'

I walked over to the window and ran my hand across the screen; it was tactile, intricate and fabulously unique. Something like this would sell for hundreds of pounds in an art shop, and it was obvious why Nat was so pleased with it. I peered through the blind at the ordinary scene below – Nat's dad washing his car, her mum raking up the soggy leaves, and her little sister riding her bike through a puddle. This was a turning point for me. I might never sit here again doing normal everyday stuff with Nat because what I was going to say about Genevieve couldn't be taken back. I was preparing to call her a murderer and say that

I had evidence to prove it. Genevieve's secret might be big, but mine was even bigger.

Nat returned five minutes later with two mugs of steaming hot tea. Her face was still shiny with make-up remover and she'd put a giant clip in her hair, making it look even more out of control. She was so cuddly and funny I nearly backed down, but I steeled myself – I had to do this. Nat slipped into a fuzzy dressing gown that was hanging on the back of her door and wedged her feet into a pair of pig slippers.

'Genevieve's parents didn't die in a car crash,' she began, and my ears immediately pricked up. 'They died in a house fire and she was in it too.'

'So why did she lie?' I asked with a horrible sinking feeling.

'She's still haunted by it,' Nat answered defensively. 'Knowing they were burnt alive and only she escaped. And that's not all . . .'

'There's more?'

'Genevieve went to live with an aunt and uncle after the fire, but they were cruel and spread lies about her.'

I felt light-headed with disbelief at the way things were unfolding. 'What sort of lies?'

She gave a deep incredulous laugh. 'That she was dangerous and needed some sort of professional help. She was only eight at the time.'

My mind was inwardly screaming but I couldn't articulate my fears because it was obvious that Nat didn't doubt her story for a moment.

What if the accusations were true and Genevieve really was evil and no children would go near her and even adults were afraid of her but now she's learned to disguise her real nature and I'm the only one who can see it?

'There's worse to come,' she continued, and I died a little more inside. 'Genevieve had been adopted when she was a baby because her real mother took her own life, so she was left with no one.'

I covered my face, trying to collect my thoughts. This had the added advantage of making me appear traumatized and sympathetic at the same time.

Nat's voice was unusually grown-up. 'I knew how upset you'd be.'

'It's dreadful,' I replied, wondering how to pump her for information without looking callous. 'I suppose Genevieve must have changed her name at some time.'

'What makes you say that?'

'Just an idea,' I fibbed, wondering if she'd picked a beautiful lyrical name so that people would remember her.

'She wouldn't say, but she did insist the person she used to be was dead forever.'

'I guess I haven't been very understanding *again*,' I said woodenly, 'but the way she behaves with Merlin gets to me.'

Nat nodded vigorously. 'I'd be exactly the same if I was dating someone like Merlin, but they're really just friends. She's been helping him with something . . . a present for you.'

'Really?' I cringed.

'The truth is, Katy, Hannah and I have both noticed . . . just lately . . . you're as prickly as a hedgehog.'

So they had been discussing me and how suspicious I'd become. I was glad that Nat had the guts to tell me, but it still hurt. 'Sorry it's been so uncomfortable for you,' I muttered. 'It's under control now, especially after the things you just told me.'

Yet again Genevieve had somehow anticipated everything I intended to do and got there first. She was pushing me to the limit now. She told me when we first met that I didn't deserve the life I had and she was going to take it from me. I had to make certain to disappoint her. I gave Nat another hug and said goodbye.

'The problem with Genevieve,' I began as an afterthought, 'is she'll never find what she's looking for and be happy.'

'That's the weirdest thing ever,' Nat breathed.

'Why?'

'Because that's exactly what she said about you. By the way . . . what *did* you want to tell me about her?'

I smiled wanly. 'It doesn't matter now . . . it wasn't anything important.'

CHAPTER TWENTY-FOUR

I prowled around my bedroom like a caged tiger. There was no way that Genevieve could have known about Luke and me being held up last night, because we hadn't known it ourselves. It was downright unreal, and I was keen to see how Luke would explain this away with his usual logic. How did she do it? And that stupid pendant had turned up again like a bad penny, this time wrapped in a note from Mum telling me not to be so careless. It must have slipped out of one of the ventilation holes in the burner. I stared at it as Genevieve's words came back to haunt me. *I don't need to follow you, Katy . . . you're marked.* I jiggled the green glass about in my hands, wondering why it felt weightier, and then lost my temper and threw it against the wall. When I examined it, the pendant was completely intact but it had made a hole in the plaster. Hastily I moved one of my posters to cover the damage.

I worked so hard and in such a frenzy that afternoon it was a miracle the paper didn't burst into flames. My phone didn't stop ringing and beeping with incoming texts, but I studiously ignored everyone, trying to work off the pent-up rage inside me.

'I'm a good listener,' Mum told me discreetly, when I eventually came down for a late lunch.

My face seemed to be set in a permanent scowl and I remembered how Gran used to warn, 'If the wind changes, Katy, you'll stick like that.'

'Thanks for asking, Mum, but it's something I have to work out myself.'

'Is it that girl again?'

I was determined not to tell her anything because she hadn't believed my story so far and I was exhausted just thinking about Genevieve.

'I'm here when you want to talk,' she said, and pressed her lips together.

Mum hadn't even reached the kitchen door when my resolve weakened. 'Honestly, we've got the same taste in everything, we like the same guy, and now we say the same things about each other. We're merging together so much I don't know who I am any more.'

'She must have very low self-esteem,' Mum replied diplomatically. 'It might not feel like a compliment, but she must admire you.'

'She doesn't. She despises me and, anyway, she's better than me at everything.'

'I'm sure she isn't. You need to have belief in yourself.'

The red mist was descending again and, once it had

started, I couldn't pull back. 'She looks like a cat, with her big creepy green eyes. Everyone thinks cats are attractive, but they're really horrible . . . cold, selfish, snooty, superior, vain and predatory . . . Only out for themselves . . .'

Gemma gave a reproving miaow as if she understood every word and idly flicked her tail at me.

'She's really under your skin,' Mum commented sadly.

'She calls herself Genevieve,' I ranted, 'but she's changed her name, although her real name doesn't suit her at all – it's far too nice.'

Mum gave an indulgent chuckle. 'Why? What is it?'

'It's Grace.'

I must have looked away for a second. Mum's cup slipped out of her hand and smashed on the kitchen floor, breaking into a hundred pieces. Her face looked so shocked that I was rendered speechless and temporarily unable to react. Our eyes locked together for what seemed like ages until she quickly bent down, with trembling hands, to start picking the cup, cutting her finger on a shard of china.

I took her over to the sink, cleaned the wound and then wrapped some gauze and a plaster around it, all the time trying to ignore the feeling of disquiet lurking somewhere inside.

'I won't go out,' she murmured. 'You shouldn't be left alone like this.'

I felt a pang of guilt. Mum had arranged to help at the church bring-and-buy, her way of trying to get out more and meet people. It might not sound like much, but it was a big thing for her and now I'd ruined everything.

'I'm absolutely fine,' I reassured her. 'Just go and enjoy yourself, and don't hurry back.'

Mum was still a little pale, but she set off with a determined face, not even going through her usual obsessive routine of checking doors and windows before she left. And she hadn't asked how I knew Genevieve's real name. For some reason I had the distinct feeling she wanted to get as far away from our house as possible.

I went back to work, counting Merlin's missed calls and taking a perverse pleasure in the number and frequency, especially when they reached thirteen. There it was again – a horrible niggle that wouldn't go away. I had to do as Luke advised, stop clouding my mind with all the hocus-pocus stuff and apply reason to the problem of Genevieve. I took a deep breath, remembering Mum's reaction to the name Grace, and Luke's words spun around in my head.

'Genevieve knows you from somewhere . . . she's targeted you because of something she believes has happened . . .'

The same expression of fear had been etched on the face of the old woman, the vicar's wife and now my own mother. Was she somehow part of Genevieve's tangled web? It was impossible not to act on this so I sent Luke a text. Five minutes later he knocked on my front door with his usual just-rolled-out-of-bed look.

'You didn't have to come straight away,' I apologized, 'but there's no one else I can run this by.'

'Tell me everything, Kat,' he said eagerly, and it seemed as if, although he didn't like to see me hurt, he was enjoying this game of cat and mouse.

I told him all about the party and Genevieve's revelations, plus Mum's reaction when I mentioned the name Grace. Luke messed with his hair, then stood up and boiled the kettle. He put two heaped spoons of coffee in a mug with three sugars, tipped the kettle with the plume still rising, stirred vigorously and took a sip. Then he raided our biscuit tin, dunked two chocolate digestives in his cup and looked at me thoughtfully.

'Why don't you just ask her?'

'Mum doesn't like talking about the past,' I reminded him. 'She never talks about my dad, or where she used to work, and I only see my grandparents once a year. It's like she deliberately cut herself off.'

'You could do it gently . . . don't rush in.'

I exhaled noisily. 'She's making an effort and I don't want to ruin it. Any upset and she'll be back where she started . . . almost a recluse.'

He raised his eyebrows at me. 'Then I don't see what we can do.'

'There is one thing . . . It's just a thought and is probably way off the mark, and I'll need some help . . .'

Luke groaned and covered his ears. 'I know it's going to mean trouble or something worse. What is it?'

'The attic,' I told him quickly. 'It's where Mum keeps all her photos, letters, books, furniture . . . all kinds of stuff from the past.'

Luke looked doubtful. 'She wouldn't keep anything secret if she thought you'd root about up there.'

'But that's the thing . . . we used to have a pull-down ladder, and once when I was about ten I climbed up there and she went ballistic . . .'

'She was probably worried you'd fall.'

I gave him my best sinister stare. 'Or she's hiding something. After that the ladder mysteriously disappeared almost overnight . . .'

'Attics are horrible,' Luke grumbled. 'I hate dust and cobwebs and creepy stuff like bats and skeletons . . .'

'There aren't any skeletons up there.' I laughed and looked at my watch. 'Mum won't be back for at least another two hours. Are you up for it?'

He nodded grudgingly and rolled up his sleeves. But now that he'd agreed I was stumped because there were loads of things I hadn't thought through. In an embarrassing climb-down I was forced to voice my concerns.

'Sorry, but we only have a stepladder . . . and it's not tall enough to reach the hatch and . . . if Mum came back early she'd never forgive me, especially for getting you involved.' I took a nervous sip of Luke's coffee. 'Maybe this isn't such a good idea after all.'

'You're not thinking hard enough, Kat. There's an

easier way to gain access to your attic, and your mum will never find out.'

I hated it when he was smug like this, but no matter how I wracked my brains there was only one way and that was through the hatch.

Luke gestured towards the door. 'Come with me and I'll show you.'

'Should I take a coat?'

He shook his head, still maddeningly secretive. Two minutes later we were climbing the stairs of Luke's house. We stopped on the landing and faced four doors that perfectly mirrored the layout of our own house. The first I knew to be his bedroom, then his parents', then the bathroom and, lastly, a tiny space barely big enough for a single bed and used by my mum as a place to do her laundry. I nudged him impatiently, but he simply grinned in his annoying way and flung open the door to the smallest bedroom. It was empty apart from a steep wooden staircase leading upward.

Luke bowed his head and did some sort of flourish with his hand. 'Dad's converting our attic to become his office and has roped me into helping him. And guess what?'

'What?'

'Our roof spaces are connected. All you have to do is step through the gap.'

I threw my arms around Luke's neck and squeezed tightly.

CHAPTER TWENTY-FIVE

The Cassidys' attic was a light bright space. Everything had been cleared out and a floor already installed. Only the walls and ceiling were yet to be constructed. There was a new sloping roof window, just like the one in Merlin's studio, and I could see a whole row of chimney pots, patches of blue sky and a couple of blackbirds resting on a telegraph wire. A glance through to my house revealed how dark, dingy and crowded it was. I stood for a minute, screwing up my eyes, trying to make out the various boxes and strange shapes. Holes in some of the slates let pockets of daylight shine through, like tiny sunbeams, and I wondered how long it was sincc Mum had had the roof repaired.

'In another week this will be bricked up,' Luke said knowledgably. 'We have to conform to fire regulations, so there won't be any more access and I won't be able to burgle your house, Kat.'

I smiled vacantly, realizing this was my very last chance to look around in here. It almost seemed like it was meant to be. There was something here that Mum didn't want me to know about, but now the moment had come I was nervous. I gave Luke an anxious look, steeled myself and moved forward.

'Make sure it's safe to walk on,' he warned as I stepped over the boundary.

'I think it's safe . . . I was up here before, remember?'

Luke followed close behind and nervously placed one of his size-ten feet. He sounded relieved. 'It's been boarded with planks of wood.'

I peeled a wet cobweb from my cheek and stood for a moment glancing around, wondering why my first emotion was an overwhelming one of sadness. It wasn't just the dust, neglect and junk; it was something tangible, and once again I was glad of Luke for support.

'Dressmaker's dummy,' he pointed out. 'And a birdcage.'

I delved into some tea chests filled with books and old toys, surprised that Mum had bothered keeping this stuff.

'What's in the suitcase?' Luke asked.

It was an old-fashioned trunk, with several bags of old cushions and curtains on top, but it was well and truly locked, with no key in sight. I tipped it up slightly and heard a dull thud.

'I'll force it,' he said.

I put one of my hands on his arm to restrain him. 'No need . . . the hinges are rusty. This one's already come apart.'

I wriggled one hand inside and felt cloth wrapped

around something long and thin. My fingers came into contact with cold metal interspersed with small holes.

'I know what it is. It's Mum's flute.'

'I didn't know she played.'

'She doesn't – not any more – but she told me she used to be really good.'

I moved among wicker baskets, fake plants, tennis rackets, an old paraffin heater and kettle, fearful that I'd been wrong and this was just a dumping ground for unwanted things.

'Some of this stuff's worth money,' Luke exclaimed, running his hand over a small oak desk with a leather top.

I went over and opened the lid. Inside was an assortment of various-sized photographs. I looked through, randomly, amazed to see photos of Mum when she was only my age, some taken on a beach, some at a funfair. Her hair was long and windswept and she was laughing and carefree, so unlike the mother I knew that the sadness came back again, washing over me in waves. Weirdly, it felt as if she'd left behind this happy smiling person to gather dust with the other things, including her dreams of becoming a musician. I sat with my knees tucked under me staring at the images while Luke continued with the search. I think he was giving me a moment to myself. It was tempting to take some of the photos away with me, but they would only remind me of how unhappy Mum was now. I carefully put them back.

My attention turned to a large black holdall, which

I quickly unzipped. 'There're even baby clothes up here,' I told Luke. 'A tiny romper suit, baby cardigan, knitted booties and a baby blanket.' I held up a white embroidered shawl which had a satin ribbon threaded around the edge. 'Wow, this is gorgeous.'

Luke pointed to some stitching in one corner. 'It's got something written on it.'

'It says HOPE. Isn't that strange? Maybe some sort of wish for the baby, like peace and love.'

'It was a name years ago,' Luke answered carefully. 'Parents used to name their children after virtues. Hope, Patience, Chastity, Mercy and . . .'

He stopped and I stuffed the shawl back into the holdall. I knew what he was thinking – Grace, the name I never wanted to hear again. I took a last lingering look at the photos of Mum and closed the desk, sitting down heavily on the floor.

'I was wrong to drag you up here, Luke . . . there's nothing of interest to us.'

'Well, it's pretty much like most attics. Ours was the same – Dad and I took four carloads of stuff to the dump.'

A feeling of despair filled me. 'This problem with Genevieve – it's made me . . . deranged. I'm always looking over my shoulder in case I'm being followed, permanently on edge waiting for her next trick, and my real life doesn't exist any more . . .'

'You're not deranged,' Luke reassured me, joining me

cross-legged on the filthy boards, 'although she might be trying to make you that way.'

I gave an empty laugh. 'Well, I think it's working. I mean, what are we doing here? It's crazy.'

'Kinda fun though.' He grinned, trying to cheer me up.

'And the worst thing is,' I moaned, 'she's shown me a side of myself I never knew existed.'

'What side?'

'One filled with hate,' I answered flatly. Luke didn't reply and my hands banged against my thighs with frustration. 'And I see stupid connections everywhere . . . even dragging my own mum into this sick game.'

'You have to be strong and focused, Kat; she wants you to fall apart.'

I struggled to my feet. 'Come on, let's go.'

When I turned round, Luke was holding up a carved dark wooden box inlaid with a paler pattern. 'These are really sought after,' he said admiringly.

'Where did you get that?'

'It had fallen down by the water tank. I saw something shining.'

'I remember that,' I breathed, thinking back to Grandad and how he would open it for me and pretend it was a sea chest full of pirate jewels.

'Whose was it?'

'It belonged to Grandad, and the lining is made of red silk.'

Luke opened the box and revealed the still-vibrant red

lining. I inhaled the familiar smell of his cigars. 'He always teased me that when I was old enough he'd show me the secret.'

'Secret of what?'

'Secret of the hidden treasure.'

'And where was it?'

'That's the thing. I never found out – he was probably just making it up.'

Luke's brow creased as he turned the box over and over in his hands. Impatiently he handed it to me. 'You try.'

I slid one finger around the rim and underneath, shaking it with annoyance. 'I spent years trying to work it out.'

He gave a cynical laugh. 'No false bottom?'

'No.'

'It's so intricate,' he pondered. 'If you look closely it's two sets of different carvings, and they fit together like a dovetail joint.'

I didn't have a clue what Luke was talking about. My face must have been blank because he took the box back and his fingers nimbly pressed different parts of the two-tone wood. This seemed to go on for minutes and I was losing interest when something moved and a hollow compartment shot out.

He grinned. 'I love puzzles. You have to press the two perfectly aligned spots or it doesn't work.'

Luke carefully handed the whole drawer to me as if it really did contain something precious, although all I could see inside was folded paper. I felt certain there was something momentous in my grasp, but I didn't want to examine it here. I began to clamber over all the obstacles to get back to Luke's house, glad of the delay because I was jumpy with nerves. We stepped back across the boundary and my stomach muscles tied themselves in knots. Luke handed me a cloth to wipe my hands on, and I noticed his face was covered in soot, which looked funny, contrasting with his blond hair. There was no more reason to stall so, with a nervous smile, I carefully unfolded the first piece of paper with trembling fingers.

'It's my birth certificate,' I whispered, wondering why Mum would keep it hidden, but then remembering the most obvious thing – the identity of my dad. I quickly checked the entry for 'Father' and my faced flushed. It was blank. I hung my head and pretended to be looking at something else so Luke wouldn't notice. A small ring of clear plastic caught my eye, still nestled in one corner of the drawer. I held it up to the light.

'It's a wristband for babies,' Luke informed me. 'There should be a name on it.'

'"Baby Rivers",' I read, 'and there're two six-digit numbers.'

'Hospital numbers,' Luke answered quickly. 'Anything else in the drawer?'

'Just a photo of a baby.' I flipped it over and could see writing on the back, but it was so faint it was illegible. 'I think Mum's been putting off the inevitable. When I'm eighteen I might try to trace my father. Maybe that's why she's been so tense. There's something about him she dreads me finding out.'

'So all this is nothing to do with Genevieve?' Luke sighed.

'It doesn't look that way. The photo must be significant, but I can't think who it is.'

His voice was gently amused. 'It has to be you.'

'It isn't,' I insisted. 'And there's writing on the back, but it's faded.'

'What about that trick we learned in the Spy Club? How to make writing reappear.'

'You wouldn't let me join,' I reminded him, sticking out my tongue. '"No girls allowed" was the rule.'

Luke playfully pulled my hair and took a pencil from his pocket. I watched, fascinated, as he carefully shaded all over the back of the photo. If you looked closely, the writing gradually re-emerged, standing out white against the grey.

'What does it say?'

He was rapt with concentration and never even looked up. 'I can just make out a date . . . 5 June, and the year . . . 1994.'

'That's my birthday!' I said, completely taken aback.

Luke peered hard. 'There's a name as well, Katy. It says "Katy Rivers".'

I snorted. 'That baby really isn't me.'

'You don't recognize yourself.' He laughed. 'All babies look alike, or so my mum says.'

'There's something we're missing,' I groaned. 'It's like when a word's on the tip of your tongue but you can't remember it.'

I looked at the birth certificate again and read all the details. 'Wow! Look at this. I was born in a maternity hospital in North Yorkshire.' I clapped my hands together but Luke didn't appear impressed.

'So?'

'That's where we've been scratching around for Genevieve's past. Isn't that a coincidence?'

'Well, it's one of the biggest counties in England, but . . . if you say so, Kat. What was your mum doing there?'

I shook my head. 'Don't know. She's never told me she lived away, and I never thought to ask.'

There it was again. The feeling that something was staring me in the face and I was too stupid to see it. I tried to join all the pieces together, but they fell apart and I could have screamed with exasperation. From nowhere, a terrible weakness seemed to descend across my whole body and I had to get out. The view from the top of the steep wooden stairs was a lot scarier on the way down and made me feel giddy, but I stumbled towards them and descended so fast that I tripped on the bottom step and twisted my ankle. Luke found me sprawled on the carpet clutching my left foot, almost glad of the pain.

CHAPTER TWENTY-SIX

'Put some ice on it straight away, Kat. It might help the swelling.'

'I can't even stand up . . . Can you help me?'

Luke pulled me to my feet, put one arm around my waist and positioned my left arm over his shoulder to take my weight as I hopped out of his front door. Even the few steps from his house to mine seemed impossible. My ankle had already ballooned and my shoe was getting tighter by the second.

'If I tickled you right now you'd be helpless,' he joked.

'Don't even think about it.' I laughed weakly, nauseous with the intense throbbing in my foot.

A loud cough made me look up and almost lose my balance. If Luke hadn't held on tightly I'd have fallen into Mum's rose bush. Why did I look so guilty, and why couldn't I stop blushing? The curse of having red hair was that once my cheeks had reached full beetroot colour, they stayed that way for ages.

'Hi, Merlin,' I managed to whisper. 'I-I've hurt my ankle and Luke is helping me inside.'

'I'll do that,' he glowered, and Luke gave me a sneaky wink and let him take over, disappearing discreetly into his own house. The problem was that Merlin was so tall he couldn't support me at all. My arm was almost pulled out of its socket and I had to let go and hop indoors, pausing only to worm my hand into the pocket of my jeans for the key. I held on to the wall all the way to our lounge and then slumped on to the sofa, cringing as I caught sight of myself in the mirror above our fireplace. My face was even worse than Luke's. I must have rubbed it, and the dirt was smeared across both cheeks. My hair had a giant cobweb nestling in it. Merlin had spent last night with a perfectly groomed, glamorous Genevieve in a killer black dress, high heels and stockings, only to come face to face today with his girlfriend the chimney sweep. Even worse, my phoned beeped at that moment so I couldn't even lie about not getting his messages.

'Sorry I didn't take your calls,' I simpered. 'We were in Luke's loft and I couldn't even see my phone. That's why I'm filthy and covered in . . . er . . . dust.'

Merlin sighed with mock annoyance and picked something out of my hair.

'You can't stay here alone . . . you might have broken that ankle. Come back to my house; Mum will look at it for you.'

'No . . . really, I'm fine, and I need to get cleaned up and . . .'

Merlin didn't give me a chance to finish. His phone was already in his hand, dialling the number for a local taxi. I usually liked it when Merlin was decisive, but today it irritated me; it felt as if he was simply disregarding my feelings. In less than five minutes we heard the beep of a car horn, and this time I was allowed to hop outside without any support. The taxi driver chatted all the way to Merlin's house, which meant that we didn't have to talk to each other. It hadn't escaped my attention that neither of us had yet mentioned the party.

When we got inside there was no sign of anyone else and Merlin sheepishly pretended this was unexpected, but I didn't believe him for a second. He took me into the kitchen, made me a cup of sweet tea and insisted on bandaging my ankle. But he didn't do a good job, because I almost tripped again as I hobbled over to the drainer with my empty cup and looked out on to the garden. There was a circle of flattened grass where the marquee had stood, and fairy lights still hung from the trees. I could see the exact spot where the photo of Genevieve and Merlin had been taken, and could still picture the look on his face as he danced cheek to cheek with her. I held on to the sink for support as the knife twisted again.

'Are you OK?'

'Yes . . . I'm fine,' I lied, and turned around, arranging my features into something resembling a smile.

'We were supposed to be seeing each other last night, Katy.'

Merlin's tone was filled with reproach. I hadn't expected that. In all the excitement of staking out the vicarage, I'd completely forgotten our date.

'It wasn't intentional, Merlin; something just . . . came up. Luke and I had to go somewhere and there was no mobile coverage and we got back really late.'

He scowled. 'After hiding all week . . . this was a chance for us to see each other and talk properly.'

I could feel his anger but I was suddenly overcome with my own sense of injustice. How dare he make me feel bad about Luke, when he had spent last night cavorting with Genevieve!

'How was the *party*?' I asked with thinly veiled contempt.

Merlin's face darkened. 'It would've been better if you were there, but we couldn't put it off. The marquee had to be taken down today so it was last night or never.'

'I understand that.'

He turned towards me. 'So why do I feel so bad?'

I stared straight ahead and came back with, 'Don't know. Why do you feel so bad? If you feel guilty about last night, it isn't my fault.'

'Why should I feel guilty?' Merlin asked hotly. 'I spent all night trying to contact you.'

I wanted to stop but it was as if a demon was inside me. The photograph of Merlin and Genevieve – I couldn't escape from it. 'Not quite all evening. You managed to find time for a long slow dance . . .'

Merlin immediately guessed my meaning and his features twisted in anger. 'That isn't fair at all. It was just one dance. Now you know how I felt about the photo of you and Luke.'

'So . . . you did it to get back at me?' I asked in disbelief.

'Don't be so childish. I'm not like that.'

'Strange though . . . almost tit for tat.'

'While we're on the subject,' Merlin growled, 'there've always been three of us in our relationship, and it isn't Genevieve. I can't believe you don't see it.'

'Well, I don't.'

'This . . . Luke – he's making up all this investigation stuff just to spend time with you.'

'If you must know,' I informed him tetchily, 'it's *my* investigation. Luke is doing *me* the favour.'

'I've seen the way he looks at you.'

'You're being absurd and ridiculous,' I replied in my most mature voice. 'Luke's girlfriend is my friend too. I've known her for years. We're always hanging out together.'

'Like when?' Merlin asked calmly.

I didn't have an answer to this because he'd suddenly made me realize that I hadn't seen Laura in ages, almost as if she was avoiding me.

'Genevieve is the one who's always in the way,' I continued, ignoring his implication.

'She needs a lot of support.'

I moved as far away from him as I could, hobbling to the other side of the large kitchen. 'Look at it from my point of view. She's just . . . everywhere, taking over my life and doing everything better than me. She's like a mirror image of me except a nicer one.'

This was his cue to reassure me.

Don't be silly, Katy. Of course she isn't better at everything than you. Nor is she prettier, cleverer or nicer. Genevieve couldn't hold a candle to you. You're completely unique and I love you just the way you are.

But Merlin didn't say any of this. Sullenly he mumbled, 'Just lately, Katy, it feels like you're never there.'

'I can't stop what I'm doing; it's important,' I replied coldly.

'Everything seems more important than me.'

'I think we need a break from each other,' I blurted out, which took me by complete surprise, but once it was said it was impossible to retract.

Merlin put his head in his hands and gave a long deep groan of dismay. Then he got up, walked towards me and took hold of my hand. 'Katy . . . I don't want that. We'll talk . . . sort this mess out. Everything was fantastic before.'

His plea had no effect; it was as if I'd completely turned to ice. At his touch I could taste her, smell her and even hear her in his speech. I stayed mute and unresponsive.

'I don't want us to break up,' he begged. 'Maybe Genevieve has been hanging around our house too much and I felt sorry for her. I won't let you go like this.'

'You don't have a choice, Merlin.'

'I won't give up without a fight,' he persisted. 'This isn't you saying these things.'

'It *is* me.'

'I still have your text on my phone. "PS I love you X". Didn't you mean it? Was it just a lie?'

I hesitated for just a moment, my eyes lingering on the way he looked at that moment; his handsome face flushed with an angry desperation, his eyes blazing and yet pleading with me.

'Merlin, I should go.'

'You can't go yet. There's something I need to give you, a kind of early Christmas present.'

I kicked myself for coming here so soon after the party. 'I can't take anything . . . really.'

'It's of no use to anyone else,' Merlin said, 'and I'll really be hurt if you don't take it. Could you manage to climb the stairs? I want you to see it in the right setting.'

He was so insistent that I couldn't protest any more. He helped me to his studio, where a blast of cold air hit me. The roof window was open and a few withered leaves had fluttered in and lay on the floorboards. Now I was here Merlin seemed more animated. He rested both hands on my shoulders and my stomach flipped at his touch. I was filled with a sense of all we'd lost, the words we'd never spoken, the things we hadn't done together. It forced its way into my throat and stayed there, choking me. Part of me wanted to push him away and the other part wanted to burrow closer into him.

I caught sight of our reflection in his mirror and was taken aback. We looked so good together. What greater proof did I need that he loved me and not Genevieve? I was the one here with him, and he was trying to make things right between us. My face turned to him, my resolve weakening, when a flash of colour caught my eye. There was something suspended from a hook above the side window, twisting and twirling in the breeze, throwing out shafts of emerald light. There was no mistaking where it had come from and I quickly pulled away. Merlin's face clouded over.

I went over to the window and scowled. 'I recognize that pendant . . . it's Genevieve's.'

'I didn't even notice it was there,' he muttered. 'She makes loads of them and gives them to all Mum's students.'

'Not like that one,' I insisted.

'She must have left it here by accident.'

'She's been here? In your room?'

'Helping me with something for *you*,' he emphasized.

I couldn't even bring myself to comment. I craned my neck to look at the fast moving sky, perfectly framed by the sheet of glass like a beautiful living work of art.

Merlin moved over to his easel and I was suddenly horrified. With all that had happened I'd forgotten about the painting but, undoubtedly, this had to be his present for me.

'I can't take it, Merlin . . . not now . . .'

'You have to,' he insisted. 'It's finished and it's for you.'

He ran one hand through his dark hair. 'It isn't something I could give to anyone else.'

'Is this what Genevieve's been helping you with?' I asked suspiciously.

He nodded.

'But . . . you said you could paint me blindfold.'

Merlin reached out and touched my face. 'I could, Katy, but then something happened . . . when I was jealous over Luke . . . I lost sight of you . . .'

'You lost sight of me,' I repeated forlornly.

'Not for long. See, I could have painted a likeness of you any time, but I had to capture your . . . soul . . . otherwise it would just be like any other painting.'

'And Genevieve? How did she help?'

His forehead wrinkled as he struggled to explain. 'You're both creative and kind of spiritual . . . her presence alone reminded me how incredible you are.'

So Genevieve had acted as his muse in place of me. I definitely didn't want to look at the painting; it was completely tainted. I tried to back out of the room, but Merlin was in the process of slowly pulling the sheet from the canvas and I was forced to watch the gradual unveiling. Somewhere along the way small details had changed – the eyes were now larger and more luminous, the lips fuller and definitely crueller, the cheekbones higher as, bit by bit, a strange hybrid image of Genevieve and me appeared, the eyes following me wherever I went.

I looked at the painting and then back at Merlin to

see if it was some kind of sick joke. Bile rose in my gullet and I thought I might be sick. His face was so proud – he really didn't have a clue. If it wasn't so tragic, I might have laughed.

'Haven't you got anything to say, Katy?'

I said just two words. 'Goodbye, Merlin.'

CHAPTER TWENTY-SEVEN

It was half-term and I was glad of the chance to lick my wounds and not have to bump into Merlin every five minutes in college. Everything Genevieve promised had come true – she'd hijacked my friends and my boyfriend and sabotaged my college course. She'd known exactly what I'd do and how I'd react. But the thing that hurt the most was the painting – the utter humiliation and shame of it. Thank goodness I'd finished with Merlin before he'd shown it to me. I had taken the lead and kept my dignity, which was a small consolation. It seemed crazy, but the uncertainty of being with him was almost harder to cope with than the realization that he was no longer mine.

There weren't many distractions to take my mind off things – Hannah had gone to Paris for a few days to improve her French and Nat had to look after her little sister for most of the holiday. For once I had plenty of time to devote to my designs, but they were all morbid, the colours flat and sombre, as if someone had asked me to sketch a whole collection of clothes for a funeral. I spent ages in my bedroom to avoid Mum, who was still acting oddly. Out of the blue she brought up the subject of us moving away to another city for a fresh start. Mum hated change of any kind, and I grew ever more suspicious that this had something to do with her reaction to Genevieve's real name.

When Luke heard the news about Merlin he turned up after work with flowers and spoke in a hushed voice as if someone really had died. I still couldn't walk properly so he came into our kitchen, put them in water for me and arranged them really badly.

'How's the ankle?'

'Still sore.'

I lifted my hem of my jeans. It was every colour of the rainbow and still oddly spongy.

Luke pinched an apple from our fruit bowl and took a large bite. Juice ran down his chin. 'You should have an X-ray, just in case.'

'That's what Mum said.'

'Is it painful?'

'Agony.'

'If you don't get some crutches, you'll miss college.' He waved his car keys at me. 'Come on. I'll take you to the hospital . . . right now . . . get it over with.'

I groaned because he was right as usual. Reluctantly I grabbed my bag and hobbled to his car. I glanced at his profile as he drove, remembering what Merlin had said about Laura, but I couldn't pluck up the courage to ask him. We reached the hospital and made our way to Casualty. I'd never been to an adult hospital before and was surprised at the huge number of people waiting to be seen.

'Good job it's not late at night,' Luke whispered. 'It's not a pretty sight.'

'I'll be fine by myself,' I told him bravely. 'Just leave me here and I'll get a taxi home.'

'Wouldn't dream of it,' he insisted, and began to whistle cheerfully.

'Laura must hate me,' I began nervously.

'Why?'

'Always monopolizing you like this.'

'She doesn't mind.'

'You always say that. You always tell me that Laura wouldn't mind.'

Luke changed position and stared at me. His eyes were usually bright and laughing, but today they looked as coldly blue and deep as a fjord. 'And what, Kat?'

'It's just . . . why hasn't she come to see me lately? We three used to hang out.'

He shrugged. 'She's been busy, and it's different now . . . I mean she used to style your hair and stuff . . . you were just a kid.'

I pondered on this for a minute. I didn't know what Luke was getting at, but it didn't feel good. Maybe she really *was* avoiding me.

'Well, just don't neglect her, Luke . . . look what happens.'

'Did Merlin feel neglected?' he asked quietly.

'Apparently.'

'It'll hurt less soon,' he murmured, 'and you'll find another boyfriend.'

'Find?' I echoed, aghast. 'I'm not *looking* for another boyfriend, and it was me who broke it off with Merlin.'

Luke was immediately contrite. 'Wow, Kat, I didn't realize. I thought you were . . .

'Heartbroken?'

'No, just cut up about him.'

I'd had no one to talk to about the break-up and it was a relief to open up to Luke, although I couldn't bring myself to mention the painting, or what Merlin had said about Luke.

'Something changed between us. Merlin looked and sounded the same, but something was missing . . . like a part of him had been stolen from me. Sounds silly, doesn't it?'

'No, it doesn't,' he answered pensively. 'It sounds . . . really insightful. You're very grown-up . . . emotionally.'

'Stop teasing me, Luke.'

'I'm not,' he insisted, and for once there wasn't any trace of a smirk. 'And what about Genevieve?' Luke sucked in his cheeks. 'You were so agitated when we left the attic. I reckoned you were on to something.'

'I've thought of nothing else . . . but it's a mental block . . . this connection with York.'

A pregnant woman waddled by just then and I looked at her with terrified awe – how could anyone's stomach stretch so far? The cogs in my brain began to whirr again, only this time an idea took shape that was so frightening I had to lean forward and almost put my head between my knees.

'Are you OK, Kat?'

'Luke . . . we're in a hospital,' I whispered. 'What happens in hospitals?'

'Er . . . people have treatment when they're sick.'

'And they have babies.'

'Yeees . . .'

I buried my face in my hands. 'Can't you see it?'

'See what?'

'It's horrific, and yet . . .'

At that moment a nurse called my name and I was glad to get up from my seat and have my sore ankle prodded, poked and X-rayed – anything to stop me from thinking about the possibility that was growing bigger and stronger all the time. I refused to say another word until we were back home, my ankle tightly strapped and a pair of crutches in my grasp. It was late and Mum's bedroom light was switched off. Luke followed me inside, quietly closing the door behind him. He paced up and down our living room, hands behind his back, which normally would have made me laugh because he looked like a member of the royal family.

'Well? Will you tell me at last?'

'There's a photo album in that sideboard, Luke. Would you get it for me?'

Obediently he knelt down, opened the doors and felt around inside. He handed me the brown leather-bound album without asking any questions. I flicked from one page to another and stopped about halfway through, angling the book towards Luke. 'This is me as a newborn baby.'

'And?'

'It's so obvious . . . you should be able to see how different I look.'

'Not really. I said before, a baby's a baby.'

I took the other photo out of my bag and waved it at him. 'I was premature and almost bald. This baby's heavier with jet black hair. I really meant it . . . this baby isn't me.'

Luke sighed. 'So your mum was tired after all the sleepless nights and labelled her photos wrong, or the lab gave her the wrong set of prints.'

'And she never noticed they were of a different baby,' I replied witheringly.

'Babies change in a matter of days. They lose weight or put it on, their hair falls out . . .'

'It's not my face,' I insisted. 'That photo was hidden with the birth certificate and wristband for an important reason, and I can't believe you haven't seen the significance. The hospital gave me the clue.'

Luke seemed definitely grouchy now. 'And what, Kat? You think you and Genevieve might have been born in the same maternity ward?'

I took a deep breath. 'More than that. I know it sounds incredible . . . unbelievable and downright crazy, but . . . I think . . . it could be possible that . . . Mum took the wrong baby home from hospital.'

Luke had to pinch his nose and cover his mouth to drown out the sound of his laughter. After a few minutes he apologized to me. 'Even I didn't see that one coming. *I'm* supposed to be the journalist, into conspiracy theories and stuff.'

I wasn't offended because I knew my idea was completely off the wall, but I tried to sound restrained and credible so he might take me seriously. 'It's the link between Genevieve, Mum and me. I was born in another city, a baby that has my name isn't me, and Mum went white when I said the name Grace. This could be the answer to why Genevieve hates me.'

'You know what you're actually saying, Kat? Genevieve is your mum's daughter and you're . . . someone else's.'

'Suppose.'

'Oh, and your mum knows all this. But why would she allow it to happen?'

'Haven't worked that out yet, but . . . you think it's impossible?'

He rolled his eyes. 'I think you've been reading too many trashy novels or watching too many American soaps.'

'Look . . . all that stuff was hidden in the secret box so I'd never find it. Mum will never tell me where I was born, and she's cut herself off from everyone, even her family.

She's been running from something my whole life, and she's even hinted she could lose me.'

'This is Britain. Babies don't get mixed up in hospital, especially with no one noticing. That's what the wristbands are for. They don't get taken off until the baby is discharged.'

I swallowed hard and spoke more to myself than to Luke. 'All Genevieve's threats suddenly make sense. She says there isn't enough room for both of us . . . she's entitled to my life because it should have been hers. She can't forgive me because she had such an awful childhood and she came to see Mum, pretending to sell jewellery but really to see her face to face.'

'How would *she* have found out something like that?'

'I don't know . . . but we do know how clever she is.' Luke drummed his fingers on the coffee table while I carried on thinking out loud. 'It would explain why Mum's always so secretive and doesn't like talking about the past. I've always thought it was about my dad, but maybe it isn't.'

'I'll have to think about this one.'

'Maybe you could do some more digging around? Access the hospital records or birth register or . . . I don't know; you have your sources.'

'We still don't know Genevieve's/Grace's real surname,' Luke reminded me, putting on his jacket. He hesitated, one foot inside the doorway and one foot out. 'There is an easier solution . . . find out her birthday. You'd have to be born within a few days of each other for your idea to work.'

'You're a genius,' I told him gratefully. 'But how?'

Luke looked at me, baffled. 'It's a simple enough question.'

'Nothing's simple with Genevieve,' I muttered. 'And she mustn't be alerted in any way. I daren't even ask Nat or Hannah in case it gets back to her.'

'Sorry, but I'll have to leave this one with you, Kat. I know you'll think of something.'

As soon as Luke left I went upstairs and slid open the drawer of my bedside cabinet. There was one thing I'd kept from him – my obsession with the pendant. It *wasn't* just my imagination; it felt heavier every time I examined it, as though it was growing with Genevieve's power. And why couldn't I throw it away or destroy it? Each time I tried, it came back to me. It was impossible to explain. I lay under my duvet reflecting on everything that had happened, the pendant casting strange shadows on my wall.

You're marked, Katy.

I remembered the vicar's wife who claimed she could still feel Genevieve's presence in the house as if something of her had been left behind all those years ago. Maybe she was marked as well? Luke had a rational explanation for everything, but he couldn't stop me from fearing this emerald glass. Mum had invited the pendant into the house and I had the strangest feeling that the only way to get rid of it was to give it back to Genevieve. I'd tried already and failed, but now I knew what I had to do.

CHAPTER TWENTY-EIGHT

Luke had to go away for a week on some type of training course, but he offered me a lift to college the first morning after half-term. He dropped me outside just as Genevieve approached, and there were a lot of students milling around. The pain in my ankle was worth it just to see her jealousy as everyone rushed to help. My bag and my folder were carried in as people made jokes about my injury and tried to borrow my crutches. My foot was too swollen to fit into my normal shoes, and I had to wear a pair of Mum's comfy flat loafers, which were like huge boats on me. But they were so ugly they were almost cool, and a definite talking point. I went straight to class and settled down with some work, glad to sit down.

Miss Clegg came over smiling. 'There's a message from the secretary, Katy, for you to report to the office. I'm sure it's just a formality to make sure you don't attempt any acrobatics while you're injured.'

I was getting used to the crutches, although they used

muscles I didn't even know I had and my arms ached like crazy. The secretary, Mrs Wright, made me sit opposite her desk and read a health-and-safety warning of all the things I mustn't do. My eyes must have glazed over with boredom because she apologized, saying that it was all common sense. As she spoke, Luke's words came back to me.

'I'm going to leave this one to you, Kat. I know you'll think of something.'

Who else would have access to Genevieve's file? This could be the chance I was looking for.

'Could I ask a favour?' I gushed, trying to get up from the chair and wincing with exaggerated pain. 'Our new girl, Genevieve, is so lovely but . . . really shy, and she won't tell anyone her birthday because she doesn't want a fuss.'

I waited expectantly, hoping Mrs Wright might take the hint and stop me having to ask outright, but her face remained blank.

'Could you tell me her date of birth so she doesn't miss out on a party? It's so sad because she's an orphan and we all want to give her a big surprise.'

She shook her head with regret. 'I'm sorry, Katy, I can't do that. It might seem a little thing to you, but it goes against the rules of confidentiality. I can't divulge any information about students.'

I got up and began to shuffle to the door, overcome with disappointment. Being in the office had seemed such a great opportunity, but I'd failed, and I couldn't see any other way. It'd be too dangerous to approach her new foster-parents in case they alerted her to my questions.

'Katy?'

I stopped, adjusted position and turned around. Mrs Wright was smiling right at me. 'If you like, Katy, you could ask me the date of *my* birthday.'

When she gave me a crafty wink I wondered if she'd been working too hard. 'You see . . . one of the new students and I were born in the same month, except that I'm close to the end and she's at the beginning, the *very* beginning.'

It wasn't hard to guess her meaning and I laughed. It was kind of her to get round the rules like this.

'When is your birthday, Mrs Wright?' I grinned.

She folded her arms. 'Why, thank you for asking, Katy. It's on the twenty-ninth of June.'

I thanked her profusely as she held open the door for me. So Geneviéve must have been born on 1 June, which meant that our birthdays were within four days of each other. This gave weight to my idea that our mothers could have been at the same hospital together. I was no nearer to finding out the truth, but this provided another possible clue and that felt like something.

There was another hurdle to face. I'd have to see Merlin sooner or later, and I needed to get this over with because I was so jumpy my stomach felt full of butterflies. My heart leaped as he came through the door of the cafeteria at lunchtime and our eyes immediately locked together. He gave me a rueful smile, which made me catch my breath because he looked so attractive and full of yearning. It felt like one of those black and white movies where the hero and heroine are forced to separate forever and they watch each other through unshed tears because they have to be brave but the scene is heartrendingly poignant as a train mournfully pulls out of the station and the sad music plays . . .

Oh, get a life, Katy Rivers.

After college I waited outside the automatic doors at the top of the steps for Nat to appear because she'd insisted that her mum would drive me home. I squeezed myself into a corner to avoid being crushed or knocked over. One minute I was alone; the next, Genevieve was beside me, putting out her arms like a barrier, with the pretence of helping me. It was a bright day and we were face to face in the late-autumn sunshine. I was mesmerized, unable to turn away. There was an almost imperceptible scar at the side of her nose and I touched my own nose self-consciously, feeling a tiny bump from a similar scar when I fell off a swing aged about ten. Genevieve brushed her fringe from her eyes and on one hand there was a peculiar arrangement of freckles that looked like a star. I had a similar mark, but on the opposite hand – Mum always said it was a lucky sign.

I hadn't seen her for a week and had almost forgotten how bad the sensation was. Today she was a curious mix – triumphant and gloating blended with jumpy anticipation.

'Sorry you missed the party, Katy. We were all *devastated*.'

'That's OK, Genevieve, it couldn't be helped. It was nice of you to organize it for Nat. She was thrilled.'

'Yes, she was.' She examined her nails as if she was sharpening them. 'I've already taken over your friends and there's only one person left.'

'You don't mean Merlin?'

Genevieve shrugged nonchalantly.

'You mean he hasn't told you already?'

'Told me what?'

'I broke up with him.'

'As if,' she drawled. '*You* finish with Merlin?'

'Ask him if you don't believe me.'

She took a few seconds to digest this and the tip of her tongue protruded from her mouth. 'You mean he wanted to finish with you but you beat him to it, to save face?'

'Not at all,' I corrected. 'He wanted to spend more time with me, but I felt a bit . . . stifled.'

She put on a high-pitched little girl voice dripping with sarcasm. 'Maybe if you'd managed to have your romantic night away together, then everything would have been different. But we'll never know.'

I moved closer to her, grinning all the time with excessive sweetness. 'He's all yours now, and everyone will know you're just a substitute . . . second best because I didn't want him.' Genevieve's face was a picture as she struggled to control her feelings and I twisted the knife further. 'He doesn't seem so attractive, does he, Gen? Enjoy him while you can.'

For a minute I thought I'd really got to her, but she

gave a laugh that chilled me to the bone. 'He was never yours . . . not even for a second. I allowed you time together because it suited me.'

'As if I'd believe that.'

She sighed wistfully and looked up at the grey sky. 'I could push you right now – just a small push, and everyone would think you'd tripped. Careless Kat, waiting by the stairs instead of taking the lift.'

I *was* careless to get myself cornered like this. I'd automatically come out of the main entrance instead of using the lift which went down to pavement level.

'It would be a relief,' she whispered.

'You couldn't even find a life of your own,' I challenged, 'so you had to steal mine. How pathetic is that?'

She made a swirling movement with her hand as if writing in the air. 'All it took was a few brushstrokes and you were completely erased.'

Was she referring to the painting? She didn't elaborate, and I hoped against hope that Merlin hadn't let her see it. My foot edged forward and I gazed downwards, the sensation making me reel. I felt helpless, all the time aware of a weight in my hand and the coldness of glass and metal. I almost stumbled and reached out to clutch her jacket, which gave me the opportunity I'd been waiting for. The pendant was slipped into her pocket, and I straightened up, immediately feeling steadier.

'Is that what happens to everyone who annoys you?' I asked with renewed confidence.

Genevieve jutted out her chin. 'Maybe you ought to be more wary.'

'So sorry about your adoptive parents,' I mocked. 'I heard your sad story but . . . it seems everyone who gets close to you dies.'

She looked almost pleased with my words and her lips curved at the corners. 'It's a good job you realize that. Other people underestimate me, but not you. We understand each other.'

The bizarre thought occurred to me that at three thirty on a Monday afternoon I was hearing a murder confession. Her hand suddenly gripped my wrist and my head was filled with her horrible thoughts. I was back there at the cottage, seeing the flames licking the wood, hearing glass shatter and the awful screams of the people trapped inside. And she was glad. I could feel her pitiless satisfaction. If she really was capable of this, then I had to act.

'Mum and I might be moving away,' I said quickly. 'To a new city for a fresh start.'

'It's too late for that, Katy.'

'Too late?' I said. 'But you wanted me to go, to leave the way open for you.'

She wrinkled her nose with feigned regret. 'Yes, I did, but now . . . it's not enough. You'd always be out there . . . somewhere . . . and that wouldn't work for me.'

'So what should I do then? Die?'

'It should be as if you were never born. That's why we found each other.'

This was her usual riddle, but I had to ask. 'How *did* you find me?'

Genevieve seemed to exhale slightly, and a gentle breeze caressed my face. One of her curls brushed my cheek. 'You know the answer . . . you just haven't realized it yet.'

I blinked and she was gone. Only Nat was beside me now, scolding me for not taking the lift.

I was so unsettled when I arrived home that I locked myself in my room. The thought that Genevieve could have seen the painting made me feel physically sick. I pulled my hair back from my face and gave a long low groan of dismay. When I caught sight of myself in my mirrored wardrobe it made me flinch – I looked so cruel and vindictive that I barely recognized myself. I exhaled several times and smoothed my hands across my forehead, cheeks and mouth, trying to get rid of this awful expression. It would have been nice to talk to Luke, but there was no point in telling him what had happened until he was home. Today felt like progress, but where did I go from here?

CHAPTER TWENTY-NINE

The train was already packed. My limp managed to buy me some sympathy and I was offered a window seat next to a middle-aged guy with a lunch box laid out on the table, munching egg sandwiches and drinking from a Thermos flask. Everyone else had probably avoided him, but I needed to think and couldn't do that getting thrown around the compartment. The scenery changed as we left the city behind – tower blocks, factories and shopping centres gave way to fields full of cows and isolated farms with only the giant electricity pylons spoiling the view. My trip had been planned on impulse, a quick call to Gran and Grandad to announce my intention to visit, but now came the hard part – working out what to tell them. I had an hour to come up with a story. I leaned against the headrest to let my mind drift, but I was so tired that my eyes grew heavy and slowly began to close.

The set of three carved mirrors was directly in front of me. Genevieve and I were positioned side by side on a cushioned stool, our movements perfectly synchronized, like some kind of strange charade. An antique silver brush and comb sat on the dressing table. As I lifted the brush to my hair she mimicked my movements as closely as if she was my reflection. I speeded up, wanting her to stop, but her timing was perfect and I couldn't shake her off. I moved faster, hoping that she'd slip up, but gradually she overtook me in the game and I realized that I was following her and had no control over my actions. She could make my hands jerk about and my head shake uncontrollably. I became confused and exhausted but still she went on, pulling at my strings as though I was her puppet. And then she clutched her head and screamed. But it was actually me who was screaming, yet I had no voice – it was a silent cry of agony and impotence.

I looked around the carriage in panic, convinced I must have made some kind of gruesome noise, but no one was looking my way. Genevieve was even invading my daydreams now. The train was about to pull into the station. I picked up my bag and composed my face to appear bright and upbeat.

'Katy!'

I was enveloped in a plump pair of arms and breathed in Gran's perfume, which always smelled of lemons. I turned slightly and my cheek came into contact with rough whiskers.

'You've been in the wars,' Grandad's gruff voice joked.

'It's nothing, only my ankle. I was on crutches a few days ago and couldn't put any weight on it at all, but it's getting better.'

'Too much dancing?' Gran smiled, dimples appearing in both cheeks.

Grandad insisted on fastening my seat belt for me before we drove to their village. Gran took my arm as soon as we got out of the car.

'Now come into the kitchen and I'll make some tea. There're fresh scones and chocolate cake and those biscuits you used to like. I hope you still have a healthy appetite. I've no time for teenage girls starving themselves and looking like skeletons. It doesn't do at all.'

The kitchen was unchanged, with an old-fashioned pantry, an ancient fridge-freezer, a big enamel sink and a marble-topped circular table where we always sat.

Nerves always gave me an appetite. I devoured one misshapen scone and then started on the chocolate cake before Gran plucked up the courage to ask, 'Your mum . . . Rebecca . . . is she . . . I mean, is everything all right?'

'She's fine,' I replied, my mouth still full and crumbs flying from it. 'She's getting out more and starting some . . . therapy, even talking of going back to work.'

Gran's face brightened. 'That's wonderful. I should call her and we could drive down one day. We always mean to, but . . . sometimes . . . it isn't that easy.'

She coughed self-consciously and began buttering herself a scone with extra care to cover her discomfort.

There was no need to explain. I knew why they didn't come to see me more often – Mum always made so many excuses.

Grandad slipped back into the room. 'Does Rebecca know you're here?'

I shook my head and he murmured, 'Ah,' as if this was significant.

I swallowed several times because it felt as if my tongue was sticking to the roof of my mouth. 'I . . . wanted to ask you something.'

'What sort of thing?' they asked in unison.

'About when I was a baby.'

There was an awkward silence before Gran spoke. 'You're growing up fast . . . we thought you might start to ask questions.'

'Is it about your father?' Grandad asked gently.

'Mmm . . . not really. It's just that . . . I found my birth certificate and wanted to know about the place where I was born.'

Worried looks were exchanged. 'I'm not sure we should discuss this without Rebecca's knowledge,' Gran said. 'It's her you need to ask.'

'But . . . she doesn't want to talk about it,' I cried in frustration. 'I know she doesn't. She never even told me I was born in another city, and if I hassle her . . . she'll get ill . . .'

Grandad got up from his chair and muttered something about 'checking on his plants', even though it was raining.

'I'll tell you what I know,' Gran said at last, 'but it isn't very much.' She refilled her cup full of strong orange tea and settled back in her chair. 'Rebecca was only twenty-one when you were born. She was studying music in York and we didn't know she was pregnant. The first we heard was a phone call to announce your birth.'

'Mum didn't tell you?' I asked in surprise. 'Did she think you'd be angry?'

There was a small sigh. 'We were a little . . . conventional, but we would have supported our daughter – any mother and father surely would. Rebecca was very independent and headstrong and I think she wanted to cope on her own.'

I thought of Mum lying in bed day after day, the exact opposite of independent and headstrong, and I wondered again what had made her this way.

'What happened when you got to the hospital?'

'Well, that's the thing, Katy. Rebecca had already discharged herself, so we went to her flat instead.'

My heart sank into my boots. 'You didn't see me in the hospital?'

Gran's face creased as she tried to remember. 'No . . . we didn't see you until you were five days old.'

'And what was Mum like? I mean, was she OK being on her own with a tiny baby?'

'She was like a duck to water, looking after you,' was the delighted reply.

'And . . . was anyone else there? Did you see any of Mum's friends?'

'No. By the time we arrived she was upset and kept

saying she just wanted to leave, to come home. She'd finished her final exams and had her bags packed. We helped her of course.'

'Nothing seemed strange?'

Gran rocked backwards and forwards in her chair laughing. 'Only the fact that my only daughter now had her own daughter and I wasn't at all prepared.'

'How did she keep it from you?'

Gran made a sucking noise with her teeth. 'That Easter she hadn't come home – she said she had to revise. And in the early stages she hid it well with plenty of baggy clothes, and we just put the weight gain down to all the unhealthy student food. And remember how tiny you were at birth.'

Then why does a photo of a bouncing chubby baby have my name on it?, I wanted to yell, but somehow this was one step too far and it didn't feel fair to burden Gran with my worries. I knew instinctively that she wouldn't have the answer to this. My grandparents were never even at the hospital and the only baby they ever saw was the one my mum presented them with.

'What are you looking for, Katy?' Gran asked kindly.

'Don't know,' I answered honestly. 'Just a reason why Mum wouldn't tell me about my birth. I thought there had to be some kind of secret.'

Gran picked up the teapot to pour herself another cup and somehow managed to scald her hand. She held it under the cold tap while I hovered in concern.

'It's all right, I'm not hurt,' she tried to reassure me, but she seemed pale and anxious. I felt enormously guilty for coming here like this and worrying her. Tears sprang from nowhere and I hastily blinked them away. It wasn't just the strain of Genevieve, but seeing my grandparents again and realizing how much I missed them. Gran must have noticed and motioned me to sit down again. She rested one of her wrinkled hands over mine.

'There *was* something else,' she began. She looked at me for a minute as if she was having second thoughts but continued hesitantly. 'The flat Rebecca was living in was . . . rundown and not in a nice area. Some of the tenants had problems . . . drugs, I think.'

'Mum wasn't . . . ?'

'Good grief, no. But . . . there was an incident.'

'What sort of incident?'

Gran cleared her throat, fiddled with her rings and folded her arms in the same way Mum always did when she was nervous. 'One of the women living there . . . she took an overdose . . . and . . . unfortunately . . . she didn't survive.'

'Did Mum know her?'

Gran nodded. 'Rebecca was terribly shaken. It took her ages to get over it, and we were worried about her for a while.'

This could be the key to why Mum had always been so fragile. I was almost too scared to ask. 'Why? What did she do?'

Gran looked out of the window and her face was etched

with sorrow. 'She was almost locked in her own world . . . so unlike the bright cheerful girl who went away. We knew she was hurting but were powerless to help.'

'But . . . Mum left you and found her own place. She must have been feeling stronger?'

Gran nodded. 'After a time the garden seemed to heal her. She spent so long outside tending the flowers, and her favourite place was under the weeping willow. She even named it after you, Katy.'

An enormous feeling of sadness welled up inside me. 'And . . . Mum never went back to the flat?'

'Never. She didn't want to talk about her time there and we never brought it up.'

'What about enemies? Did she have any?'

Gran laughed. 'Rebecca never had an enemy in the world – she brought sunshine to everyone.'

I smiled wanly. 'Can I see one of your first photographs of me?'

Gran was more than happy to get out the family album. I noted that all her photos were exactly the same as I'd always seen at Mum's, and none of them looked like the one from the attic. I had to sit for a whole hour looking at everyone in my extended family until my eyes glazed over. I made an excuse not to stay for tea by hinting that Mum needed me home. As I kissed Gran goodbye there was one question I had yet to ask.

'When she was younger . . . did Mum ever complain of strange dreams or any kind of . . . er . . . premonitions?'

Gran shook her head sadly and gave me one last hug. 'Take care, Katy.'

It was rush hour when I got back on the train and standing room only; hordes of commuters flooded the carriages and not even a limp could get me a seat. I managed to find a corner close to the luggage rack, my mind swimming with unanswered questions. What had happened in that dingy flat? And why was Mum so unwilling to talk about it? Something so awful that she was prepared to leave her home rather than face up to it. And something involving Genevieve.

CHAPTER THIRTY

It was only a week before the whispering began – a constant low hum, like white noise, that surrounded me wherever I went. It was waiting around corners, in corridors and in conversations that ended as soon as I appeared. Despite being practised at leading a double life and smiling through everything, it really started to wear me down. I overheard two girls talking in the ladies' when I was locked in a cubicle, saying that I only had myself to blame. Blame for what? What had Genevieve done now? Every nerve fibre in my body was stretched as I waited for her latest trick to be revealed.

Gradually even Hannah and Nat seemed affected, which was the last straw. I was about to confront them when they decided to take me out to lunch. It was all paid for by them, with the choice of every sugar-coated dessert under the sun, obviously to cushion the blow from something. I almost felt sorry for them – the furtive glances, tight smiles, the over-nice manners – whatever Genevieve had done now must be bad.

'You might as well just tell me what it is,' I said at last. 'You two are making me nervous.'

The table wobbled and I knew they were nudging each other underneath, neither wanting to be the one to speak first. I got to my feet. 'I'm leaving right now unless someone tells me what's going on.'

Hannah nodded to Nat, who screwed up her eyes, braced herself and let the words just pour out.

'Merlin and Genevieve are going out together, as in boyfriend and girlfriend. We didn't want you to hear it on the grapevine. It only happened after you finished with him, and he's really worried you'll think something else.'

I didn't actually know what I felt, except maybe as if I'd been hit by a bus. All the times I'd thought this was about to happen, that Genevieve would make it happen, that I'd pushed Merlin into her arms . . . yet now I was faced with the reality I was completely stunned. But that wasn't the only thing – everyone must have talking about me, pitying me, which was almost as bad.

'Merlin knows you're breaking the news to me now?' I hissed.

They both nodded feebly.

'What? As if I need to be wrapped in cotton wool and let down gently! How dare he be so arrogant and even think that I'd care!'

'You mean . . . you don't care?' Hannah faltered.

'Why should I? *I* finished with him.'

'We know that,' Nat put in, 'but . . . we thought it was just . . . a tiff.'

I went back to eating my chocolate fudge cake with dollops of ice cream and whipped cream, but it suddenly tasted awful. I hadn't been able to face telling anyone about the painting, and pride made me point out, 'Merlin begged me to carry on seeing him.'

'That's a relief,' Hannah sighed.

Nat winced apologetically. 'Thing is . . . you never told us what really happened. You were in love, going away for the night, then you were grounded and missed my party and then you broke up.'

'Was it the party?' Hannah asked. 'Merlin dancing with Genevieve?'

I actually felt sorry for them both because they seemed so innocent. Someone as darkly complicated as Genevieve was making my life hell, and they knew nothing about it. To them life was still full of trivial teenage stuff, but I could never go back to that. Genevieve had changed me.

'I was annoyed about the photograph,' I admitted, 'but it wasn't just that. Something was different, and it felt wrong somehow. I had to be true to myself.'

'Katy, you are so brave,' Hannah gushed. 'Standing up for yourself like that and refusing to compromise.'

Nat peered at us both in bewilderment. 'Have you seen most of the males around here? If we refuse to compromise, we'll die alone.'

I managed a lukewarm smile, noticing Hannah's foot

tapping manically on the floor, which meant there was more to come.

'Genevieve is mortified because of the timing, Katy . . . She hopes you won't hate her.'

I didn't even look up from my dessert. 'Hate her?'

'She's worried it seems a bit . . . hasty.'

'As far as I'm concerned, Merlin was free to hook up with whoever he wanted.'

Nat's voice was annoyingly concerned. 'It's important to Merlin that you don't think he acted . . . *dishonourably*.'

I laid my head on the table and broke into cynical laughter at her choice of word. 'You can tell Sir Lancelot his honour is still intact . . . and his *Guinevere*, of course.'

We walked slowly back to college. As we reached the steps, we saw them. Unfolding, frame by frame like a slowed-down movie, were the figures of Merlin and Genevieve, climbing the steps together, holding hands. It was a bright winter's day and it seemed as if Genevieve had shafts of light in her hair radiating outwards. Her smile was blinding as she gazed at Merlin. Their bodies moulded and curved together, and when he moved she filled the space left behind; even their clothes synchronized in a stylish way. Students actually stopped what they were doing to stare at them both – happy shiny people with the world at their feet.

'They make a lovely couple,' I managed to say, trying to defuse the moment. Two arms linked through mine and I gritted my teeth. 'Come on. Let's get it over with.'

We quickened our pace to catch up with them. Merlin

noticed me and almost stumbled as a look passed between us that I didn't understand. His grip on Genevieve's hand loosened, but she held on even tighter.

There was nothing else to do but clear the air. 'I've just found out the good news.'

'Thanks, Katy,' Merlin muttered, but he looked away. This made me feel better because he didn't want to rub my face in it.

'Thanks, Katy,' Genevieve echoed, and for the first time I couldn't read what was in her eyes – rage, triumph or her usual menace. I remembered the pendant and wondered if our connection was broken.

After college I managed to sneak out without Nat or Hannah seeing me and took my favourite route home. In the last few weeks the hedgerows and trees had changed into arrangements of sticks and branches that had a stark kind of beauty. I studied a row of terraces, realizing that in another week they'd be sparkling with Christmas lights, and tried not to imagine Merlin's house filled with all the handmade decorations his mum had been working on. The ones I wouldn't get to see. Genevieve would have my Christmas now along with all the romantic things that Merlin and I would have done together.

A mocking voice called after me, and this time I wasn't surprised; in a way I'd almost expected it. 'Poor Katy. She comes this way to be alone when she's feeling sad.'

I didn't turn round, but my heart plummeted at the

prospect of another encounter. 'Why would I be sad, Genevieve?'

'Because Merlin doesn't love you any more.'

'Congratulations,' I told her. 'You wanted him and now you have him.'

'Still think he's your cast-off?' she asked gleefully. 'That he ever belonged to you?'

'Of course.'

'Then I'm about to burst your bubble.'

She moved in front of me now, walking or rather skipping backwards, which forced me to slow down. I had visions of her tripping, but her feet seemed to anticipate every bump and crater. She artfully pointed her fingers and made a series of undulating wave movements with her hands as if this was a mime and she was acting out the story.

'He was with me from the very start. Don't ever fool yourself he was yours.'

'Merlin didn't deceive me; I would have known.'

'Oh, Katy. He didn't know, he deceived himself . . . but his canvas told the truth.'

'The painting,' I said flatly, wondering how I could possibly have imagined that she wouldn't have known.

'Glorious, isn't it?' She laughed unexpectedly and a startled flock of birds flew up out of a tree.

'The painting was of me,' I had to say.

'You're not a proper artist, Katy, so you don't understand. It's impossible to change an oil painting halfway through. It was always my face on that canvas.'

'I saw it,' I insisted, still knowing this was playing into her hands.

'You saw nothing but a few daubs on a canvas . . . an idea that wasn't even formed. You wanted to see yourself there, and so that's what you imagined. When Merlin filled in the detail, it was me.'

'Believe what you like, Genevieve.'

She stopped dead and I was forced to stop also. 'It was finished weeks ago,' she whispered, and a smile slowly spread across her whole face like oil on water. She sensed my uncertainty and her smile grew even wider. 'Even when Merlin was with you he wanted me.'

She opened her fist, arranged her lips and blew as if there was a puffball in her hand that now floated into the air. 'Now everything is almost complete, everyone is where they ought to be.'

She walked away without a backward glance.

Luke was tinkering with his car when I walked down my street, his head under the bonnet. It had refused to start this morning for the second time in a week.

'Look as if you've lost sixpence and found a penny.' He grinned.

'That's the sort of lame thing Mum would say,' I growled. 'If you mean I look pissed off, just say so.'

He wiped his hands on an old piece of rag. 'Do I have to ask?'

I hesitated. I still hadn't filled Luke in on what had

happened when he was away. I was worried about how he'd react but couldn't hold back any longer.

'Genevieve practically confessed to murder, Luke. It was like she wanted me to know . . . like she was proud of it.'

He shook his head. 'It could be a warning.'

I wiggled my eyebrows up and down, trying to lift the mood, determined not to tell him the full truth. 'She did joke about pushing me down the college steps.'

'That isn't funny, Kat.'

'Whatever she does, she wants me to know about it.'

'That's the part I don't like,' he replied worriedly. 'She's getting too close to you.' Luke was definitely unsettled and I had the feeling he wasn't as comfortable about all this as previously. 'She seems to be moving towards something,' he brooded. 'Some sort of ultimatum.'

'That might be a relief,' I replied. 'To find out what she really wants . . . better than the uncertainty.'

He half-nodded, as if he understood but wasn't happy about it.

I shook my head and heaved a sigh. 'That's not all. Merlin and Genevieve . . . they're an item. He was so *devastated* about breaking up with me he waited . . . oh, at least a week before getting together with her.'

'I'm sorry, Kat.'

'Mum was right,' I complained. 'My jealousy made it all happen, like a . . . self-fulfilling prophecy.'

'I think you had some help from Genevieve, don't you? She went out of her way to make you doubt Merlin.'

I tapped my chest. 'No, it was inside me, the green-eyed monster just festering away, destroying what we had. I can't *completely* blame her.'

Luke seemed doubtful. 'She manipulated you . . . played on your weaknesses.'

'But I had to act on it. Mum's right – if you love someone, you have to set them free.'

'Wise words,' Luke agreed lightly.

'That's the good thing about us,' I said as an afterthought. 'We don't have all those complications. We can say what we like and we'll always be friends. Friends are better than romance.'

'If you say so,' he murmured, but sounded oddly tetchy.

I stared at the workings of the car as if they made perfect sense to me. 'Wonder if she'll leave me alone now and I can forget all the stupid baby-swap theories and about Mum harbouring dark sinister secrets.'

Luke stopped what he was doing and faced me squarely. 'You think Genevieve's done? That she has everything she set out to get?'

'She has Merlin. He was the prize.'

Luke shut his car bonnet and his face seemed creased with worry. 'Maybe Merlin's just a distraction in all this. Maybe you're the real prize. Just don't stop looking behind you, Kat.'

CHAPTER THIRTY-ONE

The most incredible thing happened – Genevieve didn't turn up at college. Apparently she'd been stricken with a bad case of tonsillitis and could hardly speak, which was just about the best news ever. When Nat told me I tried not to look elated and probably failed miserably. It was strange getting used to the fact that I could get up in the morning not full of dread, sit through my lessons without her horrible eyes staring at me and have lunch without watching every word I said. The first day she was away was wonderful, the second day bliss, and by the third day I could have danced for joy. It made me remember how great life was before Genevieve came along. It was hard to believe it was less than three months ago.

Hannah, Nat and I decided to do some Christmas shopping on Thursday night when all the stores in town stayed open late. It was just like the old days – queuing for the bus and laughing at something and nothing, in this case an old lady whose lapdog tried to lift up Hannah's skirt with its nose, then teasing each other about our different tastes in clothes. We jumped from the bus, fighting our way through the crowds to get into serious shopping mode. We hit the department stores first and I bought a blouse for Mum in a gorgeous lilac colour, remembering all the years I'd had to get her a nightdress or dressing gown because that was all she seemed to wear. Nat was pretty boring and settled on slippers for her dad and perfume for her mum, while Hannah just window-shopped, claiming she never bought anything until the last minute, otherwise it wasn't truly festive.

In less than an hour Nat was weak with hunger and dragged us both into a pizza restaurant for a megalarge with five toppings. I was fascinated by the decor. The theme was 1950s diner, with red leatherette booths in a half-moon shape, an old-fashioned jukebox and the waitresses in ankle socks and flared skirts. One of the waiters had a giant greasy quiff and wore a Teddy-boy suit in an electric shade of blue. I kept expecting them all to break into song just like in a musical, with some jiving thrown in.

'It's a pity Genevieve couldn't make it,' Hannah mused.

'It *is* a shame,' I agreed, determined not to freeze every time her name was mentioned. 'Genevieve loves shopping for clothes. We both spotted a gorgeous evening dress in a charity shop, but she got to it first.'

'Did she buy it?' Nat asked curiously.

'No, it needed lots of repair and she changed her mind.'

'Why didn't *you* buy it?' Hannah demanded. 'You could stitch just about anything and make a great job of it.'

I shrugged. 'I sort of switched off after Genevieve had tried it on. She looked so good.'

For some reason Hannah wouldn't let up on the subject of the dress. 'You look as good as she does, better even.'

I gave a doubtful laugh. 'Genevieve's bound to change her mind and get it for the Christmas Ball.'

'She won't need a dress,' Nat answered quickly, and her cheeks turned pink. 'I-I mean she'll probably . . . just make something.'

'There's something you're not telling us, isn't there?' Hannah challenged.

'There isn't. Really there isn't.'

'I've known you since reception class,' she teased. 'Come on – spill the beans.'

Nat suddenly lost all interest in her pizza and glumly pushed away her plate and took a long drink of cola. 'I promised not to say anything.'

Hannah pointed to me and then to herself. 'But we're your best friends. We won't breathe a word.'

Nat hesitated for a few seconds more and I had the feeling she didn't need much persuading. 'OK . . . it's Genevieve. She probably isn't staying around here much longer.'

My knife slipped off my plate and fell to the floor with a loud reverberating clatter. 'Not staying? Are you serious?'

'When did she tell you?' Hannah asked.

Nat looked up to the ceiling as if trying to recall. 'Er . . . at the weekend.'

'What brought this on?' I managed to whisper.

'She said this town is really boring and she feels closed in. I don't think she's actually ill at all but making plans for her escape.'

'Where did she say she'll go?'

Nat spoke importantly. 'She talked about another place . . . that's better than anywhere she's ever been.'

I was having trouble taking in this news and actually massaged my temples as if my head hurt. 'And she didn't say where this other place was? Abroad or in this country?'

'No . . . but I think she'll hitch around the world, selling her jewellery and living out of a backpack. She's too much of a free spirit for around here.'

This dramatic change of heart was so bizarre – Genevieve had claimed that she couldn't let me go, yet now, suddenly, she apparently intended to leave, and leave quickly. Maybe she *had* been working towards something and this was it – to leave as abruptly as she had arrived. For a split second I felt almost envious at the picture Nat painted of Genevieve being such a free spirit, but it didn't last.

'I don't know what to say, Nat . . . it's so sudden.'

'Not for *Genevieve*,' she stressed. 'She can't wait to leave.'

Hannah frowned. 'What about the people she's staying with?'

'I don't know,' Nat admitted. 'But she did say she wouldn't be going alone.'

I resisted asking how Genevieve could just leave Merlin like this and took a great interest in my plate instead. The pizza tasted fantastic after this news. I polished off my own and Nat's leftovers. When Nat nipped to the ladies', Hannah looked at me a little strangely.

'That's a turn-up, isn't it, Katy?'

'Definitely unexpected,' I answered without emotion.

Hannah rolled her eyes. 'I'm not sure I believe it. Genevieve is great, but a bit . . . unpredictable.'

I groaned inwardly. So blinded by hope, it hadn't occurred to me that Genevieve could be lying. 'Maybe she wants us to find out because . . . it's just a joke.'

'Nat believed her,' Hannah pointed out. 'Anyway . . . not much of a joke, is it?'

My joy had turned to despair. I crossed my fingers on both hands and put them behind my back as Nat returned, whispering a silent prayer for it to be true, for Genevieve to disappear out of our lives as suddenly as she'd arrived. We left the restaurant and walked back towards the bus stop, dodging the sea of people clogging the pavements. All the adults seemed really fed up and hostile, weighed down with bags, their faces etched with tension. I wondered if Christmas shopping stopped being fun when you reached a certain age. We passed the charity shop that Genevieve and I had visited together, and the window display had been changed. Two dummies were dressed in hideous Christmas outfits – a gold sequinned dress with puffed sleeves and a black velvet number with an enormous calf-length skirt and tartan sash.

'Another twenty-five years,' Nat joked, 'and Katy will be wearing this to the golf-club dinner.'

Hannah sniggered. 'Or the Women's Institute ball.'

I pinched them both on the arm. 'I'll never dress old even when I'm sixty. I'll turn my crimplene dress into a mini and stomp around in Doc Martens.'

Nat stuck out her tongue. 'The granny from hell.'

'They had really cool retro stuff last time,' I said. 'Come in and I'll show you.'

It looked as though the shop was just about to close; two elderly ladies were emptying the till and counting the takings. I quickly flicked through the rails, searching for the mermaid dress, but it was so distinctive that I immediately knew it wasn't here.

'Someone must have bought it.' I sighed with disappointment.

A voice called over. 'I knew you'd come back for that dress after you tried it on . . . I put it in the storeroom. It shouldn't have been on display at all – it was far too damaged.'

'I didn't try it on,' I answered peevishly. 'It was the girl I was with who did.'

I recognized the assistant now, the woman whose hair was so stiff it wouldn't have moved in a force-ten gale. She walked over to me and peered hard, lowering her voice. 'If you don't want your friends to know, that's all right. It'll be our little secret.'

My voice, in contrast, became louder. 'Really . . . it

wasn't me. I was with another girl . . . medium height, curly red hair, slim and pretty.'

The woman pursed her lips. 'I do remember the other girl, but it was you who wore the dress. I might be old, but I wouldn't forget someone like that . . . I'm looking at her right now.'

I stretched out my arm and pointed with one finger. 'No. I stood over there and watched.'

'If you say so.' She laughed, and I knew she was just humouring me. She disappeared into the back of the shop and I told myself it was stupid to get annoyed about this. She was old and could have poor eyesight or just a really bad memory. What did it matter if she confused me with Genevieve? When she emerged again I sullenly took the dress from her.

Nat came towards me with a puzzled expression. 'What's up?'

'That lady got me mixed up with Genevieve,' I muttered. 'Even when I pointed out that Genevieve was slim and really pretty with curly red hair.'

'But . . . you've just described yourself,' Nat said slowly.

I swivelled round. 'Me? I'm not slim . . . or even vaguely pretty.'

She looked at me oddly. 'If you say so.'

Hannah stroked the dress lovingly as if it was a pet dog, and then pushed me towards the changing room. It was freezing in here and I stood with my arms wrapped around myself, reluctant to try the dress on because it had fitted Genevieve not me, and we were completely different shapes. It took ages to climb out of my clothes, shivering as my flesh erupted in goosebumps. The shop was old and damp and I could see mould spores on the ripped orange wallpaper. My shoes stuck to the ugly floral carpet.

'You'll have to come out sometime,' Hannah called impatiently.

The mirror inside the changing room was cracked and I had several different reflections of myself, like something from a Hitchcock movie. I took a tentative step from behind the curtain while Hannah indulgently fixed my straps and led me towards the shop mirror. With my arms by my sides the tear wasn't even apparent.

'Katy, you shall go to the ball,' she announced with a mock fanfare on a pretend trumpet.

I was rooted to the spot, gazing at my reflection as though I'd seen a ghost. The dress could have been made for me. It fitted perfectly, and the person staring back didn't look like me at all – it was a better version.

I closed my eyes, waited a moment and then opened them again, but the image was still the same. 'This is weird. I look different. Why do I look so different?'

'We've noticed a change,' Hannah answered kindly, covering my shoulders with her coat to stop my trembling. 'You seem to have kind of . . . blossomed.'

Something was happening that I didn't understand. I tried to voice my confusion. 'That lady mistook me for

Genevieve. I mean . . . I thought it was strange, but now I barely recognize myself.'

Nat seemed genuinely perplexed and twitched her nose like a rabbit. 'If Genevieve looks like you, then you must look like her . . . mustn't you?'

There was a catch in my voice. 'Yes, but I thought she was copying me, and now . . . now . . . I don't know any more.'

'Maybe . . . all this time . . . you were the real stalker.' Nat grinned.

I tried to smile, but my face refused to cooperate. At that moment Hannah decided to intervene and took charge. She helped me get out of the dress and paid for it while I gratefully slipped back into my layers of clothing. She handed the bag over to me and winked.

'We should meet up on Saturday and try on our clothes for the ball. We'll do each other's make-up and hair and stuff.'

I nodded with forced enthusiasm even though that only gave me a few days to attempt a repair. I was quiet on the bus all the way home and watched the drops of condensation running, with steady speed, from the top of the glass to the bottom, trying to get rid of the churning feeling inside. All this time I'd thought I was running from Genevieve. Had I really been drawn to her like a moth to a flame? I rested my head against the cool pane, fearful that I didn't know what was real any more.

*

Organ music is playing, wafting down those winding stairs, and it sounds like a wedding march, but my nails are clawing at the banister, leaving gouges in the wood like a wild animal would. Genevieve is waiting, as always, a secret smile on her face. She is holding a bouquet of flowers and a beautiful ivory dress for me to try on. It's delicate and intricate lace over a satin bodice. I walk into it as though it's a second skin, but the dress is ice cold and straight away I want to take it off. I pull at the fabric, but it's stuck to me, growing ever colder on my flesh. The smell in my nostrils isn't just damp any more, it's decay and rot, so strong it makes me gag. Genevieve urges me to look at myself in the mirror and I have no choice but to obey. I'm not wearing a wedding dress any longer – it's a shroud. I'm cold and still, my cheeks pallid and my lips blue. The music playing is actually a dirge. It's my funeral but I'm not dead. I'm trapped in a paralysed body, unable to speak or move. I'm about to be buried alive and Genevieve is going to watch.

It's dawn before I dare to close my eyes again.

CHAPTER THIRTY-TWO

`Katy, could I talk to you somewhere away from college? About midday if you're free? X`

I stared at my phone for ages, annoyed because my whole body tingled as I read Merlin's text. But it was tinged with resentment – I refused to be summoned as if we were still involved with each other. My reply was coolly dismissive.

`Sorry Merlin, going to lunch with Nat and Hannah, maybe some other time.`

He replied immediately.

`How about La Tasse? 12.30 X`

Full marks for persistence. I ended up agreeing out of curiosity. We hadn't been alone together since the episode with the painting, and I couldn't imagine what he needed to say. I was glad that I'd washed my hair that morning and made a serious effort to coordinate my clothes into a multilayered chicness rather than total grunge.

A long wait at the level crossing made me fashionably late and I looked around the cafe for a moment. There was a pang somewhere deep inside as my eyes rested on Merlin – he was by the window in the same booth we'd first sat in together. That already seemed like a lifetime ago. People had stared at us then because we were so newly in love, but now no one gave us a second glance. I slid into the seat opposite, feeling as though the ghost of me was still lingering there.

'You look great, Katy.'

'Thanks.'

I pointed to his laptop, which was open on the table. 'Homework?'

'Just web-design stuff.'

I knew my body language was stiff. If felt as if there was a coat hanger wedged in my back. 'How's Genevieve?'

'Her tonsils are still swollen.'

Cue the sympathetic face. 'Hope she'll be better for Christmas.'

I watched Merlin carefully but there was no reaction from him. If Genevieve intended to leave, then he didn't know about it. But why would she tell Nat and not him?

He drained the dregs from his cup. 'I'll order another, shall I? And one for you?'

I was friendly but firm. 'Merlin, we could make small talk all night and it'll cost a fortune in coffee. Why did you ask me here?'

He nodded hesitantly and studied his hands. 'Katy, I have to sort things out between us . . . Ever since that . . . last time . . . we haven't cleared the air.'

I tried to sound dispassionate and in control. 'We don't have to do this. There's no need. We'll still be friends, without complications.'

'It's not just us,' he pleaded. 'What about everyone else? It won't be the same if you and I don't . . . get things out in the open.'

He was right. It would be awkward for Nat and Hannah if we didn't move on from being a couple.

'OK,' I agreed. 'You first.'

'I have to explain about . . . the painting.'

'There's nothing to explain,' I answered, hurt quickly rising despite my good intentions.

He closed his eyes. 'I keep seeing your face when I showed it to you . . . It was awful.'

I ran my tongue over my teeth as if there was something nasty on them. 'And why do you think I was so annoyed, Merlin?'

'I think I made a . . . mistake painting your . . . eyes,' he mumbled.

'Not just the eyes,' I snapped, as my anger bubbled over. 'There wasn't much of me at all in your painting.'

'You're still there,' he insisted.

Just the remnants of me, a ghostly shadow, I reflected bitterly. There was nothing else to do but confront him. 'I think you know whose features dominate that canvas.'

He wouldn't look at me. 'You mean Genevieve's?'

My voice came out weirdly stilted and formal. 'Yes, Merlin, I certainly do mean Genevieve's.'

Merlin scratched his chin and I could tell he was struggling to find his words. 'It was of you, Katy. I swear. You and only you.'

'That's not what I saw.'

'But that's what I'm trying to tell you . . . It wasn't of Genevieve . . . not at first anyway.'

I found myself repeating her words and throwing them back at him. 'It couldn't have changed at the last minute.'

'That's what did happen,' he brooded. 'I kept refining bits here and there . . . right up to the day I showed it to you and—'

'It wasn't finished weeks ago?' I interrupted.

'No . . . I never rush my work.' He made a circle with his hands. 'It's a gradual evolving of a theme, and sometimes it takes on a life of its own.'

It did in this case, I thought morosely, but I remained silent, wondering whether to believe him or not. I was annoyed with myself that I so wanted to believe him.

'Katy . . . one minute I was looking at your almost completed portrait, and then you were in my studio looking confused and shocked. After you left . . . it slowly dawned on me why.'

I smiled politely and blinked several times. 'Maybe your subconscious was at work . . . guiding your hand. Secretly you wanted to be with Genevieve . . .'

He shook his head. 'I didn't, and it wasn't her I painted. I wish I could make you believe me.'

'Why's it so important, Merlin?'

'The truth's always important,' he answered, and I refused to look at him because he sounded so sincere. He hung his head. 'You and Genevieve are an enigma,' he complained. 'Whenever I think I'm getting close I discover you're a million light years away from me.'

I closed my eyes for a second because this was exactly how I felt about him.

'You're with Genevieve now,' I had to point out. 'She can't be that much of a mystery.'

Merlin shook his head almost in despair. 'She was always there, Katy, and you were always . . . somewhere else.'

I looked him straight in the eye. 'But . . . it doesn't matter any more.' I was overcome by the knowledge that this was the truth. I didn't think we could ever mean anything to each other again. Meeting Merlin this way felt like saying goodbye to a part of me.

'So, Katy . . . are we OK now?'

'Of course.'

He jerked his head as if to wake himself up. 'Genevieve asked me to show you a new design competition on the web. The prize is a week's work experience at one of the big fashion houses.'

I tried not to sound ungrateful. 'The details will be in college. Miss Clegg always puts them on the noticeboard.'

'Genevieve said this one was extra-special and no one else would find out about it.' He turned the laptop to face me. 'She's stored it on favourites: "For Katy's Eyes Only".'

I sucked in my cheeks, outraged at Genevieve's nerve, and clicked on the link, waiting for the screen to change.

'Slow connection?' He smiled as my face froze in sheer disbelief. I felt as though the floor was opening up beneath me and I was sinking into a black hole. I stared for as long as I dared, my eyes reading the text again and again, hoping I'd misinterpreted the meaning. I got up quickly.

'Merlin, I have to go. Something's come up.'

'There's nothing wrong, is there?'

'No . . . I just need to get home. Probably . . . see you around.'

'It might be sooner than you think,' he joked, but I was too upset to respond.

I think I must have beaten the record for running a mile and texting at the same time. I didn't slow down until my street sign came into view. My heart was thumping and there was a nagging stitch in my side. I slumped against a wall feeling sick with anxiety and exhaustion. Luke's car was outside his house, and I was relieved because I had to tell him what Genevieve had wanted me to see. His mum answered the door and my voice was breathlessly high-pitched.

'Hello, Mrs Cassidy. Is Luke around?'

'Sorry, Katy. He's taken Laura into town for a celebration.'

I was overwhelmed with crushing disappointment. 'Is it her birthday?'

Her whole face lit up. 'No, it's their anniversary. Three whole years.'

'Oh, wow, that's amazing.'

'That's probably why his phone's off.' She winked at me. 'They might not want to be disturbed.'

I was mortified. 'No . . . yes . . . of course they don't. I wouldn't dream of it.'

'Was it important, Katy?' she called after me.

'No, it wasn't anything really. I'll . . . er . . . catch up with him tomorrow.'

There was nothing to do but wait until morning. There was no one else who could possibly understand this new development. I hated myself for needing Luke so badly and tried to shut him from my mind, but it wasn't possible. I lay awake listening to the wind howling and blowing my curtains through the rotten frames. Slowly I took the photograph of Luke and me out of my drawer and held it up to the light. Each time, it surprised me more. I carefully put it back, not sure why I'd even kept it.

I can feel the heat even in my sleep. I'm back at the decrepit house but this time helpless, unable to go further than the porch. I'm forced to watch as Genevieve throws a match and the flames spread, the staircase cracking and splintering like tinder. She walks through the fire unharmed, hovering at least a metre above the ground. The only way I'll be saved is to go with her. I don't want to, but there's no choice. She holds out her hand and I step towards her, our two figures merging to become one. Her thoughts become my thoughts. She takes me to the city square to gaze at the hangman's noose suspended from a gibbet, framed against the burned-orange night sky.

CHAPTER THIRTY-THREE

It sounded like a shower of hailstones, lightly hitting my bedroom window and then growing heavier. I was hovering between sleep and being awake, but it took me ages to realize that the pattern was all wrong and someone was actually throwing stones at the pane.

Hastily I opened the casement and poked my head out. Luke was underneath my window with a hand full of tiny pebbles from his garden.

'Luke? It's so early.'

'Mum told me you called last night. I knew something was up.'

I held up both hands to indicate I'd be down in ten minutes.

I washed my face, brushed my teeth, ran a comb through my hair and pulled on a pair of jogging bottoms and a sweatshirt. Lastly I picked up a sheet of paper and stuffed it into my bag. Luke was waiting near his car with bleary eyes and unruly hair. He'd probably slept in his T-shirt, because it was warmly crumpled and smelled like his room. My nose must have been working overtime, because I could also detect garlic and a sweet lingering beer smell.

'It wasn't that important,' I said guiltily.

'Mum said you were out of breath as if you'd run a marathon.'

'Can we go somewhere, Luke?' I was desperate to get away from everything that was familiar.

I slid into his car and he gave me a mock salute and grinned. 'Where to, m'lady?'

'I don't suppose . . . you fancy going to the . . . seaside?'

Luke didn't even bother replying, but did a sharp three-point turn and sped out of our road. It was only twenty minutes to the coast and we drove in preoccupied silence until Luke pulled into a car park at the end of the promenade and told me to wrap up. The morning tide was in and the waves were huge, three-metre breakers hitting the barriers. We put up our hoods and tried to walk across the dunes, but a film of sand was soon stuck to our faces and our eyes were sore and gritty. Among the shingle and seaweed my eyes picked out pieces of sea glass, which gave me a weird feeling in the pit of my stomach. We were soon driven back to a seating area that was sheltered from the wind. There was a small catering van serving hot drinks and fast food.

I took out the piece of paper and handed it to Luke, then turned away, not wanting to read the story again.

The headline was emblazoned in my memory: 'FIRE AT VICARAGE'.

Luke was quiet for what seemed like an eternity. I listened to a pair of dogs barking and a little girl laughing as the wind buffeted her along, and wondered how everyday things could just carry on when someone like Genevieve was in the world.

'I printed it off my computer last night,' I told him.

'It might not be anything to do with her,' he murmured eventually.

'Another of those coincidences,' I answered scornfully.

'She couldn't go halfway across the country to attempt something like this.'

'*We* did. We went halfway across the country just to delve into her past, and you've got to admit it's strange that things like this just seem to follow her around.'

Even Luke seemed to be stumped by this one. 'But everyone's OK . . . I mean, it's awful but . . . they all got out in time.'

My voice was a deathly whisper. 'Only thanks to the fire escape on the top floor. If the vicarage had been smaller . . .' I shuddered, remembering that the ground floor had been completely gutted and the main staircase cut off. I'd climbed those stairs so many times in my dreams.

'If it was Genevieve, Kat, then she's settling old scores and it's nothing to do with us talking to the vicar and his wife.'

I couldn't believe that Luke could be so blind and I

wondered if he was simply trying not to scare me. 'She got Merlin to show this to me on his laptop . . . even labelled the link "For Katy's Eyes Only".'

'That's sick!' he said angrily.

'She's on to us,' I insisted. 'She knows what we . . . *I've* been up to. She always knows.'

I was beginning to learn that the more agitated I became, the calmer Luke was. 'You're upset and shocked and probably overreacting.'

I stood with my hands on my hips. 'How can you of all people say that?'

'I know you're into . . . unexplained events,' he began tactfully, 'but everything has a reasonable explanation. I can't buy into this telepathy thing between you two.'

'She's getting far too dangerous, Luke.'

'Is that why you were so desperate to get home last night?' he asked.

I pulled a strand of hair from my mouth. 'I was completely in shock . . . worried that no one's safe from her.'

'We should go back to the vicarage,' Luke suggested. 'Talk to the vicar's wife and persuade her to go to the police.'

I shook my head violently. 'She won't go. It's in the story. She blamed it on pranksters playing with fireworks . . . a joke that got out of hand. "I bear them no ill will," she was quoted as saying, which sends a message to Genevieve that she won't do anything to expose her.'

'That doesn't make sense.'

'She knows what Genevieve's capable of,' I answered mutinously. 'She believed she was truly evil and that that's why she couldn't live in a sacred place.'

Luke gave me an exasperated look.

I took a deep breath, deciding that I couldn't contain this any longer. 'I know you're into logic, Luke, and hate superstition and magic but . . . Genevieve isn't like us. She has something that sets her apart . . .'

'She might be a sociopath,' he responded. 'Someone completely amoral, without a conscience, but she's of this earth, completely and utterly.' He stared into the distance and I had to resist the urge to snuggle closer to escape the wind. Since seeing the photograph of us together I was more wary of how I behaved and how other people might view us. The tea from the vendor tasted of nothing but plastic and hot water, but I slurped it gratefully.

'It was so weird seeing Merlin yesterday.'

'Was it?'

'Yeah . . . almost like when we were together.'

'And you don't want to get back to that?'

My hood had fallen down and Luke pulled it up again and fastened the ties, pushing the stray hairs back inside. 'I think there's a lot going on with you right now, Kat.'

'He was my dream boyfriend, you know . . . the kind I never ever thought would even look at me, and when he did everything seemed amazing.'

'Maybe it was the idea of him you were crazy about and not the real him,' Luke answered with a peculiar smile.

I was taken aback by how perceptive Luke was, because, in a strange way, I'd already come to the same conclusion. I tried to explain this. 'The very first time I went to Merlin's house there was an incredible rainbow behind it, and even though I knew I could never reach it, I still tried. Going out with Merlin felt a bit like that . . .'

Luke cleared his throat and appeared slightly embarrassed. 'It must be hard for you to trust people right now, but when this is over . . .'

'We could never go back to what we had,' I told him with certainty.

'Never say never, Kat.'

I banged my trainers against the concrete, trying to get rid of the wet sand as Luke offered me a torpedo-shaped container. I shook my head politely, not wanting to make a big deal about my aversion to meat, and watched him wolf down a hot dog with all the trimmings, which was doubly gross at breakfast time. I changed the subject.

'What about you and Laura? Three whole years – congratulations!'

He didn't reply and I was worried this was too personal, but he raised his eyes as the gulls swarmed overhead desperate for scraps. 'She's so completely comfortable.'

'Like a pair of old shoes,' I joked.

Luke smiled, but seemed sad at the same time. It was ages before he spoke again. 'I don't think we'll make it, Kat. We want such different things. Laura's given me some kind of ultimatum.'

'I'm so sorry . . .'

I trailed off, not knowing what to say and shocked because I was glad at this news. I didn't understand why, because I didn't have feelings for Luke. I couldn't have feelings for Luke.

'It's OK,' he replied easily. 'We've both changed . . . it happens.'

I squeezed his hand and we studied the turbulent water fighting against the wooden sleepers of the sea wall. As I stared into the murky water with its yellow foam I felt a horrible prickly fear run down my spine about something that was to come.

'I feel like I'm drowning,' I said simply, 'and Genevieve's with me but she doesn't want to be saved, she wants me to go with her.'

Luke dug his hands deep into his pockets. 'That's just a projection of your fears . . .'

Suddenly the heavens opened. Luke pulled me to my feet and we ran to the car together, panting. He turned on the wipers and we stayed for a few minutes watching the awesome power of the rolling sea, the horizon just a grey mist of water and sky converged.

'Things have gone way too far now,' I said with unusual decisiveness. 'The burning building changes everything. I have to try to stop Genevieve. End the mystery once and for all.'

Luke raised his eyebrows at me. 'You sound determined.'

I nodded grimly. 'I've put this off for too long, Luke. I know exactly what I should do next.'

*

Mum?'

She was out of bed but still in her dressing gown. I'd been kidding myself that she was doing well, but evidence to the contrary was staring me in the face – the sunken eyes, extra worry lines that had appeared overnight and a permanent look of apprehension. She was living on her nerves, and the slightest noise made her jump out of her skin.

'Mum, we need to talk. You have to tell me what's going on.'

CHAPTER THIRTY-FOUR

Two cups of coffee lay untouched on the table as we sat by the fire together, the wind howling outside and rain lashing the windows. Impatience was making me edgy, but I knew it was important to let her do this in her own time. It took her ages to begin and I really thought she was going to bolt, but finally she took a deep breath.

'I was living close to York when you were born.'

I wasn't supposed to know this so I appeared suitably surprised. 'You mean I wasn't born here?'

'No . . . I was still a student when I fell pregnant and I hid it from everyone for as long as I could. I didn't tell you because . . . well . . . I'm not sure really.'

Mum looked at me wistfully and I wondered if she was remembering my father, whom she never talked about.

'Why did you hide it?'

She clenched her fists together until her knuckles were white. 'My parents . . . Gran and Grandad were quite strict and were so pleased that I'd gone to university; I couldn't bear to let them down.'

'Were you living in halls?' I asked innocently.

'No . . . all the places went to first years. The only accommodation I could get was outside the city, a dingy room in a big old house with five or more other dingy rooms . . . damp, mice, peeling wallpaper . . .'

Mum reached for her cup and took a gulp, spilling some on to her dressing gown, but she didn't even notice. She stopped and I realized that I was going to have to coax her and it was important to choose my words carefully.

'Did that place . . . I mean . . . is it possible it could have a connection to Grace . . . or Genevieve as she calls herself now?'

'I can't be certain,' Mum answered with a tinge of desperate hope. 'It might all be a terrible coincidence. I mean there's no proof . . . just a name.'

Her voice said one thing but her eyes told me another. There was one way to sort out Genevieve's identity once and for all. I steeled myself, feeling that I was on the brink of something immense. 'Would you remember Grace's date of birth?'

Mum reeled off the date immediately which took me by surprise, but I reasoned that it was only four days before mine so it would have stayed in her memory.

'Then there's no doubt,' I replied flatly. 'The college confirmed Genevieve's birthday from their computer records. Genevieve and Grace are the same person.'

Mum barely reacted and I figured that, deep down, this wasn't a shock to her. But my stomach lurched and wild thoughts ran through my mind as I remembered the photograph of the unknown baby: Mum had postnatal depression and didn't know what was going on; Genevieve's mother had tricked her into taking the small sickly infant and kept the strong, healthy one herself; or they'd both undertaken some strange experiment to raise each other's child and see how they turned out. This was utterly mad and I was impatient for answers, but it was important not to frighten Mum. I took a few deep breaths and composed myself.

'Did you know Genevieve's mother well?'

'I knew *of* her,' Mum stressed, and I could tell it wasn't in a nice way. Her brow wrinkled as she struggled to remember. 'People were aware she was taking drugs, but everyone looked the other way . . . We all walked by and didn't want to get involved, it was easier that way.'

'So . . . what changed?'

Mum's eyelids slowly closed and her voice faded. I had to lean my ear towards her just to catch her words. 'She became a mother . . . and now it wasn't just herself she was destroying.'

I knew the answer already but I still had to ask. 'Was I there . . . at the same time as Genevieve?'

Mum didn't deny it. She let her head fall to her chest and cleared her throat with difficulty.

'The night you came home from hospital you slept

like an angel, perfect and beautifully still and in the morning . . . you were so peaceful.' She stopped and one large tear rolled down her face and splashed on to her leg. 'And I heard the crying again . . . frantic . . . inconsolable . . . so I went down to look.'

I jumped as Gemma strolled into the room as if she owned the place. She curled up at my feet and I brushed her fur, glad of the distraction. 'What did you see?'

She stared straight ahead and spoke without emotion. 'There was a heatwave, and even at nine in the morning it was a scorching day. There was a pram parked next to bags of rubbish . . . I could see a face . . . she was dirty and had soiled her nappy . . . waving her arms frantically in the air and a wasp was crawling over her. She'd been crying for so long that she was all blotchy and her crying was hoarse . . .'

I felt prickles again and wished I could spare Mum this pain. Gran's words suddenly came back to me – she'd talked about a death from a drug overdose which had affected Mum deeply.

'Was her mum . . . OK?' I asked cautiously.

Mum shook her head and quickly wiped her face. 'There was nothing I could do, nothing anyone could do . . . I was frozen with shock . . .'

'It wasn't your fault,' I said immediately, but Mum ignored me and continued talking in the same monotone.

'But that's when I knew . . . I was in that exact place at that time . . . I was a mother too, and it was my duty. I felt it so deeply that nothing could have stopped me.'

This sounded a bit strange. 'You phoned the police?'

Mum didn't answer.

'You phoned the police?' I persisted.

'They did come,' she replied. 'I remember them coming.'

'And what happened to Genevieve?'

Mum's mouth twisted in anguish. 'I'm not sure. I was far away, back home with Gran and Grandad. It was so remote there and cut off from everything, but that was what I needed.'

Warm relief engulfed me. These were the answers I'd been seeking. Mum was only guilty of acting like a caring person. If she hadn't decided to investigate that morning, it could have been much worse. Genevieve could have died too. I felt like a balloon that had slowly deflated and I could breathe easily again. I'd been so stupid, coming up with bizarre scenarios when the explanation was so simple – sad but simple.

'You never told anyone?'

'Not until today.'

I stood with my back to the fire, warming my legs. Now I could view Genevieve as a person with psychological problems and stop obsessing about her having some kind of supernatural hold over me.

'I'm almost an adult now, and it's obvious to me you couldn't have saved Genevieve's mum. Anyone could see you did nothing wrong.'

'Anyone but *Genevieve*,' she corrected.

This was entirely likely, but it was important to offer Mum reassurance. 'She will understand.'

Mum suddenly sat bolt upright in her chair. 'That girl, Genevieve . . . I don't think she's very stable.'

This didn't seem like the time to describe how disturbed Genevieve really was. I still didn't know how she'd managed to track us down, but she must have distorted everything in her head so that Mum was somehow culpable. And it was easy to see why she hated me – I still had a mother and she didn't, which was probably why she made those threats about taking over my life.

We sat in silence, listening to the storm. It felt nice to be cocooned together like this, all the distance between us removed. I tried to drink my coffee but it had gone cold and there was a skin of milk floating on the top. Mum was still chewing something over, and I waited for her to continue.

Eventually she spoke. 'And . . . Genevieve's childhood? Was it very unhappy?'

I rolled my eyes. 'By all accounts . . . but . . . she was a problem child. No matter how many people tried to help, she always ended up alone.'

The effect of these words was startling. Mum looked devastated and her fist jammed in her mouth. She began to sob – huge noisy sobs that shook the whole of her body. 'I should have intervened, Katy. We were both young mothers, but I had Gran and Grandad to support me; she had no one. A few minutes sooner and I might have been in time . . .'

'You had your own problems,' I soothed.

'I've ruined two lives . . .'

I knelt on the floor next to Mum's chair. 'Genevieve's mum died because she didn't give up drugs, not even for her baby. She didn't take responsibility and she paid the price.'

Mum's lips formed themselves into a small O of despair. She looked like a frightened child. 'I've no right to judge; *I've* been a terrible mother . . .'

'You haven't,' I argued. 'I've never been unhappy or neglected.'

Mum was still distressed and I kicked myself for not handling this better.

'This has always haunted me,' she cried. 'You can never escape from the past, no matter how hard you try.'

'I'm going to talk to Genevieve,' I announced. 'Make her see that you did nothing wrong.'

Mum shook her head stubbornly and her bottom lip stuck out. 'Stay away from that girl. She's determined to make me pay . . . she's getting to me through you.'

'Not any more,' I insisted. 'She can't hurt me now because I know the truth.'

Mum suddenly slumped in her chair. 'The truth is not always what it seems,' she answered with difficulty.

There was no point saying anything else. Mum seemed to have gone somewhere in her mind, to that place that I could never follow. I helped her back to bed and she responded mechanically and was asleep in less than five minutes. I studied her face for a moment. I had hoped the confession would be a weight off her mind, but it didn't seem so. Even asleep, her forehead was deeply scored and her mouth twitching as if she was plagued by bad memories. But she'd opened the floodgates and maybe now she could heal.

I sent Luke a long message telling him everything that had happened and how the mystery was finally solved, and also to thank him for all his help. In a strange way, I was sad, because we'd made such a great team. He was right after all – the mystery wasn't weirdly spooky or inexplicable, just a sad tale of a woman who couldn't cope and the consequences. Mum was a bystander who got caught up in it, and the repercussions were being felt even now. No one knew how Genevieve had discovered the truth, but it wasn't really important. The only thing left was to convince her that my mother was acting in her interests and beg her to leave us alone. Closure – that was what we needed.

CHAPTER THIRTY-FIVE

The dress was so sheer that it kept slipping through my hands like grains of sand. It was going to take all my patience and endurance to put it back together again, and the colour was impossible to match because it varied depending on the light. The moment I had a piece of thread ready, it seemed to change again. I worked from the inside, making a kind of cat's cradle to support the layers of thread and gently joining the frayed edges together. If the fabric had been paler, I wouldn't have got away with it, but in the end the tear was virtually undetectable.

We'd made arrangements to meet at Hannah's at about seven. Mum wanted to see what I'd bought so I floated downstairs, doing a twirl as I reached the bottom.

'Wow . . . what a transformation. You look fabulous.'

'We're having a kind of dress rehearsal for the ball.'

Mum's face was still drawn, but she made an effort to look pleased for me. 'That'll be fun . . . I'm sure I have a pair of long gloves somewhere.'

I clapped my hands in excitement. 'Can you dig them out? And please can you show me how to do my hair in a French pleat that screams elegant and sophisticated rather than frizzy and flyaway?'

Mum found the gloves easily and a pair of black satin slingback shoes with a kitten heel, plus a great string of fake pearls and some dangly earrings to match. I changed back into my jeans and put the dress into a bag, ready to take with me. Mum went upstairs again and returned with a bag full of clips, slides, combs and hairspray and spent ages teasing my thick wavy hair into something vaguely resembling Audrey Hepburn's in *Breakfast at Tiffany's*, one of her favourite movies.

'You know . . . since this girl, Genevieve, came along,' she began tentatively, 'things have changed, haven't they?'

'Suppose,' I grunted, wincing as my head was yanked to the left.

'You seem more confident . . . less the . . .'

'Doormat?'

'No, that's not the word I'm looking for,' Mum scolded. 'More your own person.'

'Maybe,' I agreed.

'Things have changed with me too.'

'Have they?'

Mum's nimble fingers brushed my neck. 'I've realized you're almost an adult and soon you'll be making your own way. Going away to uni maybe.'

'I did think about it. The best degree course for me is probably in London.'

'Well, Katy, I've had you to myself for so long it's time I let you go.'

She spoke without a trace of self-pity, which was unusual. A seagull squawked overhead, making me start. Through the window, I watched it spread its wings and soar into the white winter sky. It almost seemed like a sign that Mum was ready to set me free to make my own way.

'You're not a child any more and I have to make a life for myself so . . . Genevieve's influence hasn't been *all* bad.'

'Not sure about that,' I replied sourly. 'If I never saw her again in my whole life it'd be too soon.'

Mum carefully sprayed my hair, studying it this way and that like a work of art. 'You dislike her that much?'

My eyes blazed. 'Too right. I know she's had a difficult life but she's conceited, underhand, sly, manipulative . . .'

'Oh dear.' Mum laughed nervously.

I glowered. 'I hope she takes herself off to the other side of the world.'

'What was that?'

'Er . . . nothing.' It was best not to say anything yet about Genevieve leaving before it was definite, just in case Mum came over all guilty again.

Because Genevieve wouldn't be there I dug out my favourite coat, and it felt wonderful to wear it again, like being hugged by an old friend. Mum waved me off and told me to watch my step because the ground was slippery and snow was forecast for the next few days. I was OK walking in my trainers but lots of people were unprepared and I watched one lady, in stilettos, holding tightly to a wall, and an old man stuck on an ice patch unable to go forwards or back, his arms extended like a tightrope walker's. Children were having fun sliding along the pavement, making everything so much more dangerous. I hit a patch of frozen water from an old leaky drainpipe and my foot skidded but I managed to stay upright.

At Hannah's house the lights were on and the curtains open. Hannah and Nat rushed to the door and pulled me inside. Both were already dressed – Hannah in a slim-fitting ivory satin gown which had been her gran's wedding dress, and Nat in a taffeta frock, shocking pink to match her hair, worn with her Converse pumps. A surge of excitement ran through me because this felt as good as dressing up as a child, trying on your mum's clothes and make-up. I didn't want to admit that I'd never had anyone to do this with.

'Love your hair,' they chanted in unison, steering me into the living room instead of the kitchen-diner where we normally hung out. 'Now get into the dress, Katy.'

'What's the hurry?' I asked, pulling the curtains across and self-consciously wriggling out of my jeans. 'We've got all night.'

'We can't wait to do your make-up,' Hannah replied, and I could sense her impatience.

I was about to strut up and down when one of her

hands forced me on to a dining chair and tilted my face to the light.

'Foundation,' she barked, and Hannah rummaged in her make-up bag and brought out a compact. It was impossible to talk as she pummelled my face and then instructed, 'Blusher followed by eyeshadow.'

'This is like having an operation,' I joked, as she went to work on my eyes. I studied Nat close up, and then glanced over to Hannah. 'Hey. How come your make-up's already done?'

'We were bored,' Nat answered, lunging at me with a mascara wand and making me blink madly. She stood back to survey her handiwork and seemed relieved that it was finished.

'There, Katy . . . you look great.'

I looked at my face in the mirror and had to admit she'd done a good job. My skin glowed; my eyes were a smoky grey, and I had razor-sharp cheekbones and exaggerated lips in a cupid's bow. I took out my accessories to finish off the look, trying not to feel a sense of anticlimax because it was barely eight o'clock.

'Well . . . I'm ready now. What'll we do for the rest of the night?'

Nat looked at her watch and then back at Hannah. I got the distinct impression there was something they weren't telling me. The doorbell chimed and Hannah jumped up and announced in a loud stagey voice, 'I wonder who that could be?'

I trailed after her as she went to answer the door, and my jaw hit the ground.

'Don't stand there gawping.' Hannah laughed. 'Show the boys through to dinner.'

Merlin was standing on the doorstep dressed in pinstripe trousers with full top hat and tails and a canary-yellow waistcoat. Adam was beside him in a black tux and a white ruffled shirt, while another friend, Harvey, was wearing some sort of weird quilted smoking jacket and cravat. They looked like something out of *Brideshead Revisited*, and I couldn't believe they'd walked along the street dressed this way, even in the dark. I looked behind them, expecting to see Genevieve making an entrance, but she was nowhere in sight.

Merlin moved forward, took my hand, encased in the black glove, and kissed it before stepping over the threshold. This already had an element of a play about it and I shadowed Hannah through the hallway and into the kitchen-diner. There were goblet wine glasses and proper napkins, with an elaborate silver candelabra taking centre stage. My gaze carried on through to the conservatory, which had been decorated with balloons and fairy lights. A disco ball was hanging from the glass roof and lots of sequined shapes were strung across the windows.

'Are things OK between you and Merlin?' Hannah whispered. 'He said they were, but . . .'

'They're fine,' I whispered back.

'Sorry you missed the party,' Nat grinned. 'It's not quite a marquee.'

'It's better,' I told her, choked with emotion, and I really meant it. 'It's completely fab.'

The table was only laid for six, and I couldn't believe that Genevieve would let me enjoy an evening like this without trying to ruin it. Hannah tapped one of the glasses with a spoon. 'Sit down, everyone, and make sure you check your name card. The seating plan is already arranged and you have to stick to it.' Hannah winked at me, because it was obvious that Adam would be strategically placed next to Nat. 'Mum's prepared all the food, so it won't be disgusting. We haven't any staff to wait on us, but Nat will do her best.'

Nat gave a loud groan but willingly went to help. I wasn't allowed to lift a finger or to move from the table and spent the time grinning inanely at all the activity and soaking up the atmosphere. The food was light and vegetarian – creamy vegetable lasagne, loads of salad, pan-fried potatoes, and ciabatta to mop up the sauce. We all sat down to eat with a noisy clatter and Nat proposed a toast to me and to friendship, which actually brought a tear to my eye, although I hastily blinked it away. Genevieve could keep her huge ostentatious party; this was small, intimate and far more special.

Hannah's dad had an old record player with a turntable that played 78s, and all through dinner we listened to a collection of 1920s music, laughing at the scratches in the vinyl and the needle which kept sticking. By the second glass of sparkling wine it seemed even funnier, and I was convinced that Hannah had laced it with something stronger. My cheeks were on fire, despite the cold, because everything looked so pretty and everyone had made such an effort for me. Merlin was seated directly opposite and I talked and joked with everyone, trying to avoid his eyes because he had that look in them that was hard to resist. If we were alone together, I feared I'd drown.

Hannah startled everyone by suddenly leaping to her feet and screaming, 'Omigod it's snowing.'

Everyone rushed to the conservatory windows and watched as the first soft powdery flakes fell. It was completely crazy, but I had an overwhelming urge to be outside in it. I flung open the patio doors and tumbled on to the grass without any coat, the snow gently settling on my shoulders, my hair and my face as I gazed in wonder at its beauty mingled with a thousand stars. I threw my head back and twirled around the garden, rubbing the flakes into my skin. I was the ballerina, the escaped balloon, the leaf in the wind, twirling and pirouetting in this blanket of whiteness. There was laughter as everyone called my name but I kept on going until I reached a row of conifers at the bottom of the garden, standing in line like soldiers on parade. It took two people to drag me back inside, as wet and slippery as a fish that'd jumped out of the river. Nat threw me a towel and I patted my arms and neck, the sharpness of the cold making me tingle.

'It looks like confetti in your hair,' Merlin whispered, and I felt his hand brush the bare skin on my back.

It was then I knew that I'd been given a second chance and this was the night I'd wished for. Tonight I sparkled and could do no wrong; tonight I wasn't invisible Katy. There was only one explanation – Genevieve had let go. There was no way I could feel so confident and free unless she was diminished in some way. She must have taken leave of me. Merlin stared as if he was seeing me for the first time and I flashed him my most radiant smile before moving back to the party.

My mood was contagious. The table was hastily cleared, with everyone mucking in to help, and the dance floor was declared open. We all swapped partners and tried the charleston, tango, foxtrot and, finally, Merlin took me in his arms for the waltz.

'Imagine if we lived back then, Katy,' he said, attempting a low dip and catching me just before I hit the floor.

'Would you have looked at me . . . in your big house?' I tried to keep it light-hearted. 'You'd have been the squire's son and I'd have been the housemaid polishing the silver or your boots.'

'Sounds good.' Merlin smirked. 'I could have taken advantage of the servant girl.'

I did a mock curtsy, although I knew what was happening and that I was encouraging him.

'I'm definitely forgiven?' he asked earnestly.

'There was nothing to forgive.'

'And now?'

'We're dancing,' I quipped.

'And now, Katy?' he persisted.

He stopped halfway through the dance, and still holding one hand, led me back through Hannah's hallway. I hadn't answered his question and he moved his face closer to mine. I didn't pull away. He began very softly kissing my neck all the way up to my ear lobe. It felt unbelievable to have this time together, and I shut everything else from my mind. Any minute now he would reach my lips and it would be as if we'd never finished. And the best thing was that Genevieve deserved this, she really did. This was my ultimate revenge.

I suddenly caught sight of my face in a small mirror positioned next to the coat stand and recoiled. I looked so hard and cruel, my eyes glinting horribly. I barely recognized myself and from nowhere the realization hit me like a sledgehammer. If Merlin could so easily do this behind Genevieve's back, then what did it say about him? Or about me? I tore myself away and rearranged my dress, livid with myself. Genevieve *did* deserve this, but to get my own back I had to sink to her level and I wouldn't do that.

'We're not interchangeable, Merlin,' I snapped. 'You can't just pick one of us up whenever the other one's not around.'

He put one hand on his forehead. 'I don't know what came over me . . . I'm sorry.'

'It's OK, but we can't go there again. You're with Genevieve now.'

We couldn't look at each other.

'I almost forgot you weren't mine,' Merlin muttered, and walked away from me.

CHAPTER THIRTY-SIX

A taxi dropped me right outside my front door. It was difficult getting out because the dress was so fitted that I couldn't stretch my leg very far without splitting it again. I'd held out at the party until midnight, thanked everyone profusely and made my getaway, refusing Merlin's offer to walk me home and using the snow as an excuse. We'd got too close, and I had to make sure it didn't happen again. The house was in darkness and I turned my bag inside out trying to locate my keys without switching on the outside light in case it woke Mum. I jumped about a metre in the air when a voice came from out of the blackness.

'I knew you'd go back and buy that dress.'

'What the . . . ? You gave me such a fright. What are you doing here at this time of night?'

'Waiting for you, Katy.'

Genevieve appeared from the shadows, her hair scraped tightly back and her face ghastly white. I was so spooked that it took me three attempts to put my key in the lock.

'Have you missed me?'

'Not really,' I whispered, and pointed upstairs, indicating that she should keep her voice down. She wasn't even wearing a coat, just a thick cardigan over a T-shirt. I could see how cold she was because her body was hunched and her hands red. I couldn't believe she'd wait outside on a freezing December night just to taunt me.

'What is it you want, Genevieve?' I asked loftily.

'We have unfinished business.'

'Do we?'

'You know we do. You should invite me inside.'

The door was open now and I could see her breath rising in the cold air.

'It's late . . . we can talk tomorrow.'

Genevieve gave a hollow laugh. 'Haven't you ever heard . . . tomorrow never comes.' She consulted her watch. 'Anyway it's half past midnight, which means it's already tomorrow.'

I had an absolute horror of her making a scene and getting Mum out of bed so I let her push past me into our porch. I followed and shut the door, nodding in the direction of our living room. I folded my arms and watched her survey the room as if she was a prospective buyer. She even ran one hand across the sideboard as if checking its quality.

'It's not what I expected,' she drawled.

I was exhausted but tried to match her laid-back sarcasm. 'What *did* you expect?'

She sighed heavily. 'I don't know . . . something

different . . . original and special, to make it all worthwhile. But to risk everything just for this . . . this suburban hell.'

'I don't find it hell. It's home.'

She grimaced with distaste. 'You don't know any different, Katy.'

'Genevieve . . . I'm tired . . . too tired to play games.'

'Maybe you'd like me to shout a bit louder. We could use some extra company.'

She knew exactly which buttons to press to make me edgy. 'No . . . don't do that. I'm OK, and we can talk. Come into the kitchen and I'll make us both a drink.'

Her contempt continued into here. 'What a nice pine kitchen with cute little flowers on the walls, a cupboard for your cereal and a shelf to stack your plates. I bet you have a dinner set for best and a few china cups stashed away in case guests call.'

She was right. Mum had both these things, but I carried on boiling a pan of milk and didn't take the bait. I handed the steaming cup to her and she sniffed, detected it was cocoa and raised her eyes to heaven.

'It's all so utterly boring. Is this what you want for yourself?'

'I don't know what I want for myself,' I came back with. 'Does anyone at our age?'

'Maybe not,' she agreed coolly, 'but you should know you don't want this. You must want something better.'

'I never expected anything better,' I told her, taking a sip from my cup.

She looked me up and down critically. 'So the dress didn't work your magic then?'

'In what way?'

She smiled the cat smile. 'You and Merlin?'

'I told you before, Genevieve, I don't want him.'

'He's just a mirage, anyway, Katy. I discovered that really quickly.

'You only wanted him when I wanted him,' I retaliated. 'It's obvious.'

She shrugged and made a noise that could have meant anything. 'I'm leaving . . . but you know that already.'

'Yes, I heard.'

She yawned and raised her arms above her head. 'It's really sad that your life isn't worth stealing. If this had been me – if this life had been mine, with your crazy *mother*, boring friends and cardboard boyfriend – I don't know what I'd have done.'

'Is that why you're going?' I asked evenly.

She nodded. 'I've had a lot of time to think, and things might have happened for the best.'

It was a cheap shot I knew, but I couldn't help it. 'I definitely *won't* miss you . . .'

She got to her feet and began studying our family photographs. 'I did you a favour, Katy. You were such a mess when I arrived – frumpy and a complete mouse. Now you're quite . . . attractive and you're learning to stand up for yourself.'

I felt at a disadvantage, sitting down with her towering

over me. I stood up, awkward in the dress, the one we had both wanted, and glad that I'd kept my coat on. I pulled it tightly around me. Our house was freezing; the wind whistled through gaps and holes in the roof, windows, even skirting boards. It was shabby and neglected and it was horrible suddenly seeing things through Genevieve's eyes. It felt as if she was a thief, rifling through our personal possessions.

I tried to make my voice firm with a note of finality. 'So . . . we're happy to go our own separate ways.'

'Yeah. Your crazy mother is off the hook.'

It was the second time she'd called Mum crazy in as many minutes. 'She never harmed anyone in her life,' I retorted.

Her face darkened. 'So you still don't know . . .'

I faced her squarely, trying to sound more confident than I felt. 'I do know. Mum told me the truth.'

The green eyes glowed dangerously. 'And what truth is that?'

'That your mother was a drug addict. My mum lived in the same house and had to phone the police the day that she . . .' I couldn't bring myself to say the word *died*, but Genevieve closed her eyes as if in pain. 'So she actually rescued you, Genevieve. You were only a few days old and crying inconsolably.'

Her lips moved silently as she digested my words. Then she spoke. 'That's what she told you . . . and you believe that?'

'Of course.'

'But that doesn't explain the most important thing.'

'Which is?'

'Us.'

'That's all in your head,' I insisted, but my stomach began to lurch again.

Genevieve studied her nails with apparent nonchalance as she spoke. 'Your favourite colour is indigo, you like to study clouds and often see faces in them, the smell of meat makes you sick, you always feel like an outsider, you have a fear of the water and hate your toes because they're bumpy . . . oh, and you prefer winter to summer but you worry this is unnatural . . .'

She stopped and I sat down again. 'Anyone could have told you those things.'

'Why won't you just face up to it?' she yawned.

'You're mistaken . . . deluded . . .'

Genevieve faced me across the table. 'Do you have the dream?' She smiled again, showing all her teeth. 'When I was little I dreamed of you all the time, sitting in front of the mirror watching me. I figured it was like Narnia, except there was only a piece of glass separating us.'

Her words cut through me like a blade. I'd never told anyone about that dream.

'Is it just too much to handle, Katy, the knowledge that we're the same?' She leaned across and took hold of my right hand. Our fingers mapped together perfectly just like on that day on the bus. 'Your . . . *mum's* still in denial,' she said softly. 'She's rewritten the past until she believes it herself . . . convinced that her version of events actually happened because what she did is too painful to face.'

Every part of my body had turned to ice. I trembled uncontrollably and my voice quivered. 'I don't want to know any more . . . you should go as you promised.'

She shook her head slowly and deliberately. 'I can't leave yet. That woman has made it impossible for me. She's still telling lies, still hiding from what she did. I have to set you free. Are you ready, Katy? Are you ready for the truth?

CHAPTER THIRTY-SEVEN

It was the longest night of my life. Every minute seemed to last a year. Mum found me the next morning sitting in her armchair. I'd been in the same spot since Genevieve had left. My face must have looked awful because she rushed over, crouched down and touched me, but I couldn't feel anything. I think I'd turned to stone. She felt my cheek, then placed one hand on the dress and seemed to crumple.

'Whatever's wrong, Katy? You're frozen and you haven't been to bed. Oh my goodness, has someone hurt you? Have you been attacked?'

I turned to her with difficulty, my eyes bloodshot and my voice hoarse. 'Genevieve was here last night. She was waiting for me when I arrived home.'

Mum flinched as though she'd been struck. 'What did she want?'

I didn't reply. Mum took a step backwards and then another. She carried on this way, as if she wanted to escape from me, until she reached the door and muttered something about going to the kitchen. A few minutes later she returned with a drink, the steam rising. She even took my hands and wrapped them around the cup in case I spilled it. I didn't protest because my fingers were numb.

I gulped a mouthful and immediately choked on scalding tea. 'She was going to leave,' I coughed. 'She'd made up her mind because it was so boring around here and my life wasn't even worth stealing, but then something changed.'

'What?'

I studied Mum as if I hadn't seen her for a long time. 'You. We talked about you, and that changed everything.'

'You should have let her go, Katy . . . out of our lives.'

'I had to defend you,' I answered hotly. 'She had to know that you were only protecting her.'

Mum grabbed hold of a chair to support herself. 'And what did she say?'

The trembling began again and my teeth knocked against the side of the cup. 'She said . . . there was a reason we had so much in common . . .'

Mum's eyes darted about crazily, her pupils enlarged. I wasn't sure I could go on with this. The overwhelming urge was to stop, pretend last night never happened and everything would be as before. Except that it couldn't be – not with what I knew. The only way I could do this was to close my eyes tightly and spew out the terrible truth.

'Genevieve told me we were related . . . not just sisters, but . . . twins . . . non-identical twins.'

'And you believe her?' Mum whispered.

I put my drink on the side table and cupped my face with my hands. 'It's so stupid and so unbelievable and horrific and sick but . . .'

'But?'

'There's no other explanation. Why we think alike and copy each other without knowing, and we've been having the same dream ever since we were small.'

I thought Mum was going to collapse, but she sat down, instantly appearing twenty years older. I saw different emotions cross her face as the minutes ticked by and the silence of the room magnified until it sounded like thunder.

At last she said, almost in defeat, 'It is true.'

'You split us up!' I accused her, my teeth clenched so tight they hurt. 'No wonder Genevieve despises you.'

'She has every reason to,' Mum answered with strange calm.

My voice grew louder and more incredulous. 'Did you toss a coin? Give away the one that cried the least? How could any mother do that?'

'What I did was for the best.'

'Don't say that any more . . .'

'I thought it was for the best,' she repeated.

She sat inert, her head bowed and hands joined limply together. I had an urge to go over and shake her. 'You can't just hope she'll go away. She's part of our lives whether we like it or not.'

'It's too late to change things, Katy. You know what she is. She'll destroy us.'

'You're only thinking about yourself.'

'No . . . I'm thinking about you and the things she's done.'

It seemed unbelievable that I was defending Genevieve. 'Maybe she can't help herself. You never gave her a chance . . .'

Mum didn't protest. 'You're right, Katy. It was you or her and it was a terrible choice to make.'

'Don't expect me to thank you for choosing *me*,' I answered contemptuously.

She stared at me for just a second and then dropped her gaze. 'I don't expect any thanks, but . . . when you know all the facts—'

'I don't want to know,' I ranted.

Mum clammed up completely, but the urge to punish her was overpowering.

'And you made up that story about a drug addict living in the room below. That was wicked.'

Her face was a terrible colour – whitish grey with what looked like a mixture of shock, humiliation and shame, but my heart stayed well and truly hardened.

'I didn't lie,' she managed to say.

'Of course you lied, you're lying even now. My whole life's a lie.' I rose to my feet, desperate to get away from her.

'Don't go. It isn't what you think,' she pleaded. 'I'll tell you the truth, Katy. The complete truth.'

I slammed the living-room door and stormed out of the house. I thought she might follow and looked over my shoulder several times, but she didn't. It was barely seven in the morning and the only car on the main road was our milkman, driving his float. He did an about-take when he spotted me in my evening dress but simply smiled and trundled on his way. There was only one place I could go. I knew that straight away. The converted barn was on the edge of our town and sat in about half an acre of land. I climbed a stile and took a short cut across a field which was thick with snow. The bottom of my dress was soon wet and torn. The delicate satin shoes were ruined, and my feet slid dangerously in them as they filled with water and one of the heels came loose. Soon I was walking with jerky up and down steps which were tiring and I was glad when the house came into view. The original barn doors were now huge floor-to-ceiling panes of glass, and as I approached I could see Genevieve sitting at a table. She looked up and waved.

'I knew you'd come,' she said simply.

'And I knew that you knew I'd come.'

We both laughed, and for the first time it seemed genuine between us, not as if we were trying to score points off each other.

'Come on in,' she beckoned. 'You can change into some of my clothes.'

The downstairs was completely open plan, with a living area dominated by a squashy L-shaped sofa, a modern dining table which seated eight, and a study area tucked away behind a screen. Even the funky red kitchen was on display, although it was so clean and shiny I wondered if anyone actually cooked in it. Everywhere was a strange mixture of old and new, but they complemented each other. There was a minstrel's gallery, stained in light oak, accessed by a matching staircase with four half-turns.

I followed Genevieve as she climbed, all the time gazing upwards and hearing our footsteps echoing in the cavernous space. Her bedroom wasn't huge, but it had views over the countryside. Today everywhere looked perfect – white frosted roofs, a snow-topped church spire, trees and shrubs with their snowy branches extended. She handed me some jeans and a sweater from her wardrobe and I stripped off, without embarrassment, not missing the irony that Genevieve felt like an extension of me now. Her clothes and even her trainers fitted like a glove.

She offered me a brush and when I glanced in the mirror I realized that my hair was still in a severe French pleat, which looked out of place with the casual clothes. I carefully took out the clips and pulled.

'Were you a tomboy?' Genevieve asked curiously. 'When you were small.'

'I nodded. 'Yeah . . . forever trying to play with Luke and his gang.'

She made a face. 'So was I, but I had to wear bubblegum-coloured dresses decorated with hearts and ribbons, and frilly blouses.'

A memory resurfaced just then – something I'd read in a magazine. 'Some twins have their own language and don't talk for years . . . but then . . . we're not identical so . . .'

'That doesn't matter,' she interrupted fiercely. 'Twins always share everything. It's right we should be together, don't you think?'

There was something about the intensity of her gaze that made me squirm. 'It's incredible that we are here . . . together.'

'I can't leave you now, Katy. You do know that?'

I nodded, feeling a familiar dread flooding through me even though she was being almost normal for once. 'You're not leaving . . . so . . . we'll see plenty of each other,' I mumbled.

'I don't want to just *see* you,' she responded scornfully. 'We were in the womb together for a whole nine months – that's how it is with twins. They belong to each other, and you belong to me, Katy.'

Her words suddenly came back to me. *'It should be as if you were never born.'* I still didn't know what she meant, but it made my skin crawl.

She surveyed the ruins of the fishtail dress. 'Did you sleep?'

'No . . . not for a second.'

'Me neither,' she admitted. 'Let's go and have breakfast.'

The kitchen was a design dream; as well as the red glossy doors there were black granite worktops and a stainless-steel range and splashback. It was obvious that the people who owned the barn lived well. They had an American style fridge and Italian coffee maker – with a choice of five different beans – as well as a juicer and other gadgets I couldn't even identify. Genevieve cooked us both scrambled eggs, just the way I like, soft but not runny, with wholemeal bagels, muesli and fresh orange juice. She seemed so at home here and I wondered how she could leave all this for a life of uncertainty.

'Do . . . the people you're staying with . . . know anything about us?' I asked, my stomach grateful for the first food of the day.

She shook her head. 'They're supportive and nice enough, but I don't let people in . . . don't confide in them. Not any more.'

She didn't have to explain. I'd spent all my life trying not to get close to people. I always thought they kept their distance from me, but now realized it was probably my standoffish vibes acting as a barrier.

'It's better not to rely on anyone else,' she added. 'Then they can't hurt you.'

It was incredible that we'd had such different lives but stayed so similar. I didn't have to tell her that I had trouble making friends – she'd cruelly pointed it out to me when we first met. I pretended not to watch as Genevieve ground pepper on to her eggs but no salt, and ate her cereal crunchy with only a few tablespoons of milk. I did exactly the same – a complete mirror image. And now for the million-dollar question. It felt like the right time to ask. I put down my knife and fork and drained my coffee cup.

'When did you know?'

She ran one finger across her lips, deep in thought. 'Forever, I suppose. Can't remember a time when I didn't know about you, but I thought it was my fault you weren't there.'

'Why?'

'My adoptive parents told me I was thoroughly bad,' she replied almost cheerfully, 'so I must be responsible for our separation.'

'And how did you find me, Genevieve?'

Her green eyes stared deep into mine and they were moist, like lily pads on water. 'It was coincidence . . . destiny . . . whatever you want to call it.'

I took a deep breath. 'Really?'

'*Really*,' she emphasized. 'I've moved around the country so much, so what are the odds of coming to the same town as you? That day on the bus did it . . . you must have felt something too?'

So it was through sheer chance that we'd met. I wasn't sure if this was harder to believe than the idea of her somehow finding out where I was and tracking me down. She thought it was providence, and it was hard to disagree.

'I did feel something,' I had to confess, 'but I didn't know what it was. I just felt these waves of . . . your emotion. I thought it was hate.'

Genevieve cocked her head to one side like a hopeful

dog. 'I did hate you. You looked so happy I wanted to wipe that smile off your face, or maybe I wanted to shock you out of your complacent little world.'

'You blamed me for what happened?'

'Yes,' she stated with complete certainty. I waited for her to qualify her answer but she didn't, she just mesmerized me with her stare. No one had ever looked at me this way before, and she could read my innermost thoughts which made it doubly intrusive.

'Is that why you did all those horrible things to me?'

Genevieve shrugged casually. 'You never had any of the pain . . . didn't even know I existed. Do you know how it felt when I first saw you that day . . . laughing without a care in the world?'

'But that wasn't my fault—'

'I'd tried to reach you,' she insisted, tapping the side of her head. 'You should have been able to feel that. You should have been responsive. I loved you so much, but . . . as the years passed I grew to despise and resent you.'

'I did nothing wrong,' I repeated. 'You shouldn't have blamed me.'

She held out her hands, palms upward, talking almost to herself. 'At first I wanted you to suffer . . . and then I wanted you to disappear . . . but then I realized . . . this is a second chance for us. Now everything will be right again.'

I made an explosive noise of disbelief. 'Just like that. You expect me to forgive and forget.'

She seemed puzzled that I was resisting her. The situation was obviously black and white for Genevieve.

'You must see how it was for me, Katy. I had nothing; you had everything. But it was pointless to hate you or to drive you away . . . now I realize we can never escape from each other and we won't be separated again.'

This wasn't going well, and her words were really creeping me out. Nothing she had done or said so far made me believe she was capable of change. She had swapped from wanting to erase me to a suffocating possessiveness that unnerved me just as much. And there was the problem of Mum and how was she going to survive this.

'Mum was only twenty-one,' I tried to explain. 'She didn't know what she was doing. No one else knew about the pregnancy, and she was probably depressed . . .'

'Why are you still defending her?'

'It's weird,' I mumbled. 'The person you know and trust the most in the whole world turns out to be someone else . . . a person who could do something so unimaginable.'

'Is anyone what they seem, Katy? We all have these faces we put on for other people because we think if they saw the real person inside they wouldn't like us.'

I braced myself for the question I had to ask. 'Your adoptive parents . . . you didn't really . . . harm them?'

I wasn't sure if she was smiling or it was a trick of the light. 'They were the most awful people . . . smug and self-righteous with no love or joy – just suffering, obedience and punishment. They left me at my home-made *altar* to pray to be a better child . . . beside two flickering candles. I opened the window and the curtain caught fire . . . it spread so quickly.'

I closed my eyes and said a silent prayer of thanks that it wasn't deliberate, but that still left the other fire, at the vicarage. 'And you've never been back there since?'

'Never.'

I desperately wanted to believe her because the alternative was just too awful to contemplate. 'I think this *was* meant to be,' I began slowly, in spite of all my fears. 'We were meant to find each other and our mum in order to be given a second chance.'

'We do have the same mother,' she agreed, but her voice sounded odd, as if she'd rehearsed it. 'No one can dispute that.'

'So . . . what do we do now?'

'I think it's time we visited her, Katy . . . together.'

CHAPTER THIRTY-EIGHT

Genevieve and I sat in the back of the car, side by side. Occasionally her head would droop with tiredness to rest on my shoulder. I didn't push it away. I watched Mum's face in the rear-view mirror, her eyes huge and haunted, but she never looked back at me. I felt that the moment that everything was becoming clearer, it slipped away from me again, like a toy boat bobbing further out to sea. We had gone to my house and I expected some sort of showdown, but it never happened. Mum didn't seem to be filled with love or remorse for the child she gave away, or launch into an explanation of why she could only keep one of her babies; she simply looked scared and apprehensive. Hushed words were exchanged between her and Genevieve, which spurred Mum into action, and within minutes she'd packed a bag with food, drink, warm blankets and a torch because of the weather conditions. I was told to put on my heaviest jacket with thick socks and boots and get into the car, without knowing why.

Mum pulled away from our house like a Grand Prix driver, despite the warnings on the TV and radio telling people not to undertake non-essential journeys. Normally she was overly cautious, yet I could see from the signs that we were headed for the motorway, although we could barely see a few metres ahead. Whatever had to be done, it couldn't wait. I must have dozed with exhaustion; mile after mile of fast-moving white flurries gradually hypnotized me and it was a relief to shut down, my mind finally giving up the fight. My eyes felt leaden and drooped, until they closed in a heavy dreamless sleep.

When I came back, it was bit by bit, with no concept of how much time had passed. My brain was telling me to wake properly but my body refused to cooperate. It felt peaceful hovering in my own twilight world. There were low voices and I couldn't distinguish between them. I wasn't even sure if they were real or in my head.

'Is this definitely the place?'

'Definitely.'

'Are you sure? It must have changed.'

'I've been back before . . . many times to visit her.'

'Katy still doesn't know?'

'Not a clue. I can't imagine what she thinks.'

'How will we tell her?'

'We won't have to. It'll be clear when we're there.'

My eyes flickered and the voices stopped. I straightened up with a loud yawn, my lids still reluctant to open. My watch told me I'd been out for almost two hours.

'Where are we?'

'We've just stopped for a rest,' Mum answered, and I saw her exchange a glance with Genevieve in the mirror.

I rubbed the steamy window with one hand and peered outside. The snow was denser here and the sky completely ivory without a hint of blue breaking through. It was early afternoon and the light was already fading. We were parked in front of a tallish, once grand building, with steps leading up to it and a massive black front door with seven or eight bells at the side. No one spoke.

'This is where you lived, isn't it?' I asked.

'Yes,' Mum replied, with no explanation as to why we should drive for hours just to sit outside.

'Can we go in?'

Mum shook her head. 'They're private flats now, Katy, intercoms and everything. We wouldn't be allowed inside.'

'There's nothing to see anyway,' Genevieve added.

'No, nothing to see,' Mum agreed.

'And there's somewhere we have to be.' Genevieve spoke purposefully, and this seemed to be the signal Mum was waiting for. She took the car keys from the ignition and put on her gloves before opening the car door. Genevieve got out of the passenger side, fastening her coat and pulling a bobble hat over her ears. I knew they were waiting for me. They were both on a journey and I was blindly following.

Despite the snow, Genevieve seemed to have wings on her feet and I soon realized that she was in charge and Mum had surrendered to this. I looked around. The place where I was born held no fascination and didn't awaken any feelings of déjà vu. Everywhere here seemed to consist of small dark streets with rows of back-to-back terraces, not even the snow able to render them attractive. The street lights had already come on, tinting the pure white landscape luminously yellow. We barely saw another person as we trudged in a crocodile, our eyes blurring as flakes swirled in front of us. They stuck to my eyelashes and I furiously blinked them away. It felt like being in an upturned snow globe.

'This is a short cut,' Genevieve instructed, as she led the way through a series of narrow alleyways. I had to make sure to walk in the middle to stop my feet slipping into the drainage channels that ran close to a high wall which was covered in graffiti. I caught glimpses of names, slogans and declarations of love, and thought about all the people who'd been here before us.

I wondered if Mum had taken this short cut when she was only a few years older than I was now, full of life and hope. My father might have stopped and kissed her here and promised to love her forever before he disappeared from her life. I gave Mum a secret glance but she stared straight ahead with no visible sign of recognition or even interest. There was an opening and we came into another road filled with Victorian town houses, Christmas trees prominent in the windows of the square bays. I almost expected to see girls and boys in old-fashioned clothes playing with wooden sledges and chasing hoops.

Genevieve stopped outside the gates of an old church: St Jude's.

She gave a bitter laugh. 'The patron saint of lost causes.'

I looked to Mum for a reaction, but she appeared distant and hurt at the same time. I stayed silent. Genevieve pushed open the heavy wooden gate and followed the path towards the church. I wondered if this might be some kind of test. Was Mum going to be put on trial for what she did, in a church that meant something to Genevieve? Such dramatic stuff was just her style, and the crack about St Jude would make sense. It was the perfect place for a confession. But she didn't enter the church. Rather she veered off to the right to where there was a stone angel standing taller than the other headstones.

It didn't seem especially weird to be in a cemetery in the freezing snow miles from home, at least no weirder than everything else that had happened recently. I carefully picked my way among the graves, trying to follow Genevieve's footsteps. Starlings were swooping, their wings beating together in preparation for nightfall. They looked like tiny black crosses.

Genevieve came to a standstill and I looked down. Even covered by snow, this grave looked neglected, with weeds pushing through. Genevieve bent down, brushed the snow from a posy of artificial flowers and then carefully rearranged them, her face animated but obscure. Usually her feelings were so sharp that I could read her like a book.

Mum's lips were moving silently, as if in prayer, and I realized she must have known this person. I was still the only one here who didn't have a part to play. I read the name on the headstone, looking for clues –

JESSICA MYERS.

'Who's this?' I asked gently.

Genevieve's eyes were focused on something far away. 'Jessica Myers never had a chance in life. No parents to tuck her in at night and stick her lame drawings on the wall. She was in and out of care, shunted about like a stray dog that nobody wanted until she found herself pregnant, still just a teenager, living in a squalid flat . . .'

'I don't understand.'

'She might have had a hope of turning her life around. She finally had someone to love and be loved by in return . . . but it wasn't enough to save her.'

'Who was she, Genevieve?'

'She was just a lonely person, shunned when she was alive and made out to be a monster after her death. Now she was of interest to *everyone* . . . that one fateful day . . .'

Silent tears ran down Mum's cheeks and glistened like ice.

'What day?' I questioned.

'The day she died and her baby disappeared. You see, there was no break-in. The pram was inside her flat, and the only person who could have got in was someone who knew their way around. But this possibility was never pursued because everyone assumed the worst. They said she'd taken her own life to cover up her neglect.'

I turned to Mum for an answer but she was frozen like one of the statues. Genevieve's voice continued as if she was reading from a script.

'She was never allowed to escape her past, judged and condemned by everyone . . . and the person who knew the truth never came forward.'

'Who was she? Who was her child?' I cried with frustration.

'I was,' Genevieve replied at last, her voice thick with emotion.

I missed my footing and almost tumbled on to the grave. 'But . . . how can you be? We're sisters . . . twins.'

'I know.'

She took off one of her gloves and pushed away the snow to expose more of the headstone. I read three words – 'Mother of Grace'.

I looked at Genevieve, who stared at me with the face of a conjurer who isn't sure if the trick is going to work. Her fingers moved again and my eyes followed them as the snow disintegrated to reveal more letters. I read the final words – 'and Hope. Rest in peace for all eternity'.

'Mother of Grace and Hope?' I said aloud. 'Who's Hope?'

'You are,' Genevieve whispered.

CHAPTER
THIRTY-NINE

The cold had penetrated my entire body and I wriggled my toes to try to return some feeling to them. I was empty inside, as if all the life had been squeezed from me and all that was left was a shell. Genevieve was telling the truth. I was certain of that. I looked at the woman who had pretended to be my mother for sixteen years.

'You . . . kidnapped me?'

'I didn't mean to,' she whispered. 'I only wanted to comfort you.'

'How did you get away with it?' I cried. 'How could you just . . . keep me like that?'

'No one suspected,' she replied with surprising honesty. 'I'd brought my own baby home from hospital, and a midwife had visited to check us over . . . why should anyone think I was involved?'

'You were so *respectable*,' Genevieve said contemptuously. 'Unlike *our* mum, who was known to social services. She was a problem, a bad example, someone to be spied on and written about.'

'And you took me far away,' I added.

She closed her eyes. 'I couldn't have stayed.'

This had all the elements of a dream. I was stunned. 'And what should I call you now?'

'I'm still your—'

'You're not my mum,' I cut in vehemently and noticed Genevieve's smile. 'I don't think I could call you that again.'

She nodded with difficulty. 'You're right, I deserve that. Maybe . . . you could call me by my Christian name . . . Rebecca.'

I gazed at her in terrible confusion and tried to recognize something familiar, but in an instant she'd turned into a stranger. She cowered under my scrutiny as though my eyes threw out darts that pierced her flesh.

'Please don't look at me like that,' she said at last. 'I'm not what you think.'

'And . . . what should I think?'

'It was a moment of madness, completely out of character. I was distraught because of . . . and after finding Jessica like that, and afterwards . . . I was ashamed and frightened of what I'd done . . .'

She trailed off as I tried to make sense of her words. She'd convinced herself it was just one moment when she lost control, but I couldn't forget the fact that she'd had sixteen years to make things right. But I also couldn't ignore that she'd loved me for the same amount of time. I didn't know what to feel any more and my head hurt – badly.

'You only thought about yourself,' Genevieve said in accusation.

Rebecca's voice trembled. 'No, that's not true. I thought I could give one of you a good home but I never stopped regretting that you'd been split up. I've lived that nightmare every day . . . consumed with guilt . . .'

Genevieve scowled and tugged at my arm. We took shelter inside the arched recess of the church, where there were deep stone benches and an ancient flagstone floor. She sat next to me, and Rebecca remained standing, sipping from the flask. I touched her shoulder.

'What really happened that day?'

She searched in her pocket for a tissue and it was a few moments before she could speak. 'It was as I told you, except for one thing. I used the spare key to get into Jessica's flat. I knew where it was hidden and thought she might be ill . . . the sound of crying was unbearable.'

I felt Genevieve stiffen beside me, but she didn't interrupt.

'Jessica was still warm, but her eyes were lifeless . . . so completely lifeless, and yet . . . they seemed to be pleading with me to do something. The pram was there, but there was only one infant. The other one must have been lying in the bed. I picked her up and told myself it was only to comfort her. Her nappy was soiled so I took her upstairs–'

'Where was your own baby?' Genevieve hissed. 'Where was she?'

Rebecca leaned her head out of the recess to gaze at the

falling snow. When she turned around her face was shiny and her hair plastered to her head. 'My own dear Katy was cold and floppy,' she managed to whisper. 'When I fell asleep she was warm with milk, but . . . somehow . . . in the night . . . she just stopped breathing.'

It was hard to reconcile the fact that the Katy she was talking about wasn't me. I'd lost my identity and felt as if I didn't really exist any more. Even my birthday wasn't on the day it had been celebrated for the last sixteen years.

'Maybe it was a cot death,' I suggested, compelled to make things easier for her.

Rebecca nodded and swallowed hard, her nose beginning to run. 'I think so, and I hope it wasn't anything I did or failed to do.'

'No one will ever know the answer to that,' Genevieve growled.

Her eyes misted over. 'But I've never forgotten about my own dear Katy for a second. I carry the memory of her with me always.'

Now I understood where her grief came from – this woman who had stolen me to replace her own child had never managed to escape from this.

'You thought it was OK to help yourself to someone else's baby,' Genevieve said bitterly.

'I'll have to answer for what I did,' Rebecca replied with as much dignity as she could, and I wondered what she intended to do now. Give herself up to the police? But that wouldn't make up for Genevieve's lost childhood.

'I was told by my adoptive parents that we were separated because I was wicked,' Genevieve began fiercely. 'And when I was older I discovered that everyone thought my mother had been . . . *responsible* for the death of my sister, my twin.'

Rebecca sniffed and Genevieve shot her a furious look before continuing.

'And then I saw you, Katy, that day on the bus and I just knew who you were . . . It didn't take long to work out what must have really happened.'

Rebecca broke down and turned her face away from us, leaning against the thick wooden doors of the church. Part of me wanted to go over and comfort her, but I couldn't bring myself to.

'You're right to hate me,' she sobbed. 'What I did was utterly wrong and nothing justifies it . . . nothing at all. I'll try to make it right.'

Genevieve got to her feet, her face contorted with anger. 'Nothing you could do would ever make it right.'

I watched Rebecca bite her lips hard and squeeze them together as if she was scared what else she might say. I looked outside and felt a growing fear. The snowflakes were now as large as fifty-pence pieces and settling with incredible speed. Our footprints on the pathway were already covered.

'We should go,' I urged. 'Get back to the car and decide what to do.'

Rebecca nodded in agreement and we both looked to Genevieve to show us the way. For a minute an amused expression appeared on her face and I wondered what she was thinking, but she pulled down her hat and adjusted her gloves before summoning us with one movement of her head. It took us twice as long to get back, and Genevieve must have had a good sense of direction because all the empty streets now looked the same. There were very few fresh footprints, which meant that people had heeded the advice to stay inside. By the time we reached the car we were all bedraggled and weary with red noses and pinched faces.

Rebecca sank into the driver's seat.

'We should listen to the radio,' I said. 'The motorway might be closed or something.'

Rebecca swept aside my concerns with a wave of her hand and I was again puzzled by her sudden bravado. It was already dusk, and since we'd set out another few centimetres of snow had fallen, yet she was prepared to battle against snow, black ice and poor visibility in a car that was fifteen years old. I had a horrible clenching pain in my stomach at the thought of the journey ahead. I wondered if Genevieve had it as well, but she had lapsed into silence, staring impassively out of the window.

'Let's find a B. & B. somewhere close,' I suggested, but my voice came out weirdly shrill.

A hand reached into the back seat and patted my leg reassuringly. 'I'll take it slow all the way back and no overtaking. It'll be fine – trust me.'

I tried to sit back and relax, but the feeling of

apprehension was growing by the minute. I couldn't believe that Genevieve could stay so calm. The scene outside reminded me of a strange apocalyptic movie, with cars abandoned at strange angles and the town empty of inhabitants. None of the side roads had been gritted, and our car felt completely vulnerable. It was making a strange squeaky clunk, and every so often the tyres spun as they got caught in drifts or if we veered too close to the kerb.

'The motorway will be clear,' Rebecca announced brightly. The speedometer hadn't moved above ten miles per hour and we were getting nowhere fast. I noticed a signpost for the local library and worried that we'd already passed it five minutes earlier.

'I don't think this is a good idea,' I said, but it was under my breath. My throat felt tight as if I was being slowly strangled. There was an inevitability about events that I didn't understand.

'I think this was the way we came in, girls. It should lead to the dual carriageway and then the motorway slip road.'

'I don't remember this bridge,' I whispered as the car began to climb.

Rebecca's laugh sounded forced. 'Me neither, but we'll see where it goes.'

Genevieve hadn't moved or spoken since we set off, and I had an urge to scream and shake her out of this inertia. It was as if she'd completely shut down and withdrawn from us. I turned my attention back to the road. There was no escaping the knowledge that we were somewhere away from the town and getting deeper into the countryside. There were no street lights and it felt like driving into hell. Something was badly wrong. I knew this for certain but couldn't do anything about it. Even when Rebecca finally admitted this had been a mistake, the feeling didn't subside. She tried to turn the car around, but the road was narrow and the snow made it impossible. She rested her head on the wheel.

'Maybe if you reverse?' I suggested.

'That's not possible. We'll have to keep going and try to reach a farm or house of some sort.'

She pressed the accelerator several times and the car rocked a little but refused to move. She rolled it backwards and forwards and the tyres made a horrible grinding sound. I was worried the car might shoot forward into a ditch, but it stayed in the one spot, diagonally blocking the road.

'Girls . . . we're stuck.'

I tried to focus. 'We can stay in the car and wait until first light. You did bring food and blankets.'

Rebecca rubbed her chin and peered outside. 'We can't stay here. Without our headlights we'll be a complete hazard.'

I remembered what Luke had told me when we staked out the vicarage. 'We have to switch off the lights and heater or they'll flatten the car battery . . . right?'

'Right,' she answered.

'So . . . what can we do?'

'We'll dig ourselves out,' she declared in a no-nonsense voice. 'I brought a spade with us because they advised it on the radio. "For any essential journeys, take a torch, food, water, blankets, a phone and finally a spade."'

We didn't *have* to come here today, I wanted to point out, but I sensed that she had been unable to stop this from happening. She had denied Genevieve so much, she couldn't refuse her this journey. I looked again at Genevieve. She appeared to be dozing, although I wasn't convinced that she wasn't faking it. Rebecca and I got out of the car together. She wouldn't let me dig, but I held the powerful torch for her so she could see properly. The only sounds around were her laboured breath and my efforts to keep warm. There should have been so much to say but I think we were both beyond explanation.

'Do you hate me?' she asked eventually, and I saw her glance inside the car as if she didn't want Genevieve to hear.

'I don't hate you,' I answered straight away. Even in my confused state I had to tell her the truth that was clear in my mind. 'I can't excuse what you did, but I think I can . . . understand why.'

This seemed to be a relief to her and I saw tears glisten in her eyes. She carried on with renewed energy and then appeared satisfied. The snow was still light and soft and it had only taken about fifteen minutes. She opened up the boot and put the spade back inside, stamping the snow from her boots. The only other thing she said was, 'One day . . . I hope you'll be able to forgive me.'

She started the ignition again and moved slowly. She managed to get the car out of the hole, but once on the road it skidded dangerously.

'We have to find a lay-by or somewhere to pull over,' she said, and I could hear real fear in her voice.

Her hands were glued to the wheel trying to gain control, but the car had a life of its own. I knew it was hopeless, and she knew it too. There were only two options that I could think of – we could stop and dial the emergency services, but we had no idea of our location, or we could stay here and keep watch in case a snowplough or tractor managed to get through. I was just about to announce this when she cried. 'I can see some kind of sign . . . there on the left.'

With difficulty she turned the car on to a dirt track and then pulled over into a clearing by some trees. The sign advertised a fishing lake, with opening times and prices per hour. Rebecca switched off the engine and I watched all the tension leave her body.

'I'll get the blankets and snacks in a moment. We'll be safe here.' She sighed. 'At least until morning.'

CHAPTER FORTY

I thought it must be a dream. There was a light somewhere in my consciousness, a hand shaking me and a voice whispering, 'Katy? Will you come with me? I'm too scared on my own.'

'Genevieve? What's wrong?' I hastily moved the torch away because it was shining in my eyes.

'I need to wee,' she laughed softly and pointed to the front of the car. I could see a sleeping figure, lying across the two seats, a blanket pulled up to her chin.

'What time is it?' I groaned.

'About three.'

I opened the car door and staggered out, disorientated and stiff. My feet sank into knee-high virgin snow although the sky was now clear of any more flurries. The flask of coffee had taken effect and I twitched uncomfortably.

'There's something I have to give you,' Genevieve whispered. She put one hand into her pocket and took something out. I didn't realize what it was until she moved closer and I felt her hands caress my neck.

'The pendant, Katy. You never wore it.'

I fingered the smooth stone and smiled nervously, knowing I couldn't take it off in front of her. I tucked it inside my coat. 'Choose a bush, Genevieve, and I'll find another.'

I had this pathetic hang-up that meant I couldn't wee unless there was no one else close by. I couldn't bear to think about having to pull down my jeans and crouch in the snow, but there wasn't any choice. Genevieve made a joke about wishing we were boys. We split up and it took me ages to find a spot and pluck up the courage to expose any flesh to the sub-zero temperatures. Genevieve had taken the torch and I couldn't see her or any scrap of light. I knew which direction the car was, but I didn't want to go back without her. I jumped as I heard rustling in the bushes and wondered if she was playing a joke on me.

'Genevieve? Genevieve?' I called into the dark.

I heard sounds but thought that my mind was playing tricks on me because they seemed so far away. I listened harder and there was definitely a voice floating through the trees.

'Come and see this. Katy, it's amazing. Katy, come and join me.'

Clumsily I moved forward, stopping every now and then to listen. Genevieve's voice was like I'd never known it – full of awe and wonder. She sounded like a child. I remembered that day at the craft fair, where she tricked me into following her, but I stumbled on, taking a minute to wonder why, wherever she went, I was close behind.

'Genevieve? I can't see properly and I'm freezing.'

'It's not much further,' she shouted. 'I can hear you so clearly.'

'You'd better be close,' I shouted back with annoyance.

The snow disguised everything on the ground. I fell into holes in the grass and tripped over stones and tree roots. It was really spooky being here alone and I tried to concentrate on the trees for comfort, unsure whether my favourites were the slim graceful firs, poised like dancers waiting for the music to begin, or the sturdy ancient oaks, their trunks gnarled and blistered. I imagined they'd been here so long and seen so much there was nothing that would surprise them; in fact, after another few minutes I could see a wise old face in one of the stumps of a lopped branch. A beam through the trees suddenly signalled that Genevieve was there, and I wondered why she hadn't done this before. Impatiently I strode on until the ground levelled out and the undergrowth ended.

'What the . . . ? Genevieve, don't move.'

My hand flew up to my mouth in horror. I'd reached the frozen lake and Genevieve was gliding on it, her head thrown back, laughing.

'I've never been ice skating before, Katy. It's great, even without boots. Come on, you can be my partner.'

I didn't want to startle her so I tried to sound completely

unimpressed. 'I'm cold and tired and I don't want to skate. Let's go back to the car.'

'No,' she protested, sliding forward and extending one leg behind her. I almost expected to see her spin. 'You have to do this. It's three in the morning and we're lost in the middle of nowhere and the lake is so beautiful . . .'

I gave a loud fake laugh. 'It might not be safe . . . Remember all the warnings about skating on thin ice . . . Come back to the shore.'

Her arms now twirled like helicopter blades and she looked so full of rapture that I was momentarily envious. 'The sky is completely black,' she sang, 'like polished jet set with twinkling diamonds. This all might be gone by tomorrow.'

'It'll still be here,' I assured her, 'and we'll skate in the daylight when we can see properly.'

'No,' she answered petulantly. 'I'm fed up of always waiting for tomorrow. From this moment on I'm going to do whatever I want when I want. And the lake will never be this magical again.'

For one crazy minute I agreed with her. It looked so inviting in the moonlight, and she seemed completely free. I'd been dull and sensible for so long and she was beckoning to me.

'Katy, think of all the things we never did together. She stole everything from us. You know you should be with me. You *have* to be with me.'

I warily put one foot on to the ice and knew straight

away it wasn't that thick. I could sense movement, an ominous creak, and it could have been my imagination but I could feel the water churning beneath. It was incredible that Genevieve had made it so far towards the centre.

'Don't go any further,' I called. 'I'm coming closer, but edge your way backwards and we'll meet somewhere in the middle.'

'I've just had a great idea,' she cried, ignoring my warning. 'You can change your name . . . like I did.'

I moved a few centimetres forward, reluctant to leave the safety of the shallows. 'Why would I change my name?'

'Because you're not who you thought you were. Katy is dead, and Hope hasn't existed for over sixteen years.'

Another few centimetres and I was physically shaking with fear. 'But I still feel like Katy.'

'Forget Katy. You can be anyone you want to be.'

It was time for the question I'd been longing to ask her since the day she walked into my life. 'Who is Genevieve Paradis?'

'She doesn't exist!' she almost screamed with elation. 'I got her out of a book. When I read that name I knew I wanted to be her. I *felt* like her. You can be anyone you want to be . . . Don't let them tell you otherwise.'

I was about three metres from the bank now and this felt surreal: the moon shining on the frozen ice, the shadowy trees reaching their twisted black branches towards us, the ghostly figure of Genevieve gliding on ice and her voice resounding in the silence. The only way I had the courage to move was to tell myself this *wasn't* real. I was still Katy Rivers, the former Girl Guide, who knew every safety precaution in the book and would never, ever walk out on to a frozen lake.

A sudden ugly noise in the eerie stillness was like a whip cracking.

'Genevieve,' I warned, 'the ice is breaking up. Lie down and try to spread your weight.'

I wasn't even sure if this was the right advice, but I dredged it from the dark recesses of my memory.

'Meet you halfway,' Genevieve shouted. 'I've wanted to be with you so much. All my life I searched for you. We're different from other people, Katy, and you owe me this.'

I searched for signs of panic on her face but there weren't any. 'I missed you as well,' I said, trying to reassure her. 'I just didn't know it.'

'Don't be afraid. It isn't the end for us . . . I know that for sure.'

And now there was another, familiar voice calling, but I didn't dare turn around.

'Move back, Katy. Slowly slide your feet back. You haven't far to go.'

I didn't even hesitate but answered with certainty: 'No, I can't leave her.'

They were the last words I spoke before Genevieve slipped under the ice with one final brutal crack, like a fault opening up during an earthquake. I hesitated for only seconds, ignoring the frantic cries in the background. I was still on my feet. It was a simple choice – retreat to solid ground while I still could, or try to save Genevieve.

Nothing could have prepared me for the cold. It was raw, clean, sharp and cut through me in all its cruelty. It didn't just take away my breath, it also closed down each nerve and every function. My clothes were heavy and sodden, lead weights dragging me under. I thought of the tale of the old man of the sea who tricks travellers into taking him across the river. They agree to carry him, but he wraps his legs around them like a vice and grows heavier and heavier until they drown. I probably only struggled for a minute. I was never a strong swimmer and neither was Genevieve. Giving up felt like a relief.

The water was surprisingly clear of weeds and debris and it was easy to find Genevieve, with her hair streaming around her head like a mermaid's. She was waiting for me, as she'd always been, and I put my arms around her lifeless neck. I'd thought it would be hard to die but it felt surprisingly easy; the light beckoned, far away in the distance but drawing me closer. I was moving gratefully towards it, guided by some unseen hand, when the calm of the water was disturbed. A hand grabbed me. I was pulled upwards, ripped from the lake in a cruel rebirth, and dragged across the ice. The distance felt immense and I kept expecting to hear that sickening crack again. Everything I wanted to escape from was still there on that bank – cold, uncertainty, hurt, loss and pain. I retched and spluttered, convinced that my lungs had burst. I was rolled on to my side and coughed up water.

Rebecca hesitated and I sensed what she intended to do next. My hand gripped her arm tightly. 'You can't go back in there.' There was determination in her face, and as she began to pull away from me it took all my strength to restrain her. 'She's already gone . . . it's useless.'

'I have to try, Katy. I need to do this.'

I shook my head, my teeth chattering uncontrollably. 'Don't risk your own life. Stay with me . . . Mum.'

As the final word left my lips she seemed to crumple in my arms and we clutched each other for support. I don't think I've ever held on to anyone so tightly in my whole life.

After another few minutes had passed there wasn't even a ripple on the water; it was as if nothing had ever disturbed its tranquillity. I stared into its shining depths. There was something floating on the surface close to the bank, a piece of green glass, in the darkness almost the same colour as the lake. It drifted idly for a few moments and then sank without a trace.

EPILOGUE

'"A rose . . . by any other name would smell as sweet".'

Luke dangled his arms along the back of the wooden bench and waited for my reaction.

'*Romeo and Juliet*?'

He gave me a thumbs-up sign.

'I'm not hung up on my name,' I answered, self-consciously fiddling with my earring. 'I still feel like Katy Rivers. Anyway . . . do I really look like a Hope?'

He shook his head. 'A girl called Hope would act demure and play the violin or the harp.'

'I'm tone deaf.'

Luke squinted in the December sunshine. 'You were really brave today. I'm proud of you.'

I didn't answer because tears were still close to the surface and I'd finished with crying. Luke handed me my sunglasses and I realized how awful my eyes must look. I changed position, the starched black suit uncomfortable, but I wasn't in a hurry to leave St Jude's. Lots of people found graveyards morbid, but I felt quite comfortable among the dead. There were more visitors here than I'd expected, but it was almost Christmas and special wreaths made of holly and miniature fir trees adorned many graves.

'It's right they should be buried together,' I said, watching two sparrows fighting over a piece of bread.

Luke was making embarrassed humming noises beside me. I knew there was something on his mind and if I waited long enough he would tell me.

'I know it's not my place, Kat, but maybe you should talk to someone.'

'About what?'

'Everything . . . You think it's all over, but stuff like that might . . . er . . . resurface later on and cause you problems.'

I turned towards him, aghast. 'You think I need a shrink?'

'Counsellor perhaps,' he answered delicately.

'It wasn't what you think,' I protested. 'I was living a life that didn't belong to me . . .'

Luke blinked madly and loosened his collar. 'You still wish you'd never met Genevieve?'

'Not any more,' I answered carefully. 'In a strange way . . . she kind of set me free.'

He put one finger across his lips. 'She tried to kill you, Kat. She saw you as her enemy, remember?'

'She was her own worst enemy,' I quietly pointed out.

'But you were right about one thing . . . she *was* only flesh and blood.'

Luke seemed confused by my sudden compassion. 'Could you have saved her?' he asked doubtfully. 'From herself?'

I considered for a moment. 'I'm not sure. Genevieve was so obsessive. She hated me, tried to rub out my life and then, finally, wanted us to be together.'

'Together *forever*,' Luke added darkly.

I gave a weak laugh. 'Sometimes . . . I hear her calling my name.'

'It still doesn't make sense,' he sighed.

I tried to explain because it was important that Luke of all people understood.

'When we set out that day . . . I think she'd known it would end badly and she was prepared for it.'

Luke moved his head slightly as if he partly understood. 'What about you, Kat? Where do you go from here?'

I clasped my arms behind my head and gave a rueful smile. I had no answer to this.

'You haven't changed,' Luke insisted.

'I haven't changed,' I echoed, 'but everything around me has.'

His hand touched my shoulder. 'You're still the same inside, and you don't need other people to tell you who you are.'

'And . . . I can be whoever I want to be.' A small shiver ran through me as I repeated Genevieve's words. I bit my lip. 'Genevieve told me something . . . right at the end. That we put on these different faces for the world and never show our true nature.'

'What did she mean?'

'I think she was trying to tell me that no one knows what they're really capable of until they're tested.'

Luke slipped on his own sunglasses and grinned at me. 'She could be right. Anyway, you'll always have me. We make a good team, don't we?'

'Not exactly Starsky and Hutch,' I laughed.

'Rivers and Cassidy? Sounds like a couple of bank robbers.'

Our eyes locked and I leaned forward and gently kissed him on the lips, something I'd wanted to do again for ages. I thought how funny it was that we only seemed to kiss in graveyards. He smiled tenderly and wiped the last traces of tears from my cheek. Looking into Luke's eyes felt like coming home and told me everything I needed to know about his feelings for me. For now we didn't need to talk about what had changed between us; it was enough to be together.

There was a woman standing in the graveyard, clutching a single rose. She had altered in the last week, her face thinner and her eyes bruised, but there was a look of peace that I hadn't seen before. I took a few steps towards her until we met where the pathway forked. We weren't flesh and blood, but she was the only person I would ever call mother. We walked in comfortable silence. It was still and oddly beautiful. The well-tended paths, the old and new graves which told of grief that was one unending cycle. Dying, crushed flowers were discarded in a metal bin close to fresh blooms still wet with tears. The dead would always be here with the living close by, and I was beginning to realize that the divide wasn't as great as people thought. Luke was now by my side. He reached for my hand as we walked away.

ACKNOWLEDGEMENTS

A stupendously huge thank-you to everyone at Darley Anderson for their support, guidance and encouragement, especially the wonderful Madeleine Buston for her offer of representation. It came by email from a train travelling towards Dorchester on 2 April 2010. I was reeling with shock and elation then, and I still am now. Thank you for making my dreams come true.

Another massive thank-you to everyone at Quercus, especially Roisin Heycock, a superb editor who taught me so much (particularly about happy endings) and Talya Baker, a fantastic project manager. I feel very privileged that *Poison Heart* was given a home at Quercus – when I saw the cover for the first time I was completely blown away.

I'm also deeply grateful to my foreign publishers for the gift of translation and for taking my novel around the globe.

To all my family and friends who've had to endure my attempts at becoming an author – I couldn't have done it if you hadn't listened

And finally to Princy, the stray cat who wormed her way into my home and my heart, thank you for the inspiration of your beautiful green eyes.